UNLIMITED DESIRES:
An International Anthology of Bisexual Erotica

Edited by: Laurence Brewer, Kevin Lano and Trish Oak

GW00808273

BiPress

UNLIMITED DESIRES: An International
Anthology of Bisexual Erotica

Published in 2000 by **BiPress**
PO Box 10048
London
SE15 4ZD

*Edited by: Laurence Brewer, Kevin Lano and
Trish Oak*

ISBN 0 9538816-0-1

Introduction

The 1990s witnessed a growth in the writing and publication of erotica. Instead of being limited to specialist outlets erotic fiction has firmly found a place on the shelves in mainstream bookshops and chain stores. The growth in the market for erotic fiction has witnessed a change in erotica as a genre in itself. Not limited to the preserve of male consumers, bookshelves pronounce the names of publishers whose niches cater for women, gay men, lesbians, fetishists, BDSMers, horror, crime, science fiction as well as the erotic romance. Short erotic story collections proudly announce collections with such titles as The International book of erotica, the Best Gay erotica, the Best Lesbian erotica ... there is even a book dedicated to Gay men writing Lesbian erotica, and Lesbians writing Gay male erotica, yet at the time of writing there was no collection explicitly dedicated to stories concerning Bisexuality or about Bisexual desire. It was if Bisexual desire did not exist or was it simply a case that it was invisible, lost beneath the covers in other collections? This book is an attempt to redress that balance, by providing a collection of stories centred around bisexual desire, behaviour and identity. We hope the stories will confront assumptions, challenge expectations but above all get you excited.

The seeds of this book started in 1997, when a workshop session on Bisexual erotic writing and readings was held at the 15th National UK Bisexual Convention in Greenwich, London. The aim of the session was to explore the existence and location of Bisexual erotic stories, where Bisexual behaviour or identity was central to the plot, narrative or characterisation and not secondary as in the case of most Bi related stories geared towards a predominantly heterosexual male reader, or transitory as in the case of coming out stories leading to a Gay or Lesbian identity. Session participants discussed stories they had read and the stories' potential Bisexual relevance, as well as discussing what an anthology of Bi erotic stories could look like. It was evident from the session that Bi erotic fiction did exist and that there was enthusiasm for a collection of Bi erotic stories to be published. Encouraged by the enthusiasm from the convention, the idea of the book was discussed on Bi related email lists, and again there appeared to be support for the idea.

A small group of us met to discuss the next stage and to write a submission guideline for the book. This is when we hit our first hurdle. Given that no Bisexual erotic anthology existed there was no potential benchmark to act as a guide. What exactly were we asking people to contribute to? Were we in the unenviable position of having to try to provide a definition of "Bisexuality"? We were aware that there was a myriad of ways in which people have attempted to define the term Bisexual. From Freud's polymorphous perversity, the hermaphrodite tradition of dictionaries and biology, androgynous transgressions of masculinity and femininity, gender identity blurring, asexuality, fluid sexual identity through time, as a midpoint between homosexuality and heterosexuality, as a man or woman who has sexual and romantic feelings towards other men and women, to the threesome or moresome, to name a few.

We were aware that individually these definitions and concepts were quite iv

limited and restrictive. So instead of trying to define Bisexuality or bisexual desire, we chose to leave the question open for interpretation. The only assistance we provided was provocatively asking in our call for contributions "What is bisexual erotica anyway? Is it a story where the characters have sex with men and women at the same time ... a piece where a woman dressed as a man hunts for sex in a public toilet ... a novel set on a planet where there are more than two sexes ... a poem for a lover whose sex is unspoken?"

We received over one hundred stories from around the world, and then started the difficult task of selecting the ones for inclusion. We wanted to include a wide range of stories reflecting as many different forms of Bisexual desire, culture and activity as possible from the stories submitted, without neglecting the erotic charge. We hope we have selected a broad range of stories which reflect a diverse range of Bisexual desires. However, saying that it was also the intention of the collective that the concept of this book would be a starting-off point, an encouragement to others to explore the bisexual erotic imagination and its possibilities, to motivate new stories and books.

Contents

Acknowledgement

Dianne Millen formulated the call for contributions for the book, and also helped with reviews of articles. Alice McKay-Ferguson also helped with reviews. We'd also like to thank all the authors of the over 100 submissions we had to the book for their support with this project.

In The Summer of the Gypsy Moths

Michael Lassell

It began in the summer of the gypsy moths. Do you remember? – how they hung in the air as thick as cream, fluttered like silent applause, muffled the normal city sound? Filtered through wings, a beer bottle crashing in an alley became a crystal champagne flute falling to a marble floor. And the rush in her throat as she neared abandon was the whisper of some pagan god offering a blessing in spite of husbands and carpenters whose hands took splinters while we played. Jack, she said. His name was Jack.

Gypsy moths. Porthetria dispar. They took the place in the air that would have been filled with moisture in any other humid coastal summer. When we made love, they gathered on the screens of the open windows. They gathered on the cars parked behind the Arthur Murray Dance Studio and on the tire swing in the rabbi's yard where children with Mosaic names chased them screaming. Around lamp posts they were a whirling nimbus, like guilt. They clung to telephone poles and were crushed under foot, petals of white roses at a wedding or coronation.

When she stepped off the silver train into a city night alive with moths, she seemed to be stepping into a new dimension. She was tan but somehow pale, wearing a peasant blouse with flowers embroidered on the bodice, white on white; rising and falling breasts, soft slow breath (I had missed her); white skirt, sandals, straw sun hat for tomorrow at the beach, canvas bag with belongings she told Jack would see her through the weekend at Michelle's in New York. But she didn't go to New York. And Jack did not quite understand the nature of her visits to Michelle.

Sometimes they landed on people, pedestrians walking from the small movie theatre near the Yale Co-op to a late-night drink, slice of pizza, sex. Usually they avoided human contact, which proved them smarter than we were. On a bare arm, warm in the evening, they felt like nothing, like a hair tangled in another. Some people flicked them off or waved them away. Others gave them a free ride a block or two. Some stayed home in fear. Indignant others wrote furious letters to government agencies and newspapers. But being disapproved of didn't stop them, didn't stop their eating, didn't stop their mating, crawling, flirting with creatures big enough to brush them to death and never notice.

By night New Haven was a wonderland of living snow. In the morning it was small again, hot and rundown. Paint still flaked from the vacant Shubert Theatre. The pseudo-Gothic cloisters still hungered for students who'd run off now to summer holidays in Europe or the Rockies. The streets were empty of everything but wings, the bodies apparently carried away by animals that feed on the carcasses of insects.

It was cooler when we met. In April-Easter in pine-covered Upstate New York. The snow had only recently melted. I was visiting Robert, my hunger for him still metallic in my mouth. She was there to see Carole (our former roommates, now living together in something like sin). We were all innocent as lambs – just friends meeting by spring chance. In the back seat of the car, she offered me a taste of her vanilla ice cream cone. It was sweet and thick. Soon I was licking the wet sugar off her full lips, and there were tongues on tongues like children touching each other for the first time. When I did touch her for the first time, her breast yielded to my fingertips like something that only came alive when making human contact. When she spoke, the words were deliberate, her voice soft, as if life were a final exam she dared not fail. She stated nothing; everything was explained.

Candles flickered in her room, white candles, the room at Robert and Carole's apartment. The sheets were white, the quilt white-on-white. Her skin was the softest I have ever known. There was nothing on it like a blemish. Nothing like a mole or hair.

"Your lips are so soft," I said in wonder as she moved them off my mouth.

"All women's lips are soft," she said. Was it modesty, the discomfort of a compliment? Or did she think I'd had as little experience with women as she'd had with men?

It was true. But her body gave my body all the clues it needed. There were no fears or objections. When I put my mouth on her, my tongue into her, she made a noise that reminded me of a dream I'd had as a child.

In the morning the flavour of human salt clung to my beard.

At breakfast, with a giggling Robert and Carole at the Bluebird Cafe – a takeout Chinese restaurant now – we were four surprises all around at a table for five. It was not until after, until we had buried our faces in each other and enjoyed the meal, that I learned she was married, learned I had helped her violate her Catholic contract of lifelong fidelity to a simple man with calloused hands who was, she said, too rough, rubbing her nipples raw night after night.

Her nipples were tiny, pink. They barely grew in size when they hardened between my fingers, lips, teeth.

"Ow," she said one night when I forgot she wasn't a man, "please be gentler."

How many men have thanked me for that lesson in the years since? How many have not? In my mind's eye I always saw him in jeans, her carpenter husband, hard and muscled over wooden sawhorses, plane in hand, rocking back and forth over a pine plank as if making love to it, shavings of pungent wood gathered at his feet and cracking under his honest boots like thin ice.

But she said it wasn't so. He wasn't beautiful, his carpentry was mediocre, his method crude and clumsy as his lovemaking. She blamed her infatuation with him on the image of miners emerging from the ground in her native West Virginia (white men covered in black dust), of miners stripped to the waist and loggers who stripped trees from hills so the burrowing men – her brothers, uncles, cousins – could more easily extract the obsolete fuel. Her father was the only male in her family who wouldn't die with coal dust in his lungs, she said. A doctor, he had escaped, had taken refuge in his mind. She idolised him. She was a daddy's girl in eyelet cotton clutching a doll in organdy ruffles, a little girl who grew so soft with womanhood it seemed that she would die, until at fifteen she wrapped her soft white self around a man and felt another being flutter inside her. She learned from it. She learned it was not the only lesson she wanted to learn.

There was nothing of the mind in Jack, nothing of the soul, she said. He was not, she said, a golden boy with soft hair who abandoned parental expectations to work with his hands. He was simply a man with ambition to be nothing more than a man whose woman loved him. She had other things in mind, things of mystery, of power and stained glass.

She hoped the moths would grow so thick we'd smother in them, she said, as we lay in the morning naked in my bed. Then she laughed, picturing our agony in bas relief, moths by the thousands flying from our gaping mouths like bats from caves with the inadvertent features of natural gargoyles.

On the second night in bed I asked if I were the first since she married. She smiled, but never answered. It was her way, her iron will exerted sotto voce (a life sentence sung by a choir of boys).

The telephone call came out of a seamless sky one late spring night while the rabbi entertained the officers of the Hillel Society: "I just got off the bus," she said. "May I come?"

The answer was yes more than once, and more than once we slipped into my narrow bed in that old house that looked like a Swiss chalet, two fugitives from our own lives holed up in a tired corner of a town that reeked of corruption. She gave me gifts, slim volumes, erotic and elusive: Les Liaisons dangereuses. When the rain came, we walked in it. We stood barefoot in the city rain on the town green beside a Revolutionary War graveyard between churches. Brown children screamed Spanish in the band shell. Pigeons roosted under the eaves of the old hotel where countless indiscretions must have taken place before plywood boards sealed up the windows. Later, stencilled fists raised in salute began to cover the posters that plastered the wood.

POWER TO THE PEOPLE.

It was an angry and a violent time.

We stood in the warm rain watching the demonstrations at the courthouse, where a black man was being tried on charges of murder and conspiracy, charges nobody believed, not even the people who brought them, government people who disapproved of the man's politics, who said he preached violence.

But only the police had guns, only the police kept files. Only the National Guard opened fire.

"I don't care if he is guilty," I said, "he deserves to be free. For what life has done to him." She willingly agreed.

It was a summer of slogans and deceit, of confusion, love, and gypsy moths. She brought Carole with her after she split up with Robert. They both met Barry and Bill, lovers for two years. Before the week was out, Carole had moved in with Barry, Bill with Andre, and we all remained friends.

"Have you ever slept with Carole?" I asked one night after making love, a night I had seen a look pass between them I could explain no other way. Her eyelids moved like gypsy moths.

"She's soft," is all she said, as if it were an answer. I assumed she did not want me to know.

The next night Canadian Jim came to my room. We'd made love once, quickly, at his place after dinner. Quickly, in the way of adolescents. Jim's way.

With the two of us, he was slower, calmer, freer, luxuriating in our mouths, taking us by turns in his, open to both of us, carried away, he said, in a way he'd never felt before. His confidence grew and so did his hair.

"Do you like him?" I asked after he'd gone off into the night.

"He's soft," she said.

"And that's what you like?"

She said nothing, but I sensed that she was thinking, planning a reply, balancing the pros and cons of truth. I felt her weigh her answer as the moths batted the window screens in their rotten frames, and then I fell asleep, or she did, drifted off with the taste in our mouths of kissing and licking in a season of salty skin.

The next night, honesty hung over our lovemaking like a cloud, like a canopy of moths in slow motion held at the corners by birds. I slid into her easily. She murmured approval under her breath. And when it was over, my head in the hollow of her shoulder – or hers in mine – she slid into the truth. She'd loved Carole at Vassar. She loved Michelle, her sorority sister who lived in New York now, the one she told her husband she was visiting when she came to see me. I would eventually meet Michelle at the party where all the people in her life came together for one drug-fuelled evening of confusion. Jack knew everything, she said, and kept silent for shame. His cabinet making did not improve. He continued drinking heavily and proved as abusive to his second wife, it turned out, as he was to his first.

I held my own truth back, an eel on a leash, voracious, attacking the hand that held it.

What could I have told her? That I held Robert's cock in my mouth in a frigid bathroom in the London winter of 1968? That I had been in bed with Barry – our one futile attempt at making love – when the call came from Judy, the woman I loved before her, Judy with the Joan Baez hair, who came to my bed the night of my twenty-first birthday, after I'd left Julius, my body still slippery with him?

Yes. That's what I could have said.

When she told me how much better it was for Jim when we were both there, I could have told her. When she told me she couldn't stay another day because she'd promised Michelle. Or Jack. Any number of times. Time and again. Time after time.

By August nothing mattered, as long as she returned. Nothing mattered but that. Then she left me alone for two long weeks in a small-minded city full of impending honesty, unmitigated hatred, and gypsy moths. Nights filled with the thick scent of underground activity. Dissident French activists masquerading as tourists, Jean Genet himself, slipped into town through Canada – Barry and I saw him on the green between churches. Prosecution witnesses changed their stories in mid-sentence. I lived in fear that she would abandon me in the middle of the truth with nothing to hold onto but wings too small for flight.

Then Boo arrived, the boy/man I'd known in college, bearing drugs, which we'd smoke or drop or just ... take. We'd lie on my bed naked and stoned and feeling every nerve end, until he rolled off onto the floor to his sleeping bag and we both jerked off in the dark, me wanting him more than God, him knowing what I wanted and himself wanting ... I never knew.

Then Bill quarrelled with Andre, and Andre appeared at my door after dark, smooth as silk, caramel accent, long thin toes. He cried in my arms and grew softer and softer, until there was no body there at all. I made love to the sound of his breathing in the dark. I put my tongue on him and his skin drank the saliva.

There was something about the memory of her on my fingers, the memory my fingers had of being inside her, the memory my tongue had of having opened her in the night, that went to work on sweet Andre in the dark. I was in his mouth, and he was as deep inside my throat as I could take him. I sank myself between the tough lean cheeks of his miraculous thighs. There was a yes in it that sang from me when he came into my eyes, and I shot so hard I shuddered the length of my spine like a snake uncoiling itself. I was making love to us all. And somewhere inside I had been touched at a place so new it was uncharted on the map she had given me inside The Four Quartets.

In the morning he seemed shy. He kissed me once, then jumped into cutoff jeans with the agility of the dancer he had been before the accident and left me, still in bed, alone with myself, the taste of sex – all our many sexes – on my hands.

The reconciliation between Bill and Andre was accomplished by noon. They got back to being happy in each other's eyes, and I got back to missing Ellen ... Yes, I missed Ellen, but I found myself looking into the eyes of boys and men on the street for traces of her unspecified sorrow. I wondered where she was sleeping. With Jack in a bed he made for them both? With Michelle in her industrial loft in New York, a well-worn mattress dropped on the floor as casually as lies.

With Barry, it turned out. With Carole. With Barry and Carole. With Boo.

Boo was the unforgivable one. I've never been generous about people I coveted and could not have.

But Barry and Carole said I should call her. I never would have on my own. She agreed immediately to appear on Friday night for a weekend at the beach. And she arrived, as white as hospitals, soft as sleep, stepping from a silver train into a blur of gypsy moths that orbited one another in pairs, like twin stars.

"What's wrong?," she asked after we made love.

"Nothing," I said, and it was true. After making love to her, there was never anything wrong on earth, no questions, no fear, no injustices done to others – just silence, flavours, the drift of a tango from the Arthur Murray Dance Studio.

"Something's different. I can feel it."

"I've been tired."

"No," she said, soft and cool, "that's not it."

"I've missed you."

"I've missed you, too."

Our secrets were important to us then.

Whenever I was having sex with Ellen, I wondered where Boo was sleeping.

In the afternoon, we could hear the usual crowd chanting on the green in front of the courthouse. In the rabbi's yard Rachel fell from the swing and her mother came to gather the howling girl-child into plump and caring arms.

We talked at cross purposes, smoked each other's cigarettes, talked of the old women who were dying around us in other wallpapered rooms, the smell of them saturating the hallways. We spent the night in the dark. If I turned on the overhead light for a moment, the moths would stir into a bat-like frenzy. We resigned ourselves to sleep and waking, a single shower between us, breakfast with Barry and Carole. I told Barry everything I knew; so had Carole. Our loyalties were complex. Co-conspirators all, we shared the illicit past (my favourite of the verb tenses).

How many years later was it? Thirty? As I stood at the bridge of a ship in the South China Sea, and the captain pointed out the pinpricks of light that were the minuscule native fishing boats trawling the shipping lanes in high seas. If he hit one, he said, he would never even know. I stood in the bow of the sleek white ship all that night looking for lanterns yellow as fireflies in the deep blackness of Asian waters thinking of gypsy moths we killed every day of our summer just by walking. How many men had come to my bed since the summer of the gypsy moths? And New England so far away I felt like Melville, a fugitive from a dank north who finds himself in a wet heat, thinking of regrets that will not stay safely stored at home with belongings not needed for Pacific travel – the night I raped Bill in his sleep, the fiery loss of Roberto, the slow disintegration of life with Ben. And how many years more would there be, I wondered – watching from the prow of a vessel not my own, hoping to warn the innocent of impending destruction?

It was a summer of gypsy moths, of love and sex – of wine and drugs, too, of course.

I don't know why I chose to drop acid that day. It was a decision I made as easily as one takes a potato chip from a bowl at a party. Or was it that I wanted to devour Boo, and this was all he was offering, his masculinity already up against its limits just knowing the intensity of my desire for him. I took half, and he took the other. It was that kind of communion.

At the beach, we spread our cotton patchwork quilt near the lighthouse on the promontory. It was the quilt I was wrapped in as a child when I was ill, threadbare with use, still holding some fresh scent in it of my mother and of the hanging of it out in the yard to dry on a clear dry day.

The carousel and the grassy hill with the barbecue grills were behind us, the sharp sand and calm blue sea in front. We could see the summer homes poking from the tall marsh grass as the coast curved out of sight. Marty and Quinn were already there with Jim and Gail, I think it was, smoking dope, as usual. Laughing, as usual – and as a result. Andre and Bill joined us later, long after noon. Boo had brought the grass from upstate New York – Geneva the place was called – with the acid and God knows what else. He'd been selling to the summer kids at Cornell.

The sun was hot, but the breeze off the water was cool. A perfect day, you'd have to call it. There were fewer moths than in the city, and those that crawled the beach seemed sluggish. We sat for a while applying oil to each other, then slept. When I woke, I was looking up at the squat lighthouse tower and thought, for no apparent reason, of windmills and Greece, as if the lighthouse were a windmill that had simply lost its blades and transformed from a mammoth pinwheel into a squat silo.

"There aren't any windmills in Greece," Ellen said, as patient as Annie Sullivan to a distraught Helen Keller, "that's Holland." She said it softly, as if telling a child its parents have both been killed in a car accident.

"There are windmills everywhere," I said, and Marty began a long discourse on Don Quixote that made everyone hungry. We ate sandwiches and hot dogs. Bill and Andre held hands on the carousel, which delighted the Puerto Rican kids and shocked a few Italian widows into dragging their disappointed grandchildren off the machine while it was still in motion. But no one thought to ask the young lovers to stop. It was that kind of time, a time for enjoying the happiness of others, a time to be brought up short by love in the young.

When Quinn opened the Monopoly board, I got up to walk to the end of the breakwater, as far as I could go without falling into the sea. Boo swam slow laps back and forth, back and forth along the length of the beach. It seemed that he could go on forever, gliding from place to place without ever landing, searching for what? The home an abandoned child spends his life missing? Some truth about himself he could bring himself to approve of? The mechanism by which all our hypocrisies could be forgiven and our desires fulfilled?

He was beauty in the sea, the northern summer light glistening off his muscles as they worked. He was as lean as an animal and as remote, something African you can only see from a distance. Something African that did not herd for protection. Something that hid in the Serengeti night, a morsel in a tree, just out of reach of nocturnal predators.

He was as hard as Ellen was soft.

"Your shoulders will burn," she said as she came up beside me and put her cool white fingers on the red heat of them. I had been squatting there for ... hours? Acid will do that to time, twist it into Möbius strips of recurring experience that happen for the first time over and over again.

Had Boo been swimming all afternoon, or only for moments?

"I don't care," I said.

She said nothing, the way she does, did, and slipped her arm through mine, watching Boo swim.

"He's very good," she said.

"Yes," I said. "He is."

"And beautiful," she added.

I looked at her, her soft brown hair playing with her soft white skin, looking like someone I could kill for, even die for. "We dropped acid this morning," I said, "but it's pretty mellow stuff."

"Yes," she said, in that breathy half-voice of hers, that voice that suggested her errors weren't so much mistakes as a failure of proper aspiration (moments lost for a lack of breath): "I know."

The silence that followed was more uncomfortable than it should have been. It occurred to me to say nothing, but I was suddenly angry.

I was walking away from her just as the afternoon thunderstorm began to gather on the horizon. It wasn't her fault, of course. None of it was her fault. There were just too many possibilities. Boo was struggling up out of the water, clutching his leg. Blood ran down his calf from a gash six inches long. It ran through the sparse hair of his lower leg, across the knotted veins of his vein-corded feet, slid between his toes and ran into the sand, where drops of it seemed to balloon on contact like sponges in water.

The lifeguard said it looked like a horseshoe crab had slashed with its spiked tail across the flesh of his leg. Perhaps he'd stepped on it unwittingly, as he did most everything else. It was a mess, and it made me glad. An ambulance came to take him for stitches. He was wearing nothing but his tiny red bathing suit, a bathing suit the red of neon EXIT signs. He was, as usual, completely unabashed, and seemed as curious as the kids that gathered around him about the length and depth of his wound, the quantity of blood. But his face was a grimace, and I could tell he was determined not to cry, so I decided to do it for him.

She kissed him as he was lifted into the ambulance and told him we'd come get him later. Then she kissed me, as the rain began to fall in those huge drops summer has a way of letting loose from the sky.

Back at the room she wanted to make love. Easier for her than thinking or talking, it was always her answer, and I rarely disagreed. But I wanted to sleep. My sunburn was killing me and we'd already agreed to meet Barry and Carole for dinner.

She took off her black bathing suit standing by the sink, one foot up on a chair, her back to where I stretched nude on the bed. She put her diaphragm in place while I watched. I don't know why it struck me as funny, but I had to keep fighting off laughter. The foreplay was perfunctory, and when I pushed inside her I just couldn't control myself. She slapped at me while I convulsed with laughter and threw me off the bed and onto the floor where Boo had slept more than once (my body awake all night with my unabated desire for him). Under the bed, on the dusty, threadbare Persian carpet, a single moth walked delicately among the debris.

I still don't know what got into me. Maybe it was the acid. That excuse was always at our fingertips in those days. Were we insane or just young? Were we onto something new, as we thought then, or was it simply a question of the time it was being the time it was?

It was a quiet dinner. Barry and Carole did most of the talking. Ellen ordered enchiladas but didn't eat them. She just sat there biting into taco chips, dipping them into the bland salsa, washing them down with beer. For some reason, I remember bitter coffee, cup after cup. From where I sat, I could see the rain pouring down the front window, washing the gypsy moths from the glass. She went to the ladies room and was gone a long time. We let the waitress take her food away. We drank and grew embarrassed. Carole went to see if Ellen was all right. She was gone.

By the time I'd gotten Boo from the hospital and taken him home, her things were gone from my room. All that was left was her clear plastic toothbrush hanging upside down in the holder like a West Virginia 'possum by its tail.

She was not at the train station, or at either bus depot. She was just gone.

I stood on the front porch of my rooming house, under the green wooden overhang cut with leaves, and watched streams of water rushing in the street, carrying the corpses of moths along in their currents like the dead leaves of birches. I remember wondering which way she'd go: Jack ... Michelle ... someone or someplace new?

On Sunday, I asked Carole to call Jack.

"There is no Jack," she said, simple as clean sheets and dishes.

I wasn't even surprised. Just annoyed. I dialled the number Carole had for Michelle. It had been disconnected.

Carole said she would let me know when she heard from Ellen, as she was sure she would. Then she and Barry broke up, and both of them moved to other cities. Boo stayed with me one more night. His leg was bandaged. He had taken a lot of something and went to sleep on the floor. I pulled the blanket off him, and touched him. He started to get hard, but it was too ... ridiculous? pathetic? exhausting? By the next afternoon, he was gone, too.

So maybe she just had her fill of fence-sitting in a dirty New England town full of white moths and men who found in her answers to questions they'd never asked. Maybe she just knew how it would end, as the moths must have known in the silent beating of their wings that someday their time would come and a violent summer storm would flush them away, an entire city cleansed of an ethereal presence in one chilling downpour that left behind an emptiness more solid than the presence of most things I have known since.

If she had called, I don't know what I would have done. I would have asked whether she'd have stayed longer if I hadn't gotten angry at the beach, if I hadn't laughed when the rain began to hit the gypsy moths on the screens and I entered her body and took her breath in my mouth.

In the end it didn't matter and I knew it. None of it mattered a damn. I knew it when Andre was killed, and when Quinn was tried and convicted, when Marty went on to become an assistant to the Republican governor of Maine, when the people who decide such things decided it was no longer ... acceptable to be a lover of women and men, not even when Robert – who introduced us – died some decades later of a plague that had killed so many others, or when Carole died of a cancer in her ample left breast. What did any of it matter anymore?

It was only life and death.

Maybe Ellen went back home to the hill country of West Virginia – back to resume her incestuous fantasies about her father and her readings in Renaissance literature, a spectacled spinster draped in mosquito netting for an African safari, disappointed, alone. Or perhaps West Virginia and the Renaissance were lies, too, like Jack and loving me.

I hope she's happy, but that's hard to imagine, unless it's dressed in white – not in summer, but in snow so cold it squeaks under foot before melting.

Years pass and memories fade. They pass in the night while I sleep and accumulate in dreams that I dismiss with a shrug on my way to the shower alone.

I lived in California for many years, where the weather is warm and women wear white all year long. There are butterflies there of brilliant yellows and golds, intricate patterns of black and orange, splashes of green like a single Irish eye. But I never saw a gypsy moth. Not for all those years in California. Not after. Not ever.

In Praise of Contempt

Paul Cowdell

Marla Brast was a creature of her age: she was vacuous, and obsessive in her vacuity. It would be wrong to think her as mentally-damaged as she appeared. Marla was desperately and genuinely afraid that there was a void in her life, but she lacked any concepts with which to understand it. Worried that her life was shallow and meaningless, she filled her life with glittery surfaces – a new bathroom, a new wardrobe, a new face, but still, depressingly, the same old Marla.

She had repeatedly flirted with eastern mysticism; as an acolyte of evangelism she had been exorcised by three purulent and virginal co-worshippers, one of whom had already ejaculated into his nylon underpants; she had practised oriental muscle-control exercises in the belief that this made her not only more sexually supple but also more intelligent; the frequency of her rebirths was surprising only in that it had taught her nothing of life; and she had communed with trees until they had withered with boredom and embarrassment.

And still, inexplicably, she was unhappy. She had no real friends. She lacked judgement even about when to make her next sudden lurch of faith. She wanted to blame her parents for the failure of her spiritual odyssey (although it was hardly much of an odyssey – the one thing she had repeatedly failed to pack in her spiritual luggage was a personality) when they only wanted her to have a white wedding and give their grandchildren the names of saints or characters in current popular fiction. They were liberals and had thoroughly imbued her with their liberality – her spiritual idealism meshed totally with a material pragmatism. She was a middle-class professional with a veneer of other-worldliness. In short, she admired all hand-drummers, and thought that 'Bridget Jones' Diary' and 'The Celestine Prophecy' were great books.

But perhaps I do Marla a disservice. After all, her search for fulfilment was genuine enough to force her to turn inwards eventually. She sat in silence for ten minutes with a Lacanian analyst before he told her the session was over and demanded his fee. When she queried this he told her that that too was part of the therapy. She decided not to return, not because her confidence was shaken but because he had spent his ten silent minutes drawing an erect penis. It made her feel cheap.

She felt surer of Doctor Freuten. For a small and self-important middle-class group around an insignificant part of south west London he was the man to see. He was spoken of almost like a brand of furniture. One's personal experiences with him were irrelevant. What mattered was the name. His was a probing and brilliant mind. Marla was not afraid of him, however, because she was there to talk about herself, and he was there to listen.

For the first two sessions all went smoothly. Marla told him in maddening detail the minutiae of a life of boredom and he took her money. At the beginning of the third session, though, Doctor Freuten told her that he was going to try something different. Instead of talking, she would listen, and answer his questions. She lay on the couch as usual, and he asked her what frightened her. She began to talk airily, abstractly, about being alone. He suddenly snapped at her.

'Of course you're not afraid of being alone. You pay no attention to anybody else anyway, why would being alone frighten you? Turn over'.

Marla did not at first understand the question. He gave her no time to understand it. He grabbed her by the hair and pulled her up to a kneeling position, pushing her sideways so she slumped face first over the side of the couch.

'Now. You may settle yourself there, but for the rest of this session I want you to remain in that position'.

Doctor Freuten was a very brilliant mind, so she did as she was told. His voice was harsh (but still brilliant).

'Listen to me, Marla. Don't you think that listening to patients – a selfselecting group of people who think they have enough money to warrant problems – might have some effect on me?'

No reply was forthcoming so he yanked her hair back. 'Eh?'

'I've never thought about it like that'.

'No, of course not. That is the problem with your world view, Marla, if I may say so – and of course I may, I am the doctor in this relationship'. He gave the small laugh of a man pleased that a joke of his has gone down well over the canapés. She felt his hands push her long skirt up the insides of her thighs. He rubbed the rouched fabric over her cunt.

'But everything I hear, everything anyone ever tells me, has some effect on me. Of course it does. The world proceeds through interaction, Marla, through substance a coming into contact with substance b, interacting, and producing substance c or d or e'. His long fingers were threatening to tear the fabric as they pushed deeper into her cunt. While one hand continued probing, pinching, the other started to pull the skirt aside, finding only her knickers in the way.

'I obviously am detached from my patients' experience, but not in some remote kind of way, Marla, not how you might perhaps think, if you were capable of that at all. I manage to remain detached from them because they are for the most part meaningless. Oh don't get me wrong, I'm not unprofessional. If I have a patient with a problem I will listen, I will provide therapy. That is my job, and I feel satisfied. But the patients with money and no problems, Marla, what do I do for them?'

He tossed the length of her skirt up over her back, revealing her buttocks. He slipped one hand inside her knickers and found her cunt uncertain in its dampness. He stroked her hypnotically.

'They are looking for something that can't be found. They look inside themselves, or out in the cosmos, for something which properly belongs in their interaction with others, in the social world'.

He had a badly-manicured finger inside her now. She could feel the nail scratching her, but he was more intent on peeling off her underwear. He pulled her knickers down to her knees. She started to lift herself so he could remove them entirely but he slapped her buttock sharply with the palm of his hand.

'Enough! You move when I tell you, and only then, and you speak only when I expect you to speak! Do you understand?'

'Yes, doctor'.

His voice calmed down slightly. She could hear the scrape of a zip being undone, the rustle of fabric as his trousers slid to the floor.

'You see, I meet people like you every day, people searching for something which they think is lacking from their lives. What can I tell you? If I say that you have everything you could possibly want I would stand accused of ignoring your feelings. That would be a dereliction of my duty'.

He took his hand from her cunt. She heard a tearing of foil, the smeared sound of a condom being rolled on. His hands, greasy with lubricant, took hold of her buttocks and spread them apart. His fingers mashed down into the folds of her labia.

'I have to take my patients' anxieties seriously, Marla, even when I don't feel they merit it. But in order to cure them, I also have to offer them a glimpse of a world they perhaps don't realise is only just outside them'.

She felt the head of his prick nose into her labia. He pulled them further apart with his thumbs, and then thrust deeply into her, catching hold of her hips with his sharp nails. She moaned. He pulled back almost the length of his prick before thrusting again, more deeply.

'The world's not such a difficult place to understand, Marla. There's no real need to search for an other-worldly solution to it. It's all here if you actually want to put it together'.

He was pumping deeply into her, reaching right up to the neck of her womb with each thrust. She could feel his balls swing, slapping against her with every stroke. She was biting her lip not to cry out, because the doctor had told her not to speak. His voice dropped to a seductive whisper.

'But I have to take seriously the ways in which my patients attempt to evade an understanding of the real world'.

His thrusts became gentler. He withdrew until he only had the tip of his prick inside her, describing small circles against her cunt lips.

'Like you, for example, who have looked everywhere but in reality for life. Which is why I asked what frightens you. I want you to confront something real, something external which affects you'.

He pulled his prick out of her. She arched backwards in an attempt to stay in contact with it. He slapped her hard again.

'Naughty, naughty. How are you going to be cured if you won't help in your own recovery?'

She heard the sliding sound of a condom being removed. So there wouldn't be any confusion about what he had done, Dr Freuten threw the prophylactic on the floor in front of her.

'At the risk of cheap sensationalism, Marla, I want you to think of that as one of your intellectual, or at least spiritual, crutches'.

His hands were back on her buttocks. He slid a finger quickly into her slick cunt, then forced her arse cheeks apart quite violently. She felt his naked prick brush against her cunt lips, then rear up. Before she could object, Dr Freuten's prick was buried deep in her arse. She involuntarily let out a gasp. He grabbed her hair to balance himself.

'No, you shut the fuck up. It's bad enough that I have to listen to you during the sessions, but it won't happen now!'

He had one hand in her hair, the other roughly stroking her clitoris. He was pounding her arse with short, brutal strokes.

'Your big problem, Marla, is that you have no imagination'.

He pounded her in time to his words. 'No imagination!' She whimpered.

'Am I hurting you? Am I?'

She nodded. 'A little'.

He thrust more violently still. 'Good. At last, this is something real, something tangible, something suffered.' His thrusts described the rhythm of his speech. 'I want you to remember this, to remember the physical sensation of pain'.

His prick scraped rapidly into her, its way only slightly smoothed by sweat. She felt the scald of his come as it gushed up her. She felt light-headed with the burning sensation of her rectum. He pulled his raw prick out of her and stepped round in front of her. She looked up at him, trying to look pitiful. He slapped her face.

'Now keep still, Marla, and watch'.

His foreskin was red from the friction of the fucking, but he massaged it brutally with his hands until his erection was firm again. He brushed her face with the tip of his prick. She parted her lips with a resigned expectation. He laughed and pulled it away from her.

'Keep still now'.

In silence Marla watched the great genius pull violently at his stiff prick, still slick with come and sweat and fecal matter. Suddenly, unexpectedly, he pushed it close in to her face. Come splashed across her cheek and eyebrows. She had closed her eyes when he came. When she opened them again he was still stood before her, breathing heavily, his prick a wilted mess of sperm and shit.

'Get dressed Marla and go home, you're cured'.

She wiped at her come-smudged face. 'May I use your toilet?'.

He looked tired.

'No of course not. Fuck off'.

Gavin Strafford was 24 years old. He was good-looking in a polished sort of way, with a lucrative career just starting in financial services. Dr Freuten expressed surprise, in his charmingly disingenuous way, that someone so obviously successful should be sitting on that couch. Gavin blushed. His problem was an embarrassing one, he explained. He had, you see, been watching a pornographic video. He had been, um, masturbating in front of it. Dr Freuten nodded sagely, with understanding. Gavin had been (the blush reached his scalp, where it was visible through his overly-expensive coiffure) using baby lotion to lubricate his penis. At a scene of oral sex he had put a drop of baby lotion on the forefinger of his left hand and had inserted this finger into his rectum. He fell silent for a moment (either collecting himself or savouring the recollection, Dr Freuten guessed) before shamefully acknowledging that he had then 'come like an express train'. Dr Freuten knew that it is always too soon to write off a patient's capacity for self-destruction, but he failed to see a problem here. He waited for the wrap-up. Gavin looked mournfully at him.

'I'm worried that this might mean I could be gay.'

Dr Freuten took some time in formulating an answer that would prevent him from laughing in Gavin's face.

'Was it a homosexual video?'

It was not, but with the realisation that he liked having things inserted into his rectum had come the doubt that he was aroused not by the heterosexual sex, or by the sight of naked female flesh, but rather by the sight of the erect penis plunging into that flesh.

'Physiologically, of course, it would be extremely surprising if you did not reach orgasm when something is inserted into your anus. It stimulates the prostate and is bound to have an erotic effect. That is not in the least bit odd. What is perhaps strange is your response to this. Why would you think you were gay? And, more important, why would you think it worthy of comment?'

'I beg your pardon?'

'Why would it be strange if you were gay?'

Gavin looked perplexed.

'Well, I guess, um, I don't know. I mean, I suppose there's nothing wrong with it, but it'd mean changing my whole attitude. I mean, I like a laugh with the boys, and some of that gets pretty – um – laddish. About gays, too, you know. How would all that work?'

'I think, Gavin, we might be going a little fast here. Are you sure you're gay, after all?'

'Well that's what I came here for, doc. I mean, I was turned on by the sight of that knob, you know ... '.

Dr Freuten switched on his desk light and pulled the blinds.

'Right, undress'.

'I'm sorry?'

'You heard. Don't think, just do it'.

'But ... '

'You want to know? Just do it'.

Gavin stripped reluctantly. His penis looked like a family dog in a roomful of strangers, unsure what was expected of it. Dr Freuten switched on the television in the corner of the room (he had cut down on his outgoings by living here in the office) and put a video on. Almost immediately there appeared a scene of two men fisting a third man while wanking themselves and him. Gavin stared. It was the middle of the scene. The men sent arcs of semen over their companion's belly. One awkward jump cut later he was thrusting deep into the first man's anus while fucking the second man off. Dr Freuten's voice came as a surprise to Gavin, who had almost forgotten where he was.

'Is that exciting you?'

It is true that Gavin's prick had started to bob like a punch-drunk boxer. It would not be fair to say that it had reared up like a buckish young colt. He turned to see Dr Freuten naked, his prick stiff and in his hand.

'You seem to be concerned about the ridicule of your friends. If they are true friends, of course, they will support you. However, they aren't, they're just people you know. That's not the end of the world, that's just the way you live, so you need to see that their lives are not your life'. And Dr Freuten, still massaging his own foreskin, swooped down and sucked Gavin's uncertain prick into his mouth. The first thing Gavin noticed was how nice the sensation was (his prick hardened instantly). As the doctor's tongue flicked over the head and rippled down the shaft, as the whole body of his penis disappeared into the warm mouth and he felt the lips on his scrotum, it occurred to him that nobody had ever volunteered to do this before, let alone done it like this. It was magnificent.

Freuten sucked hard on the cock, feeling it twitch excitedly in his mouth. He pulled his head up and suddenly kissed Gavin. Gavin, his mouth still open with pleasure, found the doctor's cock-flavoured tongue flickering around his gums. He started to respond as he felt a hand tug at his prick. Suddenly there was a damp sensation. He pulled his head away and looked down. The doctor, with his free hand, had slapped lubricant all over Gavin's prick.

'What's that for?' he asked breathlessly. The doctor did not answer, but slid his arse over the head of the prick, then expertly dropped his weight onto Gavin's cock. Gavin had no time to register his surprise before he found his cock being swallowed deep into his therapist's arse. He felt Freuten's sphincter tighten sweetly around his prick. He was ashamed to feel his orgasm coming way too soon. He tried to hold back but the doctor was relentless: his arse muscles clamped onto the cock as he rode up and down, grinding the foreskin brutally. Gavin let out a cry and came for the first time in another man.

Freuten waited until he felt Gavin's spurts slow down then relaxed and lifted himself off the virgin cock. Although his anal muscle control was exemplary, the doctor allowed a fart to escape him as he stood, hoping that it might leave some residue. Gavin was still too stunned to move, and his lips were parted in surprise. Freuten pushed his prick between them. Gavin choked a little as the cock passed into his mouth, but Freuten was holding him by the ears to prevent him pulling away. He thrust into his patient's mouth. He was so aroused by the situation that his orgasm was not long in coming, and he fired his scalding come against the back of Gavin's throat.

He waited until he had ejaculated all he needed to before releasing Gavin's head and stepping down off the couch.

'Oh I nearly forgot to ask' said Dr Freuten. Gavin looked up.

'Do you enjoy sex with women?' Gavin, his throat stung with come, was hoarse and could only nod.

'Well you might be bisexual then, but you're not gay. See you next week, leave your cheque with my receptionist'.

(iii)

Gavin and Marla, who had not known each other before, met by accident at the party of a mutual friend. It was not love at first sight, or anything asinine like that. In fact they had both seen Dr Freuten dancing drunkenly in a tent in the garden and had retreated as far from him as they could. (Gavin had had his attention drawn to the doctor's behaviour by a friend who had told him about 'some div in a marquee out the back'). They had chatted witlessly for a while and Gavin had fetched Marla a drink before she said that she would like to dance. There was no one else in the room.

By that happy combination of alcohol, relief at having escaped an awkward situation, and the enjoyment of a conversation as stupid as your own both Marla and Gavin, though not dancers, found themselves quite comfortable in their rhythmless clinch. She noticed that his stomach was flat and his aftershave was expensive. He noticed that her breasts were soft against his chest, and she was wearing no bra. When he noticed this he noticed that his erection was quite prominent. The song they were dancing to finished. He pulled away, embarrassed largely because he felt he ought to be, although he was quite pleased she knew. She asked him to come home with her. He went.

Marla only lived a couple of streets away. It was a spacious flat, mostly decorated in vanilla shades. They started kissing as soon as they got the door closed. She took him to the bedroom, all festooned with scarves and hangings. A dreamcatcher was suspended over the bed. He looked up at it. She smiled.

'It's to make you sleep well. It catches your nightmares'. He smiled too. It might just make her sleep soundly, he thought. He watched her light candles around the room and then she was back in his arms again and they were undressing each other, playfully, sensitively. They stroked each other gently, then he lay her on her back, parted her legs and entered her.

Privately both of them felt their recent demons leave them as he entered. He started thrusting, gently at first, then harder. She flung her legs apart to let him in, to let him take her over. He kicked back the bedclothes so he could push deeper into her. In their passion and their concentration neither of them noticed the candle that he knocked over onto one of the scarves. As she was screaming out her orgasm and he was grunting sweatily, neither of them noticed that the flames had reached the corner of the duvet cover that was over their legs. Gavin pushed once more to ejaculate deep inside her when he felt the pain on his calves. At that moment another hanging caught light and fell from the wall onto Marla's dressing table. Her aromatherapy oils fizzled as they burned, spilling pools of scented flame across the pillows and the carpet. Marla and Gavin stood no chance. The whole room was an inferno within three minutes.

Dr Freuten was thrown out of the party. He knew that his stock with these people had run out at about the same time as his patience with them. He was stumbling home when he saw the house on fire. The smell coming from it was strange, like burning meat overlaid with perfume.

He found that the smell relaxed him, so he decided to go home and masturbate.

After The Light Changed

Carol Queen

I was looking pretty boyish that evening. Maybe that's why he looked twice at the stoplight when my car pulled up next to his motorcycle. Usually guys like that are moving; you just see a gleaming blur of black and silver. But here at the light was a real done-up daddy, sitting stock-still – except for his head, which turned in response to my eyes fixed on him and found what he saw noticeable enough to make him turn again. When boy energy gets into me I look like an effete young Cambridge faggot looking to go bad: round spectacles framing inquisitive eyes and a shock of hair falling down over one. Not classically daddy's boy, something a little different. Maybe tonight this daddy was looking for a new kind of ride.

A real done-up daddy, yeah. His leathers were immaculate and carried that dull gleam that well-kept black leather picks up under streetlights. Black leather cap, high boots, everything on him black and silver except the well-worn blue denim at his crotch, bulging invitingly out of a pair of chaps. I eyed that denimed expanse quite deliberately; he noticed. He had steely-blue daddy eyes and a well-trimmed beard. I couldn't see his hands under the riding gloves, but they looked big, and from the looks of him I bet they were manicured. I love these impeccable daddies, they appeal to the femme in me.

And his bike! A huge, shiny animal, a Harley, of course – nothing but classic for this daddy. The chrome gleamed as if he did the fine polish with his tongue – or rather, used the tongue of some lucky boy. I'm more for polishing leather, myself, but if this stone-hot daddy told me to do his bike, of course I'd get right to it.

Ooh, he was looking right into my eyes, taking in my angelic Vienna-choirboy face and my leather jacket, much rattier than his with all its ACT-UP and Queer Nation stickers. Did he think I was cute enough for a walk on the wild side? I could hear him dishing me to all the other daddies: "Yeah, this hot little schoolboy, looked real innocent but he cruised me like he knew what I had and wanted it, so I let him follow me home."

On the cross street the light turned yellow. I did want what he had. This was it. I leaned out the window and said, just loud enough to be heard, careful to keep my voice low-pitched, "Daddy, can I come too?"

The daddy grinned. When the light turned green he gunned the Harley, took the space in front of my car, and signalled for me to follow.

A South of Market apartment – oh, this was perfect. At three A.M. on any given night he could probably open his bedroom window and find a willing mouth down here to piss in – I'd heard about this alley. The entryway was dark. Good. I parked my car and caught up with him there. I fell to my knees as he pulled his keys from his belt. By the time he had his door unlocked I was chewing on his balls through the denim. He let me go on that way for a minute, and then he collared me and hauled me into the dark foyer. I barely had time to grab my rucksack, which I'd let fall beside me so I could get both hands on his hard, leather-clad thighs.

Inside, I pulled off my glasses and tucked them away safely in my jacket. In the future, I guess I'd remember to wear my contacts. Daddy pushed me back onto my knees, and I scrambled to open the buttons of his Levi's. I wanted his cock, wanted it big, wanted it down my throat with his hands fisting the hair at the nape of my neck, giving it to me hard and rhythmically. I wanted to suck both his balls into my mouth while he slapped his dick against my cheeks. Cock worship in the dark. Use me, Daddy, no, don't come yet – I have a surprise for you.

I don't know how long I went on. I get lost in cocksucking sometimes; it's like a ritual that disconnects me from my head, all the more so when it's anonymous. I hadn't even seen this cock I was sucking, and that made me feel I could be anyone, even an adventurous gay boy in a South of Market alley, sucking Daddy's big, hard dick. Any second now he could realize that I was no ordinary boy, and that gave me a great rush of adrenaline, a lust to have it down my throat. Until he discovered me I could believe this illusion myself, and with most men this was all I could expect to be, a cock-sucker until they turned the lights on.

Daddy was moaning; guess as a cocksucker I got a passing grade. I felt the seam of my Levi's, wet where they pressed into my cunt. Jesus, I wanted it, I wanted it from him, I wanted him not to care. The scents of leather and sweat filled my head. Finally I pulled my mouth away from his dick – no problem speaking in a low voice now, shit, I was hoarse from his pounding. "Daddy, please, I want you to fuck me."

He pulled me up at once, kissed me, hard. That was a surprise. I was swooning, not feeling like a boy now, whatever a boy feels like, but all womanly, my brain in my cunt. And I was about to be discovered. His hand was sliding into my jacket; any second now it would fall upon the swell of my breast. This was when most guys freaked out and sent me home to beat off. That was ok, usually, but God, it would kill me to break this kiss.

But the kiss went on even when his fingers grazed first one breast, then the other ... when his other hand followed the first under my jacket, then under my shirt, as if for corroboration, and he felt my nipples go hard under his touch. He squeezed them, eliciting a very unboyish moan, thrusting his tongue deep down where his cock had been, so that even when he twisted my nipples into the shape of morning glories, furled around themselves, I couldn't cry out.

The kiss went on even when one hand slid down my belly and started undoing the buttons of my jeans until there was room for him to slip a finger down between my pussy lips, root its way, almost roughly, all the way into my cunt, pull the slick finger out again and thrust it into my mouth, where our tongues sucked it clean. The kiss lasted while he slid his fingers back in and fucked me, so slowly, so juicy and excruciating, until I finally broke away to beg, "Oh, Jesus, please, make me come!" He stroked in faster, then; I came like a fountain into his hand. He rubbed the juice all over my face, licked some of it off, kissing me again, then pulled me down the hall into a lit room. I felt weak-kneed and wildly dishevelled; he was immaculate yet, but his cock was out and it was still hard. For me.

Those steel-blue eyes were lit with more than amusement, and when he spoke, in a soft, low, almost-drawl, I realized it was the first time I'd heard his voice.

"Well, little boy, I must say you had me tricked." He laughed; I guess I looked a little proud. "Do you make a habit of fooling guys like me?"

"Not very often," I managed. "And most men don't want what they get."

"No, I would imagine not. A little too much pussy under that boy drag. A man wouldn't want to get himself ... confused. Hey, where'd you learn to suck cock? A bathhouse?"

"My brother taught me. He's gay."

"Shit, bring him with you next time you visit," said the daddy. "I'll die and go to heaven." He pushed me back on the bed then and knelt above me. His big cock dangled above my face and at first he held me down, teasing me with it, but I begged and he lowered it to my lips, letting me have just enough to suck on like a baby dreams over a tit. "Good girl," he said, smiling a little, running his fingertips over my skin in a most enticing way. The boy energy was gone, but I didn't want to stay a little girl with a man this hot. Anyway, he wasn't acting like a leather daddy any more.

I don't know what gets into me. When I cruise gay men as a boy, I know full well that I have to stay a boy the whole time. Unless they send me out at the first touch of curves, the first smell of pussy, they'll play with me only if I can keep up the fantasy. I lick Daddy's boots and suck his cock and get on my face for him, raise my ass up at the first brush of his cock on my cheeks. I beg Daddy to fuck my ass and promise I'll be his good boy, always. But deep inside, even as he's slam-fucking my ass and I'm screaming from the deep pounding pleasure of it, even though I love being a faggot for him, I secretly wish he'd slip and bury his meat all the way deep in my cunt. I love being a boy, but I don't like having to be two separate people to get what I want. I really want the men I fuck to turn me over and see the whole me: the woman in the boy, the boy in the woman. This daddy, this leatherman whose name I didn't even know, was the first one with whom that seemed possible – and I wanted to make sure. I wanted to know if he would really play with me.

So again I let his cock slip from my lips. "Daddy, will you let me up for a minute? I want to play a new game, and I really want you to like it." He released me, looking at me quizzically as I reached for my bag and pulled the last of my clothes off. There. A femme hates having pants bagging around her ankles.

Feeling sleeker already, I took the bag into the bathroom, promising I'd be right back. Everything was there – shoes, clothes, makeup. It was time to grow up.

The dress was red and tight and hugged my small breasts into cleavage. Its backline plunged down almost to the swell of my ass. Black stockings and garters (the dress was too tight to wear a belt under, only a black g-string would fit), and red leather pumps with high, high heels. The kind of shoes drag queens named so aptly "Come-Fuck-Me-Pumps." You're not supposed to walk in them – you're supposed to offer the toe to a worshipful tongue or lock them around a neck while you get pounded. Which is what I hoped would be happening to me shortly.

With some gel and a brush my hair went from boyish to chic. Powder on my face, then blush. I darkened my eyebrows and lashes, lined and shaded my eyes with green and violet, and brushed deep crimson into my lips. An amazingly changed face, all angles and shadows and eyes and cheekbones, looked back at me from the mirror. One last glance: I was sufficiently stunning. In fact, the sight, combined with the knowledge that I was about to emerge from the little room into the leather daddy's view, had me soaked, my heart pounding, my clit buzzing. I get so very narcissistic when I'm femmed out. I want to reach for my image in the mirror, take her apart and fuck her. No doubt I'd be riding this energy into the girl bars tomorrow night, looking for my image stepped through the looking glass, out looking for me.

One last flourish, a long, sheer, black scarf, sheer as my stockings, flung around my shoulders, hiding nothing. I stepped back into the leather daddy's room.

He'd taken his jeans off from beneath the chaps. His jacket was off too, hung carefully over a chair. His dick was in his hand. He'd been stroking it, staying hard. Bands of leather drew my gaze to the hard curves of his biceps. Silver rings gleamed in his nipples. I felt like a Vogue model who'd stumbled into a Tom of Finland painting. He was gorgeous. He was every bit the spectacle I was, body modified and presented to evoke heat, to attract sex.

He looked at me hard, taking in the transformation. I saw his cock jump; good.

"So, Daddy, do you still want to play?" I said "Daddy" in a different voice this time, let it be lush with irony, like a 40's burlesque queen. A well-educated faggot ought to pick up on that.

There was a touch of wonder in his voice. "God damn. I don't believe I've ever picked up anything quite like you." Then suspicion. "So what's your trip? Trying to turn the heathens into hets? No wonder all those other guys threw you out."

A new rush of adrenaline hit. Go ahead, I thought, be uncomfortable, baby, but don't stop wanting it. I took a couple of steps, coming near enough the bed that I could put one foot up on it. I moved into his territory, gave him a view of the tops of my stockings and the wet, pussy-redolent G-string. I narrowed my eyes. "Did I suck your cock like a het? You think I can't take it now I have a dress on?"

He persisted. "Why waste this on gay men? Straight boys must fall over for you."

"Straight boys don't know how to give me what I want." I ran my eyes
down his body. "Besides, your cock says I'm not wasting this on you."

He made no move to try and hide the hard-on. His voice was more curious
than accusatory when he said, "You get a perverse charge out of this, don't
you?"

"Yeah, I do. But I really want you to get a perverse charge out of it." I
moved to him, knelt over him so that only the insides of my knees touched
the smooth leather of his chaps. He was close enough to touch; I had to stop
from reaching. This was it, the last obstacle. His hard cock almost touched
me. "I'm no ordinary boy, Daddy, and I'm no ordinary woman. Do you want
it? Just take it."

There is so much power in being open and accessible and ready. So much
power in wanting it. That's what so many other women don't understand.
You'll never get what you want if you make it too hard for someone to give it
to you. He proved it: he lifted his hands to me, ran them once over my body,
bringing the nipples up hard through the clinging dress, pinned my arms at
my sides and brought me down into a kiss that seared and melted, a kiss I felt
like a tongue in my cunt. I felt myself sliding along his body till his cockhead
rested against the soaked silk of my G-string, hard and hot, and he stroked
against my clit over and over and over. When he released my arms, one big
hand held my ass, keeping me pushed against him.

The other hand was fisted in my hair. He held me fast, and once again my
cries of orgasm were muffled on his tongue.

When his mouth left mine it went to my ear, talking low.

"pretty girl, I want your cunt so hot you go crazy. You got all dressed up
for me, didn't you? Pretty bitch, you want it rough, you like it like that?"

"Yes!" I gasped, still riding the last waves of come, wanting more.

"Then tell me. Ask for it. Beg me!"

He pulled the scarf from around my neck, threw me easily onto my back.
He pinned my arms over my head and bound my wrists with the scarf, talking
in his low daddy voice, playing my game:

"You want it, pretty bitch? You're going to get it, Miss Special. So you
think your cunt is good enough for my meat? Can't get what you need from
straight boys? You're gonna need it bad before you get an inch of me, baby.
Spread'em, that's right, spread for me, show it to me, let me have a good look,
I haven't seen one of these in a real long time ... You know what I usually
do with this cock, don't you? Is that what you want, is that what straight
boys don't give you? Want it in your ass, make you be Daddy's boy again,
hmmmm? ... No, you want it in your pussy, baby, I can feel it. Just shove it
all inside you, you want to feel it open you up. Can you take it?"

Now he was reddening my ass with slaps, the dress was pulled up to my
waist, and from nowhere he clicked open a knife. I gasped and whimpered, but
he just used it to cut the G-string off and it disappeared again. He slapped my
pussy with his cock, scattering drops of my wetness, stopping short before I
came, whispering, "Want it, pretty bitch? Want it all?" And I writhed against

him and begged him:

"Jesus, please, give it to me, Daddy! Please ... please!"

He was a consummate tease, this daddy; I wondered dimly if his boys tried to wiggle their assholes onto his just-out-of-reach cock the way I was trying to capture it with my hungry cunt. Not so much difference between one hunger and another, after all.

He reached for a rubber, worked it over his cockhead and rolled it down the shaft. The encasement made his big cock strain harder. As he knelt between my spread-wide legs, I murmured, "Give it to me, give it to me, give ..." – and in a long plunge, he did.

It felt so good to be filled so full, and to smell the hot leather and cock and pussy and feel the chaps against my legs. The second thrust came harder than the first, and a look of sexy concentration played across my leather daddy's face as he settled in for a long, hard, pounding ride.

It was my turn to talk to him as I met his strokes with thrusts of my own, letting my pinned-down body fill with delicious tension that would build up to even more intense peaks.

"... Oh, yeah, just like that, give me your cock, baby, fill up my pussy, yeah ... Give it to me, give it to me, you know I can take it, hard, yeah, come on ... Fuck my cunt like you fuck your boy's asses, make me take it from you, yeah, don't stop, don't ever stop, just try to outlast me, Daddy – you can fuck me all night, fill that rubber with a big hot load and I'll come just thinking about you, just give it to me ... Just give it to me, make me, make me ... come ..."

And it was all lost in cries and sobs and breath taking over. Somehow he'd untied my hands, and I held him and came and came and came, and the wild ride was over with half a dozen bucking thrusts. I heard his yells mingle with mine, and I reached down to pull cock and rubber free from my cunt and feel the heft of jism in my hand as we lay together in a tangle of sweaty limbs, not man and woman, just animals, two sated animals.

I drifted off to sleep and woke again as he was working the tight, sweaty dress over my head and off. My red leather shoes glowed against the white sheets.

"Hellion," he said as my eyes opened, "faggot in a woman's body, bitch-goddess, do you intend to sleep in your exquisite red shoes?"

I held them up for him to take off, one and then the other, and he placed respectful kisses on each toe before he set them on the bed.

"No," I said, "that's too femmy, even for me."

"And what does a man need to do with you around," he continued, pulling off my stockings, "to get fucked? Call your brother?"

He hadn't seen all the contents of my trick bag. I reached for it and spilled it onto the floor: three dildos, a harness, and a pair of long rubber gloves fell out. I promised that in the morning he could take his pick. I was dying to show Daddy what else a femme can do.

A Different Hunger

D. Franklin

For once my white blouse, black fitted jacket and short black skirt feel like Parisian chic rather than office-wear as I go inside the arts centre. Even my heels seem to ache less. Knowing that I'm going to see The Hunger with you tonight helps, since you're into vampires, and I love anything featuring Catherine Deneuve. I head for the cafe, and buy a tomato juice since its bloody colour puts me further in the mood for the film. I nab an empty seat with the best view of the whole cafe and take out my copy of Marie Claire to read until you arrive. You've warned me that you had a meeting with a horror zine editor who might want you to do a front cover, so I don't mind waiting. I feel better off assuming you'll arrive late after some successful negotiations – you could do with some more recognition for your artwork.

In the meantime I can indulge in some erotic daydreaming while I glance through my magazine. I'm looking forward to seeing The Hunger in the cinema again after so long. I remember inventing all sorts of erotic scenes beforehand when it first came out. I wasn't disappointed, despite all those billowing curtains and David Bowie. I wonder for a moment whether you'll say it's not as good as Interview with the Vampire. You know me well enough to know that I'll only have eyes for Deneuve, as I've had ever since I first saw her in the film.

I glance up from Marie Claire and take a look around the cafe. There are a few people dotted around. I imagine that the elegantly-dressed woman at a nearby table is accompanied by a cute-looking, well-hung toyboy rather than her stroppy teenage son. My eye then lights on a middle-aged man on his own carefully eating soup. Small build, dark brown hair with a side parting. A grey-green tweed jacket, white shirt and dark green tie. He eats with a precision that is somewhere between good table manners and fastidiousness. I immediately wonder if he's going to see The Hunger too. Perhaps he has been told to see it. I smile to myself at the thought of how nervous he would be to be seen in public attending the film under orders from his Mistress, a helplessly enthralled Renfield to her Countess Dracula. I imagine that she has made him wear women's panties underneath his clothes to humiliate him, and to remind him of her complete control and ownership. I begin to sense the delicious terror coming off him in waves, the carefully-controlled eating the

31

result of his acute consciousness of what he is wearing beneath his trousers, and why he's at the arts centre in the first place. Doubtless he'll have to report back to Mistress after seeing the film, and describe what he saw. Mistress, having seen the film herself, would instantly know if he had got a detail wrong. Mistress would then demand to see the panties he'd been wearing. She would inspect them as if handling particularly nasty toxic waste – since they had, after all, been worn by a pathetic slave – and she would wrinkle her nose in disgust at the inevitable sight of dried pre-come on the frilly pink cotton.

Or perhaps it would be even worse than that, and he has come in his trousers. He was unable to resist the erotic pull of the film and had secretly brought himself off in the cinema, only to realise with horror moments after his ecstasy that he would have to confront Mistress with the evidence. The fear is written on his face as Mistress excoriates him for his disgusting behaviour, and his infidelity in finding someone other than Mistress even remotely attractive. His timorous protest is ignored as Mistress swiftly decides on his punishment. She selects a cane from the rack on the dungeon wall, and commands him to bend over and count off the dozen strokes she will give him – and thank her properly after each one. The stripes sear across his buttocks as he complies perfectly – only to come on the very last stroke, his body shuddering with delight and torment as his cock spurts onto the dungeon floor. His failure to control himself will result in her giving him a further stroke for every minute of the film. He really is in trouble now ...

I feel a pleasant tingling between my legs from the thought of the man's hapless fate at the hands of his imaginary Mistress just as you arrive with the editor. You look like a studenty couple. She is in a baggy black jumper, a long mauve tie-dye skirt and black DM's; you are in a tight black denim jacket, skinny black jeans and 70's-style trainers. You've both got long hair: yours is still fair, slightly wavy and down to just past your neck; hers is longer, straighter and dark brown with a hint of black. Despite the fact that you are at least a head taller than she is, you look as if you belong together. You and the editor finally sit down by the big front window without you spotting me: obviously you're still too busy discussing ideas even for coffee. Luckily for me, you sit in profile. She has an oval, madonna-like face, and no make-up. I think I catch a glint of what might be a pierced eyebrow – very modish: she could be a Goth in daylight conditions. You still seem to have kept the best of a teenager's smooth clear skin despite the fact that you're only a year younger than me. I notice how tight your black X-files T-shirt fits over your skinny flat torso. I begin to wonder if you're still too good-looking to be straight, that you're the special best friend of a girl who finds lads a turn-off, but then I think perhaps you haven't told me you and the editor are a couple, and it's your feminine side that attracts her.

As you talk and share jokes, I realise that I really need to see the two of you late at night, when you're both dressed up for a night out. She would be transformed into a creature of the night; skin pale, eyes dark with heavy seductive make-up, ringed with black. She'll have swapped the baggy shapelessness of her daywear for something floaty in black lace; or possibly the slimness of her body would be revealed by the tightest of clinging black, maybe even rubber or leather, matched by high heels and long black velvet gloves, fat silver jewel-studded rings on each finger. You would compliment her dress sense: your eyes would be lined and shaded, your face powdered and rouged, just enough to blur any clear distinction between male and female. The black string T-shirt over your smooth flat chest would be echoed by fishnet tights, but disrupted by leather shorts and big flat boots. Anyone would have to look twice, and look again to be sure whether you were a tall, athletic girl or a fey young man, and even then they would remain unsure. The confusing deception would be part of the fun for both of you, seeing how many people would assume you were both female when you were out on the town.

In private you would blend and blur genders and roles as you make love. The spectrum of your sexual games would start with her riding you, imagining that the hardness thrusting between her thighs belongs to her and not you. Perhaps you would even change positions so that she lies between your raised knees in a parody of missionary sex. My fantasy of the two of you then blurs into a scene of faux-lesbian embraces, where you are her secret Sapphic lover. She is about to initiate you into the joys of oral sex, the slick salt taste of a woman's lubricious cunt, the universe of pleasure that originates in the tiny pearl of her clitoris, the endless delight of reaching climax after climax. Perhaps you both have separate fantasies of that encounter as you go down on her. For her it is a long-held, favourite dream that enables her imagination to soar and her body to let go completely, expressing its liberation in the way her hips move and undulate against your lips and tongue, urging and demanding all you can give and more. For you, the illicit thrill of imagining yourself as female lies at the tip of your tongue, not yet expressed in words but in every lick and caress of her wet sex. You discover a skill in pleasuring her that comes from some secret feminine part of yourself that you long to express with her someday – and the hope makes you lap at her sweet sex even more greedily.

At the far end of your erotic play, both your secret wishes would come true. A total reversal of roles and identities. She would scrape her long hair back, pin it all up to tuck beneath a severe military cap. A black rubber catsuit simultaneously lends her a masculine toughness and a feminine curvaceousness, reinforced by her black knee-high boots and the strap-on dildo thrusting menacingly from her crotch. You would be fully feminised; a matching black bra, panties, garter belt, seamed stockings and cheap, tarty heels. Your hair would be teased and back-combed to a big, southern-belle girlishness. Secretly, your sex throbs with the pleasure of how convincing you appear when she makes you look in the mirror – so intensely feminine that you lose your sense of who you really are. Only the tug of her fingers on the black silk choker around your throat breaks your erotic rapture. You turn to face her and notice the slight mocking smile at the corners of her mouth. She orders you to your knees. Your eyes draw level with the sex-toy jutting from between her hips. Your big, lipsticked mouth slackens with lust as you're forced to take the phallus down your throat. The magical transference of the male sex you've both imagined becomes that much more real as your head rocks back and forth on her hardness. Your tongue, more used to pleasuring her woman's sex as you imagine yourself as a woman, now must pleasure her as she demands it like a man. The path of your imagination twists and turns like the action of your tongue, and flows like the saliva you lather onto her cock. You feel her hands tangle in your hair as her hips begin to pump, forcing you to take that little bit more, to swallow that little bit deeper. You feel your body grow hot in response, hotter than it's ever been, as though this encounter is more real than any sex you've had before.

She pulls out abruptly, as if she were about to climax in your mouth. Mixing lust and new-found aggression, she turns you round and makes you kneel on all fours. Stripping aside your flimsy panties, she kneels and positions her slickened sex at your rear opening. You groan with lust tinged with fear as you both ready yourselves. Then you feel her easing her way in, a little at a time, until she is inside you to the very hilt. For both of you the fantasy is now made flesh completely. Every sensation of penetration is both shared and felt, known and imagined. Her thrusts into your yielding body are steady and relentless, driving home her possession of you time and again. You are both lost in this fantasy, my fantasy, of the two of you fucking in the mirror image of your everyday selves, until you both come from the warped, ecstatic sensations of filling and being filled that do not usually belong to your original genders.

My fantasy of your complex gender-fucking makes me feel very horny. I sip more tomato juice and read Marie Claire while my mind toys with fading images of cross-dressed erotic power-games. A random image of the editor queening your face, lipstick smeared across two pairs of wet lips, stays with me for several moments before I realise with a jolt that I'm supposed to be getting the tickets for tonight. I quickly finish my tomato juice and check the time: I've several minutes to spare. I consider slipping off to the ladies' to bring myself to orgasm since my clit is pulsing like a virgin's inviting vein and I feel as aroused as if I've actually watched the two of you at play. Unfortunately for me, I see the two of you stand up. The editor gives you a peck on the cheek, and leaves – a pity. I leave my seat, pick up my Marie Claire and walk over. You finally notice me and smile warmly.

"I didn't see you over there!" you tell me after we've exchanged kisses. "You should've joined us."

"You looked busy," I reply with a smile. "Were you planning something kinky?"

Your face turns the same deep red as your lips were in my fantasy, and I feel myself climaxing quietly at the sight and the memory.

"How did you know?" you eventually ask.

I smile enigmatically, deciding not to tell you that I spanked the editor at a fetish club a fortnight ago. One day I'll get her to play Susan Sarandon to my Catherine Deneuve too.

Unless I can seduce you into the idea first.

Alice

Piglet

I thought I'd found my ultimate truth, only now I'm not so sure. It's all a bit of a let down really. And not for want of trying to make it work. I did what I could, I wanted to be accepted. It seemed expected that I should cut my hair – I cut it, bought a labyris to show my conviction. Now I discuss issues in wimmin-only discos with these people who wouldn't even approach me when I had make up on.

Still, I guess I'm getting some credibility.

I'm here, with Suzanne, who is nice to look at – all baby features and hippy scarves. We had sex. Well I think we did. She was very gentle. She played with my clit and went down on me a bit. I didn't want to do anything to her – it felt like I'd have to ask permission in triplicate or something.

What's it like for the rest of them? I search for clues in the way they interact, the way they touch. I look for hunger and passion in their eye contact. Do they make love differently to Suzanne or is it the same gentle squishing and fondling? I don't get it. Perhaps I'm just made wrong.

I watch Suzanne talking now, in this room full of her friends. Her face is baby serious, baby round and baby wise. Someone has draped a scarf over the lamp and the light is mellow in here. Mellow on round, attentive faces.

Someone has some dope and the wine is cold. Never mind the curious faces at the door now and then, as the other partygoers peer in: "Look at the dykes in there."

"Oh yeah."

Never mind. I feel good. I am a woman-loving woman now. I hear my name in the conversation. Didn't I once have a really bad time? Suzanne's friends look towards me offering sympathy for old hurts. Focusing some kind of healing energy my way with anxious and caring faces ...

... This is the wrong time to be captivated by someone beautiful in the kitchen, just through the gap in the door, but you know what it's like – just a glimpse and you have to go and take a closer look.

I lean over to squishy Suzanne who puts her hand supportively on my shoulder. "Who's that woman, Suzanne?" I ask. It becomes plain that I haven't been paying the conversation much attention.

"I beg your pardon?" she says, closer now.

"Who's that woman through there?"

Now, as if to a child that's behaving in a way she can't comprehend, she tells me: "I think her name's Alice."

Someone's coming out of the kitchen: they hold the door wide. I see Alice. Alissss. Goth creation. Dark eyes. Freaky black hair. Red lips. Black velvet gloves and lace. Exudes femininity in fishnet stockings. Leather boots laced up tight, laced up high.

She sees me looking. Under her gaze I am a non-entity. She tosses her head with an indifferent air. Holds herself so I get her profile, her parted lips.

"She's very attractive," I hear myself saying. It is the understatement of understatements.

Suzanne is watching me nervously. "Think of all she has to do to look like that," she says. But it doesn't put me off. She's like a fine instrument that's been worked on and tuned – every detail elaborate, every note perfect.

"Excuse me" – sometimes you have to say that and just get up and go. It saves explaining.

I step over the women hugging on bean bags and cushions. When I'm through the door I make for the kitchen and search for an empty glass. Is she watching me? I'm trying not to look stupid. I rinse one out under the tap. I'm high on fear. She could leave any minute.

My bottle going so I just have a sip of water. I make my way back, smile at Alice on the way out as if it's nothing. I hear myself say "Hello". She glares.

I crawl back to Suzanne and ask her for a hug. She says "Good" because she says she has something very important to tell me. "I'm changing my name," she says, "I'm going to be called 'Orchid' from next month, Orchid Moonblossom." She goes on to explain the significance of the change but it goes over my head and is lost.

An hour later the bathroom mirror shows me my pale little face in triplicate. I wail at my shorn hair, T-shirt and jeans. At least my T-shirt is black. Now if I mess my fringe up at the front ...

Someone's knocking to come in. Hell, quick, do I need to pee? It can wait, someone is obviously more desperate.

I unlock the door. It is pushed open roughly and to my surprise in marches my goddess, Alice. She rushes over to the toilet to pee. "Shut the door," she tells me.

I go to open the door properly and leave, but she calls out again behind me: "Don't open it. Shut it! Lock the door." And keeping my eyes politely averted, I do as she says. I hear the flush being pulled. Now I dare to glance behind me. Alice has decided to sit on the edge of the bath. I feel I need permission to leave, or is it just that she's so beautiful I want to tempt fate as long as I can? Facing the door I wait for something to happen.

"What does your girlfriend do?" comes Alice's voice abruptly.

"She's a yoga instructor," I say, my voice croaking, sounding awful. I turn around slowly, feast my eyes on this beautiful woman. Her dress is a dark green velvet hugging bulging curves. Her eyes sparkle with mischief.

"Are you into yoga then?" she asks me.

"Not really." I hang my head.

"She hasn't taught you any yoga then?" Alice persists.

"I don't think I'd be any good at it." I say quickly. She's making me feel so uncomfortable but I can't just walk away, can I?

From her perch on the bath-side, she smiles and says: "Do me a headstand."

Oh come on. I turn and put my hand on the door handle. "The floor's too hard." I say and I'm going to leave. Then she's behind me and her hands are on my belt.

"Use your jeans as a cushion for your head." She smiles, her hands are quickly unfastening my belt, my button and zip. I can't move. My hands are stuck to the door. I can hear the music being turned up louder in the living room, the rest of the party carrying on without us, as Alice quietly goes about sliding my jeans down my legs, releasing them to the cool air of the bathroom.

She takes me by the hand and throws my jeans down in a little heap next to the bath. "There," she says, "Against the wall. Get down." So I kneel on the floor and put my head down.

It takes a few attempts for me to kick my legs up. When I've straightened them against the wall I'm about to laugh and say "There!" but Alice's hands are suddenly sliding down my legs and spreading them apart slightly.

What's she doing? I can't see properly. She's reaching over into the bath. Now I jolt in shock and hear my own gasps and grunts. She has the shower head between my legs and is blasting my cunt with cold water. I lose my balance and tumble painfully onto my knees.

"You'll flood the floor!" I say and throw the shower head into the bath. Alice is sitting back and laughing. Her dress has got splashed a little, but I'm soaked.

There are little puddles of water on the floor now. Alice wades her hands in them and flicks more water at me as I try to sit up properly. I grab her wrist but she is stronger and throws me off with a sneer.

"You ever been spanked?" she asks me, matter of factly.

"What?"

"Have you?"

"Yes." Well, it was a long time ago.

"By a woman?"

"No, men," I tell her. Something I'd never dared tell Suzanne.

"Get over my knee, girl," she grins.

She puts the toilet seat down and sits there. I place myself across her. My feet just touch the floor and my head is low. The water still gushes from the shower into the bath. Alice's hand strikes my arse hard and fast. It stings like hell.

"Try to take it. You're taking it fine," she says.

But I'm not. I'm yelping with each blow. She doesn't let up until her hand is too sore to carry on.

She gets me down on my back on the floor and leans over me on all fours. Her long hair falls across my face as she comes closer. White teeth gleam from softest dark red lips. Now her face against mine and a teasing tongue at my mouth. I hold her round the waist and guide her down on top of me, press those sumptuous breasts against mine.

There's a knocking in the background, it gets louder and more insistent. Someone's calling my name. I can't make out who it is because the door is thick and the shower is still running. I ignore it, so does she. Then we hear the louder thud of someone apparently attempting to break the door down.

I tap her arm and she gets up unsteadily. "I'm coming, okay," I yell, but whoever it is outside probably can't hear me. I unlock the door and open it a tiny crack. "What?" I ask, without looking out.

Now the door is pushed open wide and Suzanne is there in the doorway. Her little mouth opens wide as she looks at me and Alice and the state we're in. Her shoulders heave and her face goes red. She lunges at me saying "You ... !" but some of her friends are there to restrain her.

"Orchid," they say, "Calm down."

But Suzanne is looking into my face with pure hatred – a change from the political correctness and understanding. What can she say to me? Insults have never been her forte, though if carefully and coldly placed I give them much respect.

Not Suzanne, no style. She just looks bitterly at me ... and flings them.

What he did

Thomas S. Roche

John liked guys; there was no question about that. But in guys, as in everything else, he had perverse, somewhat decadent tastes. And he had always liked to put people in situations that would test their boundaries, destroy their resistance, take away their feigned innocence. He liked to see people, particularly men, lose control. That's why he did what he did.

....

Adrienne and I worked the same shift, at the comic shop, five to eleven, four days a week. So she and I were getting to know each other pretty well. Adrienne was a fag hag to begin with, that was for sure. You can always tell by the comics a girl reads. And she knew I was into boys. Maybe she just wanted something safe, a guy who wouldn't want to own her, or maybe just a guy who wouldn't bellyache about wearing a condom. She knew I was bi, not gay, but she also knew John and I were together. That night John came in, he stayed for the half-hour after closing while Adrienne and I cleaned and locked up and counted out the drawer. The two of them talked like old friends, about Wonder Woman and Captain Marvel, sexual innuendos periodically drifting into the conversation. I could tell he was baiting her. I was sure that he and Adrienne were flirting, which didn't quite add up.

"That chick has a crush on you, Paul," John told me as we walked home up Haight street, through the mid-November chill.

I responded without responding. "Maybe she has a crush on you."

"Nah. She's a fag hag, but she's not a glutton for punishment or anything."

I considered Adrienne in my mind's-eye. Adrienne had the look I so adored, the waiflike black-clad pose, the deathrocker bob dyed black, the studs in her lower lip and nostril and the eyeliner and tattoo of a bat on the back of her neck, the rings of silver around her ears from top to bottom. Her sexuality was just overt enough to snare my interest, not brazen enough to strike me as that of a *poseur*. Plus, she had great tits. I like guys fine, and I had been monogamous with John for over a year now. I was totally into him, but of course I still looked. And John knew who got my attention.

"Maybe you should ask her out on a date," I said. "And find out. You could take her to the drive-in and fuck her in the back seat while you watch *I Was a Teenage Fag Hag* or something. I hear it's playing down in Serramonte."

"I don't have a car. Besides – you'd go mad with jealousy," he told me, leaning over and whispering into my ear. "You'd take a meat cleaver to the

40

both of us. It'd be a tragic affair. In all the papers and everything." I snorted in disgust. We let it drop, and that was that. But the matter didn't go out of my mind, and hours later I was still thinking of her as John fucked me from behind on the futon, the two of us tangled in the black sandalwood-scented sheets, his hands on my waist, groaning his midnight pleasures in a cloud of incense and pot smoke. I thought about her as I came: I imagined her stretched on the bed next to us, my fingers inside her as our tongues intertwined.

And it was afterwards as John lit up our post-sex joint that he whispered to me, his breath all fragrant clouds and intoxication, "you were thinking about her."

....

Adrienne was a hell of a flirt. John had been right, she had a crush on me. She wasn't necessarily interested in doing anything about it, though – not at first. At least, that was my reading. She just liked flirting with me, and of course I responded in kind. Her body continued to impose itself on my fantasies, especially when John whispered to me about her. After a while I stopped complaining when he did it, and just let the images flow into my mind when John said he wanted to watch me fuck her, taste her cunt on my cock. John had never even fucked a chick, and had never expressed an interest in doing so. But it seemed that my desires fascinated him even more than his own.

I began noticing things about Adrienne, little details of the sort you only notice about someone when you have a crush on them. Like what sort of bra she wore, how she stood when she leaned up against the counter, where she bought her shoes. How the rings in her nipples would show through her baby-doll dress when she moved her shoulders just right. The way she smelled when she got close enough to me. The feel of her ass brushing slightly against me as she squeezed past me in the close quarters behind the comic-store counter, maybe just a trifle closer than she needed to be. The way she would blush afterwards.

"You're fucking her, Paul. You're on top of her, pounding into her pussy. You like that, pussy? I hear it tastes real good to some guys ... you got her tits in your hands ..." This while John was behind me, fucking his rubber-sheathed prick into my ass. His lips up against my ear, his hand around my cock. Jerking it. After I came in slick streams all over his gloved hand he told me that one day he was going to bring me home a sweet treat and share her with me on this very futon.

"All walk and no talk makes a gayboy dull as fuck," I sighed good-naturedly. But I didn't take him seriously.

Adrienne became more and more of a fascinating creature, the shape of her body seeming more exotic every day, the curves of her hips like those of some elaborate statue, the shape of her ass like harem pillows ... she paid more and more attention to me. It had gone beyond a "crush." For both of us.

I knew she'd been dumped a couple of months before, and her boyfriend sounded like a real creep. She had had a couple of things going with girls, but that was at least a couple of years back. I knew she was on the rebound, and rebounding hard, and that spelled bad news to me. I didn't want to encourage her. It seemed sort of unfair to do so. Maybe it was just a bit too easy when I got that other job at the art store, and the $1.00 an hour more wasn't so much the draw as the fact that I wouldn't have the perpetual sexual tension of being close to Adrienne. She seemed sad at my passing, and we promised to keep in touch and have dinner some time.

I was glad to be away from the desire. It wasn't that I felt guilty or anything – it was just a perpetual confusion, a desire I felt easier living without.

Still, I missed her. I missed the flirtation, the attention, the chance to look down her shirt when she leaned just so. I missed her sense of humour, her friendship. But I knew it couldn't work, us just being friends. That's what made Adrienne so hot to me. There was a sense of urgency, of a need that could not be denied.

John was disappointed. He kept talking to me about her, and the fantasy grew more intense because I wasn't seeing Adrienne every day. John would work my cock with his hand while he told me, in excruciating detail, how Adrienne was jerking me off. It always got him totally hot.

Maybe John's suspicions and fetishes were encouraged by the fact that I only read straight porn, and sometimes got off reading hetero sex manuals like *The Sensuous Woman* and *Total Sex*. I don't know, it was something weird about me, the thought of all those married straight people fucking like weasels in their suburban houses always got me going. So I probably knew as much about women's bodies as I did about men's, though I'd only been to bed with two women in my entire life, and those were fleeting romances.

I was quite happy in my relationship with John. But when I read about tits and clits and cunnilingus and hetero anal sex, I found myself invariably thinking of Adrienne.

I missed her, all right. I missed the possibilities, and the knowledge that I just *might* lose control of myself in the stockroom and tear Adrienne's clothes off and fuck her wildly amid stacks of *Love and Rockets* and *Sandman* and *Hothead Paisan*. And she might do the same to me.

John missed her, too. He missed what Adrienne did to me, how she made me feel. That's why he did what he did, the fucker.

....

When I arrived at John's place I smelled the telltale scent of sandalwood incense. I knew something was going on. John was well aware that the smell of sandalwood made me desperately aroused. But he was also aware that I associated sandalwood quite intimately with Adrienne, who used to wear sandalwood body oil. Perhaps that's why I wasn't surprised when I found her on the futon, sitting cross-legged and smoking a clove cigarette. John was across from her in the big easy chair, the one he'd found at the thrift store. His legs were crossed and he smiled at me devilishly. "Paul ... we were wondering where you got to. Adrienne came by. Well, actually I invited her ..."

Adrienne smiled at me sheepishly. "Hi, Paul," she said. She looked a little nervous. She was as cute as ever. She had on a pair of black jeans and a tight lace top, outlining her breasts and making the rings in the nipples oh-so-slightly visible. I sat down at the opposite end of the futon from her, and we hugged awkwardly. The scent of her body made me very nervous. Plus, I knew something was up. John hadn't just "invited" Adrienne.

There was awkward small talk, as I tried to figure out what was going on. Then John decided to dispense with the pleasantries.

John was behind her smoothly, quickly, without missing a beat. Adrienne seemed to melt into his arms as he coaxed her head back, and she presented her lips for him. He kissed her, deeply, parting her lips and teasing out her tongue. Adrienne let out a little moan of abandon as John's arms came around her and one hand rested absently on her belly just below her breast.

John glanced up at me, but only for a second. I noticed a smirk as he went back to kissing Adrienne.

John had never kissed a girl before in his life. But he seemed to be doing OK. I felt a momentary wave of anger as I realized that he was doing this for my benefit. Then, suddenly, there was nothing. I was freed from my responsibility to fight off my desire for Adrienne. John was giving her to me. She was the most succulent of gifts, the willing one. I moved closer to her as John and she kissed. Tentatively, I leaned forward, feeling the pressure of her body against mine.

John released Adrienne, her lips slick with his spittle. She turned to me, her eyes sparkling and terrified, her face pale and ashen. Her lipstick was smeared. She took my hand in hers, and begged me with her eyes to kiss her.

As I did, I tasted her lipstick and felt the stud in the center of her lower lip. The lipstick struck me as much stranger than the piercing. It was the first time I'd tasted lipstick in years. Adrienne's whimper was faint, distant, as I descended upon her. John's hand closed around her breast and his tongue explored her left ear, as Adrienne and I kissed. Her smell overwhelmed me, sandalwood and roses. Her hand trailed invitingly up my throat, then her fingertips cupped my face. John reached out and took my wrist, holding me insistently. He placed my hand underneath Adrienne's shirt, and her eyes opened to me as I felt her nipple harden. I slipped my other hand into her hair, stroking her cheek with my thumb. John leaned over Adrienne's shoulder and began to kiss me, his hot tongue sliding deep into my mouth. Adrienne seemed buried in ecstasy, snuggling deep between the two of us and arching her back to press her breasts more fully into my grasp. I stroked the slick metal rings, fascinated by the way they felt. I had a boyfriend once who had rings in his nipples, but they felt nothing like this. The excitement was much more for me, the implied sense of bondage or submission being overwhelming. Then again, maybe it was the way that Adrienne squirmed underneath us. John nipped at my lower lip, biting gently, his breath coming sweet and hot as he nuzzled closer and placed his lips against my ear. "She's yours," he whispered, telling me what I wanted to hear. John could enjoy our tryst, could be part of it. I would even make sure he came, and that John must have known. But this fuck was for me, his gift to his lover. He had brought her to me for the pleasure of watching me have her.

The sandalwood incense had burned down, so the three of us went into the bedroom.

....

John and I began by undressing Adrienne. First came her lace shirt, very goth, peeled away to reveal a matching bra. She had larger breasts than I had expected. The bra opened in front. The rings in her nipples were thick and stainless-steel. I bent forward and took one in my mouth as John removed Adrienne's shoes and socks. The two of us helped her struggle out of her black jeans. She didn't wear underpants, which I found somehow fascinating. She stretched nude amid the tangled sheets of the futon, her face buried in the sweat-scented cloth. She breathed deep, as if the fragrance of the two male lovers was more to her than anything. John came up behind her, his shirt gone, his arms finding their way around Adrienne's waist as I played with her breasts.

John and I began to kiss again, and Adrienne just lay there, naked underneath us, watching wide-eyed as we kissed. I ran my hand over John's bare chest and Adrienne just watched me, her breathing short, her face growing bright red. She squirmed a little underneath us, unable to contain herself. But she wasn't asking for attention. She wanted to watch us. That excited me more, and so I relinquished my hold on John's lips and slipped my tongue into Adrienne's mouth. She put her arms around me and sank into my grasp as I kissed her, deep, toying with her tongue. I was fascinated by the feeling of that piercing against my mouth. Fascinated, too, by the feel of Adrienne's naked body between John's and my clothed bodies, rubbing against us, her bare thigh curving over my waist and pulling me closer, harder against her, her breasts pressed tight to my chest. She slid her hands under my shirt and ran them up my back, one on each side of my spine. Adrienne whimpered and moaned slightly; John had slid his hand between her ass-cheeks and was touching her cunt. I guess she liked that. John looked down at her body, watching with fascination, exploring the ways his touch made her feel.

John looked up at me, then, his eyes sparkling. He could tell I was enjoying myself, and that was enough for him. He bent forward and offered me a tender kiss.

His tongue tasted of Adrienne's lipstick. My hand, resting gently against Adrienne's hips, slid to meet his wrist. It felt the juices running along his fingers, and joined them. The two of us began to feel her up, toying with her lips, tormenting her clit. As we did, we continued kissing, and I felt Adrienne unfastening my belt.

Her hands circled my prick as John and I shared her sex. The curve of her thigh was so different from John's. Adrienne ran her black-nailed fingers up and down the length of my cock, rubbing her thumb on the underside of the head. John slipped his fingers out of Adrienne and lifted them to my face. He stared into my eyes as I did it, licking his fingertips one by one, then slipping them into my mouth, tasting her sex. Adrienne, watching, leaned forward to touch my cock with her lips.

She licked up the shaft, and I moaned softly. John looked at me hungrily, and I knew what he wanted me to do. He wanted to see it, wanted to know the texture and the feel of having it done in his presence, but John wasn't going to do it. I began to struggle out of my pants, easing Adrienne back before she could take my cockhead in her mouth.

Adrienne slid further back onto the futon, relaxing into John's arms. He had quickly gotten his pants off, and now the two of them were naked against each other. His cock pressed up against her ass. Adrienne turned her head and the two of them began to kiss again, John's hand lazing gently over her breasts, playing with her nipple-rings. Now the three of us were naked. I lowered myself to Adrienne's belly, kissing her soft flesh and toying with her navel-ring. Adrienne's body went taut against John's, her ass snuggling against him as I parted her thighs. Memories flooded back to me as I tasted her cunt. I licked slowly into the silky wetness, breathing her fragrance. I flickered my tongue across her lips and made my way to her clit. I closed my lips very gently around it and began to suckle. Adrienne choked, her mouth filled with John's tongue. I began to feed off of her cunt, drinking the taste and smell of it, swallowing hungrily. I curved my hand under her ass and began playing with her asshole, almost before I realized what I was doing. Adrienne's body stiffened again, but then she relaxed as she gave herself over to the sensations. So I didn't stop, but explored the feel of a woman's asshole as opposed to a man's. John must have liked that; between deep kisses with Adrienne, he looked down at what my hand was doing and smiled at me approvingly.

John reached out to the nightstand and handed me a rubber glove. Obediently, I put it on.

John next held out the bottle of lubricant, which he poured into my palm. I worked it over, getting my gloved hand slick with it. Then I began to work one finger into Adrienne's cunt.

Adrienne whimpered approvingly, reaching out to take John's cock in her hand. John slid an unlubricated condom over his prick and adjusted his body so that Adrienne could take him into her mouth. She lay on her back, head turned to the side and propped up on a pillow, as John eased his hips back and forth, sliding his cock between her parted lips. Her hands tangled in the rumpled sheets. Adrienne's ass lifted off of the futon, pressing her cunt hard into my grasp. I gave her two fingers, and from the slow, rhythmic fucking motions she made with her hips, she wanted more. I got three in there, which was the most I'd ever shoved up John's ass. It felt tight in her cunt, but somehow secure, inviting, hungry. I began working my fingers in and out.

Guided by my memories of *The Joy of (hetero)Sex*, I started pressing against Adrienne's clit with my thumb. Her hips began to rock faster. She was jerking John off while she sucked him, her lips closed tightly around the head of his cock. John was watching me as Adrienne went down on him. He looked like he was about ready to do it in her mouth. I had no idea the sight of me fingerfucking a woman would get him so hot. Adrienne was really into it, her whole body moving with the two of us. I really had no way of knowing what I was really doing to her, but I could tell from the spasms and contractions of her cunt that she was coming. But she didn't lose her grip on John's cock for a moment.

When her hips slowed down, I was struck by a sensuous and perverse urge. I eased my hands out of her cunt, reaching awkwardly to get more lube from the nightstand. John knew what he was doing. He grabbed the lube and poured it for me as I held out my rubber-gloved hand.

Adrienne stiffened again as I parted her ass-cheeks and touched her tight hole. I could sort of guess from the way she moved that she'd never really been touched much back there. That was what turned me on so. I'd spent so much of my adult life getting fucked in the ass that I couldn't let her go without, though I guessed it wouldn't feel the same for a woman as it did for a man. She continued sucking John's cock, making him sway and moan as he crouched over her. Adrienne once again relaxed into the sensations as I worked the lube into her crack, feeling the gentle "give" of her asshole. I gently pressed one finger in, imagining that I was with a virgin guy, being as tender as possible. Adrienne sucked her breath in sharply as the finger slipped into her. She seemed uncomfortable for a second, and then it was all right.

"Oh, fuck yeah," breathed John, watching me intently. I went very slowly. By the time I had two fingers inside her ass, Adrienne was moaning and John was ready to come. He did so with a groan and a forward slump against Adrienne's body as I managed to squeeze a third finger into her ass. Adrienne writhed underneath him, her hand thrust up between his legs and playing with his ass, middle finger stroking the outside of his asshole, up and down in quick strokes. I knew from experience what she was feeling. The pulse of John's cock as it spurted his come into the condom. The warm feeling as the tip of the condom filled. The squeeze of his buns as the spasms went through him. The rush of terror at the warmth in her mouth and the feeling: what if the condom breaks. Then the wave of momentary regret, usually just for a half-second, and then, the delicious sensation as the thought flowed through you, "so the fuck what ..."

I eased my fingers out of Adrienne's ass, knowing she was ready for something else. I managed to get the glove off and toss it into the garbage without splattering anyone. Adrienne looked spent, but I knew there was at least one indulgence she hadn't yet been granted. She bent forward as John, panting and flushed, handed her a Trojan red unlubed. John reached out and took my shoulders, guiding me back onto the bed. I stretched out as Adrienne got the condom over the head of my prick and started licking down the shaft. She paused over my balls, licking them hungrily, taking each one into her mouth. John joined her, putting his mouth over the head of my cock and pushing the condom down. Then she and John began to kiss, sharing my prick. For a while they worked bottom to top, John at the balls while Adrienne swallowed me, then vice versa, then back again. Finally, John eased his body up against mine and started kissing me while I moaned and writhed. His arms went around me and he stroked my chest and face, nibbling on my lips and sucking at my tongue as he squeezed and kneaded my nipples. All the while, Adrienne had her way with my cock.

Adrienne swallowed me again, her fingers curved around the base of my cock. She rubbed the latex over her face, smearing her cheeks with her saliva while she looked up at me. She stroked the cock between her tits, something I really didn't expect a chick to do anywhere outside a porn movie. But I had to admit it was pretty hot. Then she went back to sucking my cock. I could feel the ridge of the stud in her lower lip, pressing against the condom, smooth but somehow threatening, exciting.

She slipped her hand between my legs, sliding the fingers under my ass-cheeks. I felt her finger going home, stroking my asshole, bringing on my climax. Adrienne knew how to make me come. I wondered if John had had a talk with her.

When it did come, it was like a lifelong need suddenly overwhelmed in an explosion of brilliance. Adrienne's mouth was hot around my cock as she worked my asshole and milked my prick.

Adrienne kept her lips closed on the softening knob of my cockhead for a long time. Tiny spasms went through me as she suckled on my soft cock. Every movement of her lips and tongue made my body twitch in agony/ecstasy. It was too much stimulation, but somehow I liked it. And Adrienne was enjoying herself pushing my limits. After a while, she stopped sucking me, slipping the condom off and tossing it into the trash. John slipped away from me, running his hands through Adrienne's hair as the three of us curled up into a complicated ball. I faded in and out of consciousness, losing myself in the warmth of the two bodies surrounding me.

....

I slept deep and hard, exhausted. I dreamed hard, too, hot and deep like it was reality, the way you dream when you're horny as fuck. But I found myself awake, in the middle of the night, not sure at what point I'd dreamed of myself fucking Adrienne and at what point I'd actually done it. Not sure if the taste of her cunt and her asshole, the smell of my come as I smeared it over her body, was real or imagined. Adrienne's body was pressed against mine, every inch of our naked flesh seeming to touch. I was in a dazed stupor, hardly aware of what I was doing. Adrienne's legs were spread around my belly and she was rubbing herself hard against me while she kissed me violently.

I could hardly breathe, the excitement was so overwhelming. I had completely forgotten, for a moment, that John existed. I felt no guilt, no danger. Adrienne's body felt so good against mine, it never occurred to me to stop for a moment. Suddenly Adrienne, who must have been more awake than I was, got a condom open and over my cock. Then her thighs were spread around me, and she was sitting up over my body as she rubbed the head of my prick between her cunt-lips. She worked the head into the notch of her cunt and sank down on me, her breath coming short. Her cunt felt tight, as if she hadn't been fucked for a while. I knew she hadn't been, but there was still plenty of lube in there from where I'd fingered her earlier. Adrienne pressed her hips down, pushing my cock into her as deep as it would go so the head ground against her cervix. She bent down and began to kiss me, moaning softly. She started rocking her hips back and forth. I choked on her tongue and on the smell of her hair and body. My cock seemed alive inside her. She pulled on me hard, rolling me over on top of her – over the edge of the futon. The two of us fell the six inches from the futon to the floor and I came down hard on top of her, pushing my cock inside her, fucking her slow and deep. She dug her teeth into my throat, holding on to my ass. She started playing with my asshole as I fucked her. The sensations joined somewhere deep in my body, and it was almost like being fucked by her. I kept fucking her, holding back my orgasm, feeling Adrienne keep the muscles of her cunt tight around my shaft and milking my prick. I rested one hand on her breast, squeezing gently, teasing her nipple with my thumb.

"I'm going to come," she whispered, nuzzling my ear. "Don't come yet. Please don't come yet. Keep fucking me."

I held back, feeding her long, slow, hard strokes into her cunt, keeping the rhythm. Adrienne's thighs closed tighter around me with each thrust, as she got closer and closer. She whispered again and again, "Please keep fucking me ... keep fucking me ..." and so on, letting me know that she was getting there slowly. Just knowing that she was about to come while I fucked her was enough to keep me working, pumping my hips up and down on Adrienne's supple, spread body, begging her with my cock to cream all over me.

Then she came, a silent exhalation – no moan, no scream, just a long, low breath and a spasm of her cunt on my prick. I started fucking her faster, trying to bring on my own orgasm. Adrienne, satisfied with her climax but wanting mine, started stroking my crack, feeling for my asshole, working me into a frenzy. I finally was able to let myself go, and I came inside her, kissing her hard.

I reached down, holding the filled condom as I pulled out of her cunt. It had been so different than fucking a guy's ass.

Adrienne and I squirmed back onto the futon. I was still half-asleep. I realized in my stupor that John was laying there, awake, eyes wide. He had been watching us the whole time.

Adrienne got out of bed to go to the bathroom. John leaned over and started kissing me, just a few deep, hard, possessive thrusts of his tongue as his hand drifted over my soft cock. He rubbed me down around the base, where my pubic hair was damp and matted with the juices of Adrienne's cunt. Then John rolled over, leaving his back to me, leaving Adrienne and me to sleep entwined like straight people. But I saw there was a smirk on his face as he turned.

The three of us curled up and slept the rest of the night. I felt totally happy. When the sun broke through the sky, Adrienne was gone. She'd let herself out.

....

John and I fucked long and hard that Saturday morning, him sucking my cock while he played with my ass. As he did me, I smelled her on the sheets, a feminine scent mixed with ours, but strangely, her memory didn't overwhelm me the way it had. I was content to be with just John.

John spread my ass cheeks, entering me from behind and fucking me for as long as either of us could stand it before tossing the condom and letting himself go all over my back. He licked his own come up, smearing it into my smooth skin and whispering to me that he loved it when I played submissive. Which was par for the course.

Adrienne and I talked a few times on the phone over the next week. We were going to have lunch together, and soon. Eventually I asked her if she'd had fun that night.

"Of course," she told me, her voice dropping to a whisper. "Having sex with two guys – two queer guys. It was everything I'd ever wanted in the whole world."

I froze, unable to ask her the question that begged to be asked – whether she'd like to come back.

We sort of lost touch, calling each other every few weeks but never managing to get together. I figured she was afraid. I was, too. John didn't mention her much, but one night he whispered to me, jokingly, that I didn't give head as well as Adrienne. I didn't pursue it, and I wasn't really hurt. Just a little lost.

That was the way it went for a while. For many weeks. The other day, Adrienne and I ran into each other on the street. We went and got coffee. She was as gorgeous as ever. She kept leaning toward me, her delicious smell drifting into my mind as I watched her, and a couple of times I really thought she was going to kiss me. But she didn't. We promised each other we would get together sometime soon, and as we parted we hugged longer than we were supposed to. I had a hard-on on the bus later, thinking about Adrienne. It was good to see her. It was really fucking good to see her.

I felt a strange melancholy later, as I thought about what John and Adrienne and I had done that night. John and I had never really talked about it that much. I knew that John had enjoyed it as much as I had, maybe more. I was sure that blowjob he got from Adrienne wasn't exactly just a fringe benefit. It's taken me months after the actual event to understand it, but I knew that in bringing her home, he'd acknowledged an intense attraction for her as well as an intense attraction for me. But even if what got him hot about Adrienne was what she, and her female body, did to me, by the very nature of the situation it did something to him. *That* was why he did what he did, the *fucker*. And now every once in a while I catch him slipping. He's not the faggot he's always pretended to be, though he still fucks me better than anyone. His brain and his balls are more complicated than anyone might have suspected. I'm only now starting to figure the fucker out, and he keeps throwing me curve balls. I even walked in on him reading my copy of *The Sensuous Woman* once, when he thought I was asleep in the other room. He had a hard-on.

Gubei Lover

Rachel Martin

After four months of extended dinners, traipsing about bars and lying on his couch watching his lips chain-smoke Cuban cigars, Ash gives up. It's over. She's heard about the Hong Kong wife, the ex-wife, the 10 year old son, the 19 year old Shanghainese boy lover, the boss, the box-making plant, the endless trips to Beijing, Hangzhou, Tokyo and America. She's heard the continuous declarations of trust and comfort and all about the growing feelings of intimacy he has for her. She's stomached his ready admissions of wariness concerning her, her being western, white, tall, big, outspoken, up front and completely unchinese. How it's hard for him to get his head around the concept of her being his lover when for 36 years he's viewed white woman as only friends. She's heard that these things take time. That he needs to get to know her ... that he likes her increasingly but he takes a long time to warm up. That his body is still not interested – she even stomached that. She steadied her automatic flinch when he admitted that it was only recently he could bring himself to look at her. She knew it but it crazed her to hear the words drip so unselfconsciously from his curved lips ...

Tonight he has lapsed into the same self-doubt which encased their beginning. She stretches her limbs and looks out through the half drawn curtains, focusing across at the Gubei apartments. Anton is transformed into a hazy foreground silhouette, the cigar leaving a warm glow on his face and running shadows up through his eyebrows to paint his forehead. He stares towards the wall behind the stereo, apparently comfortable with the silence. She admits she's focused on him again as it hits home that he is unaware of her presence, her slumped form peripheral to his inward turned thoughts. It's two weeks since she decided to let go of the fantasy but too early to control her jealousy when he talks about Leon all night. Is it wise to be so infatuated with him? Is he being taken for a ride? or is it the other way around? ... what would his son think? Looking at it that way he must be crazy and he should just give up on Leon for the last time ... if only he didn't find him so compelling, so attractive. And then there is the added fear, the boy is so young and what if he breaks his heart? But then again we are all searching and it's true they have a lot of fun together, maybe they could be happy. Maybe even he should commit completely. But just 19 ... and Leon shows no sign of leaving his Gigolo 23

49

year old barman. Anton casts an inquiring glance at Ash who dwells on it for a long moment, pondering her function in his life as a front covering what he deems to be his questionable path of preference, an appendage suitable for sporting at business functions.

Reluctantly Ash re-resigns herself to the role of mid-life crisis psychotherapist. She encourages him, asks questions ... feels her gut turn and takes his cigar to settle the bile. She smokes quietly, relishing the wet softness where the tobacco leaves had melted between his lips. He makes the coffee and she changes the music to Tracy Chapman from Dire Strait's Communique ... refills her whisky glass and balances it on her stomach, closes her eyes. In another moment she will stand up suddenly in disgust and tell him she's leaving. She'll walk out the door and refuse his offer to accompany her to the gate. He'll protest at her considering walking home alone and try to hail a cab ... then he'll wander back up the six flights of steps and finish his cigar before sleeping. Meanwhile she is enjoying the uneven crumbling paving so characteristic of all Shanghai's streets. She follows Sheuicheung Lu for 15 minutes before turning left into Honggu Lu and now she's close to home. All the way she half expects him to come after her, to ask her what's wrong ... it's bitter remembering her decision and that after all he is not her lover.

Three am and her thoughts labour alongside the rattling dust-covered trucks. The workers sit high on the load watching her and she stares back. She could be in communist China during the Cultural Revolution and these Soviet army trucks from before the war. That's from her eyes ... from theirs she is as out of place here as the European glitsiness of the district Gubei in rubbish strewn Shanghai: Tailor made trousers, boyish short hair and an immaculate suede coat. But the farmers too are losing their continuity with the rotting stench of the streets. They watch the development warily and the trucks become restricted to the night.

Next week at AD's they eat Italian and when he asks her why she left she explains her jealousy. Her choice of words is blunt, reckless ... "Fatika" Shanghainese for "give a fuck", whatever ... she's lost already and has nothing to hide.

After he reads her manuscript he tells her she shouldn't give up on him. He explains again that he just needs more time. That he is almost certain now he'll end things with Leon. Ash listens and acknowledges inwardly that for her it is already too late for restraint. Karaoke until 4 am and after his friends leave they sing CALIFORNIAN DREAMING and she runs her palms to the inside of his thighs. He sinks back against the plush booth and she presses her cunt against his groin ... holds his neck in her hands and feels his tongue against her lips. His hair is short and thinning, grey bristles playing at a halo over his dark temples. His eyes are intense control, wary again – and for the first time she notices his contact lenses. She looks down at his face and imagines it between her thighs, his eyes watching her caught breath.

On his couch she almost falls asleep to Rod Stewart and the undulation of Anton's voice in Mandarin talking to Leon. Tired words, reassurance, defensiveness, encouragement ... She moves her head against his stomach to listen to the coffee mix into the Rum. Stomach walls protest and extract the little moisture they can – beginning the daily ritual of dehydration, ridding his body of the booze. When she wakes the phone is dead and he can look at her for the first time slowly, deliberately, unafraid because he no longer lacks desire. "I'm getting used to you" he tells her. "I can look at you now." She is silent, stomaching the resultant implications concerning their recent past ... that she'd thought she'd already accepted. He slips his hands through hers and she covers his fingers with her palms. She turns his face towards her afraid he'll notice how tiny his hands are compared to hers. He kisses her throat and face, his tongue touches her ear and she drags her teeth through his lower lip. Within his mouth she can lose consciousness and relinquish all control, all thoughts, just experience this pleasurable sense of well-being. Even the twinge of remorse she'd held for him melts ... if he needs his control he can keep it. His hands between her thighs and she swallows him burning for this intimacy. Desperate for him inside of her.

The first time they had been dancing and he pulled her towards the bedroom tearing off her clothes. Her head spun across an evening of Mahjong and Chivas and the exhausting trek up the stairs. She pushed back his shirt and unbuttoned his belt. The bedroom environment alien and the overhead light burning her eyes. She glanced nervously at her white expanse of flesh against his dark muscular body, spider veins knitting whole garments to her telescopic eyes. Does he see it? Or does he see just Leon or just the absence of Leon? Now she is inside his eyes, peeling back his retina, sliding over the gel which forms his faltering vision. She is Leon and now she is looking up at him from a matt of gelled, unkempt hair. The skin of her biceps pass frictionless against his buttocks. Male, she slides over and around him, competent, same, familiar and sure. He is no longer afraid of kissing this sleek thin form. He pushes her head towards his groin and she kisses his cock ... gently ... uncertainly, aware of his eyes burning with intense and ferocious protectiveness of his flaccidity. Soon she gives up and they talk. Just words. He writhes with discomfort and she walks home for the second time.

After the first failure all impetus for seduction drops by the wayside, frightened away by self-doubt, anxiety that the object of desire is after all not desirable. So they grow closer, abandoning all talk of time limits, of Leon, all that really matters now is the price of the wine. He feigns no knowledge and asks her to choose for them: Italian or French? Australian or Canadian? As long as it's red and not Chinese. She takes her place opposite him in the Charr Grill on the eighth floor of the Peace Hotel. The table small and tucked in against a window overlooking The Bund.

They arrive late, just after 10pm and feel lucky to find the restaurant still serving customers. When the Chipa dressed waitress hands Ash the menu she fingers her way through it warily, unable to pass off the feeling that it's a trap. Anton tells her again to order anything, he doesn't know wine and really usually just goes by the price. She wonders about this. Afraid of what he'll think if she orders the most expensive bottle and afraid of what he'll think if she doesn't. Easier to pass the ball back into his court. French, she tells him, after all we have to think of where we are. She leaves him to impress her with the price and watches the waterside couples meander along down below. Later they walk through the great hall and the ballroom and pretend to be lovers in the 1920's. He lights up a cigarette and she leans tipsily against his arm. As they walk along Waitan by the water she kisses him and slips her hand through his. He is always so warm she can feel him burn into her skin. Skin, she longs for his skin to slide over hers – wet with desire. When they kiss together on the way home in the taxi he grimaces wryly at the ridiculousness of it all. It's like we are teenage lovers with nowhere to go ... I have a home you know. But he doesn't extend any invitation.

The second time she kisses him there he is hot with desire for her and she feels relief that his erect penis is not as tiny as she imagined. He pulls off her clothes and she helps him clumsily, forcing his fingers to her clitoris, crying. His cock against her wet cunt rubbing, throbbing, almost inside. She towers above him on the vinyl couch, crouching, his head wet with sweat and her velvet cardigan sticking to her breasts. She clutches one of his hands against her nipple and rocks her clitoris against his left hand. Her cunt drips onto his leg and he pushes up against her ... straining to enter. She slides back and forth feeling him hard against her vulva, slipping against the hollow depression of her anus, sliding firmly down towards her cunt almost entering, almost touching her fully, almost reaching into her and then she will lose breath, lose the outer, lose consciousness and he will be lost to her. She feels herself starting to shake uncontrollably and he is sliding back, pushing against her rectum, entering wherever it is soft and wet. She inches her body upwards and tucks her feet to either side of his arse, dipping, rubbing, closing her eyes against his stare which is almost a sneer. Now as his body starts to shake against hers he pulls his hands out from her clit grasping her sides, gripping her buttocks and forcing her down onto his cock. Ash screams and he drags his teeth over her collar-bone, into her throat. She wants to cry from the irresistible pain which isn't pain, from the unravelling knot of her tight flesh as she feels him push deep inside, her cunt swallowing him like a python does a rat. His hands slide up her arms to pin her wrists behind her back and he is surprisingly strong, but now she is surprisingly weak. She strains back against him luxuriously, letting the slow sweat start out of her skin, helplessly pleasured by the feeling of her cunt oozing stickily against his legs. Then he's on top of her and her mouth is open, engulfing his hand. Her tongue coils around his fingers and her awareness flows after his other hand: sliding down around her arse, fingers slipping around the base of his penis into her anus. He is fucking her hard inside and his tongue is circling her ears, his knees forcing her thighs apart and she is wide wide open. She closes her eyes and squeezes all of her orifices tight shut upon him in waves, rocking her body within a universe of his touch. Inside her mind there is three of him, six of him, penises secreting all over her skin, rubbing inside her mouth, sucked within her tongue, her ears, rubbing wet against her neck, in her anus, her cunt, against her clit. Her body is wet with the caresses of tongues, of hands, and his eyes have run glasslike into her mind.

Then she remembers. She pushes him back and crouches over him, letting him slip out slowly, her cunt holding him, releasing him reluctantly. This isn't wise. What do you mean? It's not safe. What? – you mean you're not using anything? *Fuck you! Fuck this YOU not using anything! what about us? AIDS? diseases? pregnancy isn't the only question!* ... No, I'm not, don't you have any condoms? Condoms? Anton sounds incredulous and stares at Ash with what looks like – almost – growing dislike. Don't you ever wear them? No. He pushes her away and stares blindly at the ashtray where the last cigar long since crumbled into ashes. Tracy Chapman adds her bit of advice to the situation and is flipped over by the machine in favour of Wong Fei. Ash rolls back her shoulders and eases out her leg, increasingly confused. When Anton gets up and takes her arm she begins to feel cold. He steers her towards the bedroom away from the fading music and into the harsh overhead light ... maybe it's his eyes that he doesn't notice. He is behind her rummaging in his bedside cabinet drawer, peeling back the silver foil from a white tablet. Her first shudder is drowned by a growing curiosity of desire ... amazed that he will proceed this far without consulting her. He trips her onto the bed and pushes the tablet inside her vagina, following it with his penis. He holds her and closes his eyes – silent, drawing her towards him in waves, deeper, thrusting harder into her contractions. She can feel him press against her cervix and pushes out to open wider, to clench, to trap him inside.

Then she remembers ... She rolls over and pushes him back against the pillows. *No*, I can't do this, it's not safe. What do you mean? well, what about diseases? we've got to talk about this first. Diseases? Anton's eyes are colder now and he grabs his clothes. She slips on her jacket and they talk. Leaning against the pillows, she relaxes her mind slowly around his inflexibility and enjoys brief incredulity at her own presence of mind. She no longer has a choice but to keep the pact with herself. Anton shivers and finds a jacket, pulling it around his shoulders with one hand as he lights up another cigarette. Ash turns off the light so he looks gentler, shaded in softly from the balcony light. He has no choice either. This is his contraception, getting to know people first, caution. He doesn't know any other choice. And what is compromise? Without intercourse he has lost the desire for other intimacies. Ash can't help her smile as she looks away.

Anton disappears into the bathroom and she stretches out languidly for the last time on his couch – finishes off her whisky. A taxi edges its way gingerly through the driveway far below, beneath the arch ... leaving behind a young man, the shiver of an elegant suit falling lightly over his slightly built form. He brushes back his silken hair and glances up at the window, passes under the arch ... Ash looks down at his fading wake for a smooth moment and slips on her shoes, clicking the door shut behind her to walk home for the third time. Free.

Reversal of Roles

Katherine Park

It was amazing, the way I changed when I first strapped it on. Or maybe I just became more myself. Power is a strange thing, after all, something the sophisticated play with but don't always truly understand. I was never comfortable with the power traditionally assigned to me, that of being admired and courted and finally propositioned, of being the object of a gaze rather than the gazer. I derived more real pleasure from wringing it out of some wet, exhausted, almost sore individual who in their turn was almost reluctant to give up their desire to my hands, than from laying back and offering my desire to someone else's fingers.

So perhaps it was only natural that one day I would grow tired of sucking someone else's hardness and want to force someone on their knees before my own, that I would finally disdain the intrusion of another inside me and seek to press myself into them. Perhaps the day I finally plucked up the courage to enter the store, try out the merchandise and imagine the moment when I'd finally pack it into my faded jeans, handing over the untraceable cash with a hand as steady as the one which would reach out to you later, was marked out for me since I first figured out that I was different.

We'd flirted with power games before, like any other pair of worldly bisexual sophisticates, but nothing like this. Of course, we had to do it properly, so there was no casual unveiling of my new toy in a house with thin walls or a phone that never stopped ringing, an unveiling subject to any manner of interruptions from random friends to my suspicion that I'd giggle uncontrollably when I actually tried to use it, more from force of feminine habit than any actual nervousness. I was almost afraid to actually enact such a potent masturbatory fantasy, and embellished it for days over the phone, in letters and in whispered words while I pleased myself on top of you. Was it just me, or did your urgent whisper of the degradations to be visited upon you, my lazy answer almost contemptuous in its verbal pictures of your helplessness, make you harder, lend extra urgency to your rasping climax?

I was not entirely submissive, even in the normal run of events. I loved to play with the limits of my influence over you, a whispered improper suggestion at a time when nothing could be done about it, a hand sliding inside your zip in a darkened street outside a pub just as our friends piled out behind us. There was a deliciously sleazy streak in you, the playful sordidness of your sexual preoccupations shading into a dark unexplored place where your occasional need to control everything might reach the limits of pleasure and even legality. Inside the scientist, ever explaining, with the hands that could take anything apart and fix it again, the same hands that coaxed an arrow to a target and a guitar string to its perfect pitch, lurked a schoolboy with his first stolen porno mag concealed under the mattress (a priapic schoolboy who also used his hands for less acceptable occupations and wished someone would come along and catch him at it so they could spend the rest of the day and night punishing him in all manner of unrepeatable ways). And such unrestrained sexuality gave me freedom, freedom that I gradually explored, freedom unencumbered by the myriad bonds of obligation and gratitude and dependency found in more conventional relationships, freedom to discover more of myself.

So I strapped on my curious appendage, and with the physical enhancement came an extension to my personality: my secret vulnerability became buried deeper and my sexual persona became varnished, hard as my artificial cock, harder than any real one. And as I strutted from home to the appointed place, feeling taller, broader and laughing a coarse laugh into the harsh wind, you were huddled draughtily in the local gay cruising ground waiting for me to come in and ritually seduce you. I didn't wait long, for fear I'd turn up and have to haul your face off someone else's crotch, waited only for the time it would take to spark your anticipation into flame before sidling in and holding your gaze for that fractional second too long: before I leaned against the inside wall of the toilet stall, unzipped my jeans (so tight and bulging) with the hand not holding a cigarette and made you roll the condom on with trembling hands, before you swallowed as much of it as you could take. Then I knew that one form of power, the most basic and true, is to be able to invade the body of another, even with consent. And in turn there was power in the way you teased that object, technically inanimate but so charged it might as well have been connected to me by blood and flesh, an elongated clitoris, sensation flooding its base as you ran your tongue round the rim, a hint of teeth as your mouth closed over its length. You were showing me how it felt, and I appreciated the lesson.

Artificial penises have their advantages and disadvantages. They're always hard, and they don't deflate if there's a knock on the door, or someone comes into the building, or if a stray thought wanders into a guilty mind. And if neither of the sexual participants has a real one, they are almost essential for certain sensations (the sorts of sensations that chafe the seams of jeans the next day and send secret thrills through you as they do). On the other hand, they don't transmit pleasure directly to the wearer (although the non-pervert might be surprised how much raw desire can travel along a length of latex) and they don't, in general, produce any tangible evidence of fulfilment. So as I leaned ever more unsteadily against that wall, I couldn't look down and see my fluids leaking from the corner of your hungry mouth as you strained to taste every last drop of me, or pull myself out of you at the last second and see you frantic with desire to catch the jet, then beg to lick me clean. Half of the pleasure of seeing you on your knees before me was in imagining your insatiability for cum, longing to force my fluids down your throat as my hand knotted through your hair and imposed a cruel rhythm with your wet mouth around me, almost choking on my length. (I think it was on that day that the first fleeting fantasy of seeing you kneeling before a real cock slid into my mind, never fully developed but tantalising me as a frame of the film would pierce my conscious mind at the oddest of moments, as the names of suburban railway stations flash past almost imperceptibly from a speeding express train.)

No, nothing in this life is perfect, however far you plan in advance, but if you happen to have been born with a set of genitals designed to be invaded, a warm slash of slipperiness rather than a smooth jutting cylinder, these small operational inconsistencies must be tolerated. And while there is much power in being open and enticing, from the second I strapped on my new toy I knew the other sort of power was the one I truly understood: from the second you dropped to your knees and placed obedient hands behind you to be tied before I fucked your open mouth with a ruthless precision I didn't know I possessed, I knew that I loved to strap on my counterfeit genitalia, claim the alternative power and give you the chance to try on mine.

You wore it well, too. Later, when we'd started breathing normally again, when I'd grown too cold to slide my fingers around my own wetness as you knelt and watched with envious eyes, when I'd hustled you to your feet without letting you clean yourself and taken you silently home, I vowed to show you the rest of what power was all about. An hour of possessing the power to penetrate had emptied my mind of worries, of concerns and of morals or perceptions, left me with nothing but the need to see this through to its logical conclusion, to make you the one lying there, wet, open and ready to receive as I thrust into you, to be the one who gives and takes away rather than she who waits, begs and persuades. When you were stretched out on the bed, harder than I'd seen you in a long time, breath coming ragged as you watched me lubricate this strange attachment, longing to lubricate it yourself in your own mouth, there was power in watching how much you longed for it, and power in feeling you complete the penetration of your tender orifice as I paused gently at the tip. You strained up at me to get as much of it in as possible, as quickly as possible, free to move since my control over your desires was so total, you didn't even have the excuse of being tied. And every time I withdrew my unaccustomed length almost entirely before ramming it abandonedly back in (as you howled, unusually vocal in your pain and pleasure) was a revenge for every time you had hovered above me stroking your unfairly real cock and watching me writhe in my own wetness, knowing I'm always too inhibited to hoarsely beg for what I want more than anything else in the world at that moment – for you to slowly press into me, then slide all the way in and all the way out as slowly as you can stand, building the tension until neither of us can stand it any more and the instinct to thrust hard, as hard as possible takes over, as I finally give up and mutter incoherent, disjointed, meaningless words, as I can't stop myself from crying out in my desire and pleasure.

No wonder you almost passed out when you finally came, your control over your own response unusually tested. Part of the reason I wanted to see you splashed in fluids, flushed and wet lips parted, was to disturb your perfect control, desire pushing you to the point where the sheer pleasure overcame your need to achieve satisfaction without involvement. Why should I be the only one to ask and cajole and reach up for you, the one who always broke down first and promised undreamed of favours and services if only you'd do this one thing for me? I wanted to hear your voice coarsened by desire, see your mouth form words of entreaty, to tease you to the point where either I couldn't bear to deny you any longer, or you used your superior strength to flip me over and take what we both wanted you to have. With my new persona, my new extension, I could do this: not only had I become an annotated copy of what you really wanted, now, but having it isolated the cool, detached parts within me and banished the tenderness elsewhere, concentrated and distilled me to a single bright point of desire and control. In satisfying – eventually – your hoarse pleadings, I took back some of the power that the world would take away, based purely on physiology, although only within the world that stopped at the edges of the pool of light from the bedside candle.

I had snatched back power before, had pinned others to the bed with knee, hand and fist before slaking their desires, whatever they were, but this was a different flavour of power. Then, we had both pretended that the power was mine, though paradoxically, it was only so for as long as I satisfied the others' wants whilst pretending what they mattered meant nothing (it meant everything). Here, I had the power of intrusion. To someone less fascinated with the many ways to penetrate and tease, this might have seemed a lesser sort of power. To me, it was everything, it was like blowing the sand and earth away from a beautiful pebble or shell to reveal the diamond-hard gloss beneath. It was throwing aside the suits and heels I wore to work and revealing the boxer shorts and gym-honed muscles beneath them at the end of a conventional day. It was the moment when mind and muscle work together to produce a perfect motion without conscious thought – being more intensely myself than ever before.

You wanted to borrow it, when daylight had blushed the sky and we were retreating back inside our usual personae. Did you ever understand just why I'd never let you?

New Orleans

Alice Blue

Dappled sunlight made hot spots on my tummy. Leaves flickered and twirled above me; the flashes of their revolutions making my eyes ache. A coupla beers and a shot of Jack Daniels boiled me. I was grumpy. I was twisted and mean with the forces of worked dykehood. I was leather without lace, twisted with spirits. I was one of three bitchin' dykes and two flaming fags set to bruise our knuckles on no-one in particular, but too tired and hot to move.

The party was only an echo: a hot sun and aquarium weather had bleached Mardi Gras into nothing but die hard drunks and pathetic cruisers. Our kingdom was a sad willow and the porch of our sad cottage with the thumpa-thumpa of pre-Columbian disco leaking to us from a bar next door. Through the narrow slats in the fence we could see the flashes of the milling, aimless THEM and their funny hats, clever t-shirts, "Show us your tits!" and vomit. We were invisible behind our fence, a wall of hostility and heavy, tired flowers that smelled like very cheap wine. Among us, nothing moved but the flies. Nothing doin' anything except feeling the sun on my warm tummy.

Downy and I shared the nest (a pile of leather jackets on the complaining porch) with a cute girl (Sal?) I let in because she reminded me of Dixie and a pair of Jack's friends – a bleached blond ornament and a leather and Crisco-greased Chicago boy. All of us, the boys and the girls, lay in the hot undersea air and watched the world flicker by through a flowers and wine choked fence.

It was hard to say where the undersea climate ended and the penis began. But there it was, round and white like a short slug, on the side of one of the Chicago boy's leather pants. "What do you use that thing for?" Downy asked, feeling it, running fingers over the sticky skin, ringing the head, gently flicking the tight vein underneath.

"Some guys like it sucked. Some like fucking with it," Chicago said in a heat-drunken voice, a rum-drunk voice. He watched the dyke play with his dick – drunk and hypnotised by her fascination, her brown-eyed wonder of it.

"Little boys?" Sal (I think her name was) asked from her sprawl on her back. The cock was almost hard now. She stared at it: amazed, disgusted and drunk.

"Big boys, too," he said smiling too wide and too pleased.

59

The cock got hard. Downy looked at us, her sisters. A What do I do with it now? flickered across her face. Hot day, rum and harder, boredom, comfort – I don't know. Sure, I was there, that day, but I wasn't her, wasn't Downy. I didn't know what was tripping through her head, I was just watching – as she took the unlubed condom (blue, I noticed) that he offered, rolled it down, then started to suck the Chicago boy's cock.

"Watch me be a boy," Downy said, pulling away for a second, to speak.

The sun blinked down on them: the dyke sucking cock, the leatherboy with girl-lip on his meat. It blinked down and made everything hotter. As the haze of the Louisiana afternoon settled down over my brain and wrapped everything in an undersea bed, I found myself slowly, geologically, rolled over and lifted up so I was on hands and knees. It took some work, and I didn't get help, to get my leather pants down, but it happened. Sudden air, slightly cooler air on my sweaty ass. "You know straights, how do they do it?" asked another girl-girl voice, a smiling voice, a playful voice, a festive voice – Sal's voice – from behind me.

"I think I can figure it out," the pretty boy said from behind me, and above.

Sal stroked my pus from behind, coaxing me open with girl fingertips, knowing the buttons to press, the silk to stroke. I felt myself yawn, a falling feeling under my warm tummy.

"You big enough, girl?" Downy said, taking her lips from Chicago's cock, concern sprinkled over her words, silver spit threads going from cock to her mouth – or was it the other way around?

I can't remember if I nodded or I just gave permission with silence. Either way, I was committed – my ass was naked in the hot daylight and I heard the sound of something tearing open and "– never done this to a real one before" from Sal as, I knew later, she rolled a condom onto pretty boy's cock.

A real one – I'd never thought of it like that before.

I'd played with his rubber kin, his silicone brethren, but never one of the real thing – or, at least, the flesh and blood thing. Then, there on that porch, though, I was saying ah! with my other mouth and, before even I knew it, I was full.

Boy, was I full! At the end, when I felt his furry thighs press against my ass, and his cock tapped me deep inside, I thought I was going to unzip from the pressure, that overwhelming filling. But then he pulled back, and it faded – only to come back again with the next stroke.

"Tisk – tisk," Downy said, absently stroking Chicago's blue-covered cock, "what will the girls say."

I put my hot forehead down onto the coat I'd been stretched on, breathing in black leather, boy armpit stink and spilled beer and harder. In and out in and out was all I could really think about – not what I was doing, what Downy was doing, what tomorrow would be like, what even tonight would be like (let alone in a hour or two). In and out in and out in (ouch!) and out (ooooh!) was all that easily moving boy-cock managed to let into my brain.

I didn't try to come – didn't really want to. I was trying something new, that's all, and the newness was all I really wanted to feel (in and out in and out). I was being doggy-humped on black leather by a pretty boy – that was quite enough. My clit was tight, yeah, and hard (yeah!) but I didn't feel like stroking it, touching myself or even having Sal or Downy down there with hands, lips, whatever, doing it for me (even though they'd both done the same and worse). I was just then, there, getting fucked by a boy and that was quite enough.

I didn't plan on coming, but that's what happened. I didn't try, but I came, the coming came, and I did. It was weird, unusual – deep and pressurised, not lightning bolt like fingers and lips and whatever else on throbbing clit. When it came it boiled up from my cunt, building like a can of beer casually shook and shook and shook then popped open. I popped, that's for damned sure.

One minute I was just fucking, just being fucked, and then, like the filling overflowed, I was coming – grunting like a pig into the leather jacket, biting it: tasting polish, dust, and my own stale breath. I must have collapsed after, falling down into the warm porch, the hot leather. Must have, but don't remember doing so.

Then someone was speaking. I blinked away the sparkles and the heavy exhaustion that had fallen on top of me and ground my head to the left.

Dancing green eyes; a spotlight, toothy smile – Downy's cheeks creased with warm laughter: "So, little one, get fucked by girls and you get fucked by boys – so what are you?"

I closed my eyes, feeling the weight again. I don't know how long I had them closed, maybe a blink, maybe a much longer blink. When I opened them again the sun was passing behind the fence and the world was becoming deeper colours.

"Tired," I said to Downy's naked back as a bar across the street flashed its first neon of the night, "and happy."

The Doge's Daughter

Gabriella West

I grew up in the Doge's Palace in Venice, among priests. My family disposed of me at a very early age – I have ten brothers and sisters and was just another mouth to feed. When the cleric came offering money and saying that their son could have a brilliant career as a castrato singer, my family was not shocked, but honoured. My parents trusted the Church, though I knew that trust must be misplaced when the kindly priest who had so smoothly negotiated with my mother and father almost immediately ordered me to pleasure him as we crossed the Grand Canal towards the Doge's Palace.

It was a strange scene – a windy, rainy night, the figure of the gondolier barely visible ahead of us. We were in the cabin, supposedly to shelter from the rain. I crouched down by the priest's feet. He opened his garments. I was eleven years old, tired, miserable, afraid, but some spirit took over me that night and I skillfully moved my mouth over his member until he was satisfied. Luckily, he was not large.

The next day, it all seemed like a dream. The priest effusively introduced me to my peers – other sheepish children who looked as if they were sleepwalking through their lives. The actual cutting was done unexpectedly one night – they dosed me with warm wine and tied me down. What shocked me the next morning was that they had left me some of my equipment. I had confusedly expected everything to go.

We were trained to sing, but some of us were more adept than others. I enjoyed being part of the group of singers, yet I knew I was not one of the stars. I wondered what would befall me.

On one occasion about a year later we sang before the Doge, his wife and daughter. It was the Lady Elisabetta's birthday, in the year 1627. There she was, a shy and chubby twelve year old with a mass of brown hair and gentle eyes. She clapped excitedly after the performance and asked if she might speak to us. To my surprise, she headed straight for me. She stopped in front of me and smiled.

I looked at her silently, unsure of what to do or say. "But why are you among these boys?" she asked curiously, with that bluntness that the nobility often have. I found it charming, actually. Coming from a lower – much lower – class, I had to be cautious, indirect, always thinking of my survival.

I blushed in confusion. "What do you mean, my Lady?" I said. My voice was high and some of the others tittered.

"But aren't you a girl?" Elisabetta asked in wonderment. "Those long lashes – they're longer than mine." She reached her hand into her pocket and brought out a sweetmeat. Before the priests could interfere and take it from me, I put it in my mouth. I could not help but smile as the delicious morsel dissolved on my tongue.

"That pleases you," she said with satisfaction.

"He is a boy, my Lady," one of the priests said gravely, standing by her elbow and giving me a patronising look. "As if your kind didn't make me what I am!" I thought contemptuously.

"Thank the lady Elisabetta," the priest ordered me.

"Thank you, your Ladyship," I said, lowering my lashes and bowing.

She giggled. Perhaps that wasn't the right way to address her? "And what is your name, then?"

"Piero, your Ladyship."

"Piero," she repeated caressingly. The priest looked stunned. Perhaps, I thought, he was annoyed that anyone else should find me attractive, even in such an innocent way. He had had me brought to his room last night – no doubt he was afraid I would blurt out the sordid details of our encounter. I never would. I knew better than that.

We smiled at each other. "I shall ask for you," was the last thing she said before she moved down the line, politely greeting my friends.

As we walked back to our quarters in the Palace I was surrounded by a teasing crowd. "Oooh, she likes you ... she thinks you're a girl!" was one of the kinder comments. Yet my friends were good-natured. We all hated what we were, and knew we could do nothing about it. Better to accept it and to allow others to admire us, misplaced and exploitative as that affection almost always was. Most of us were being used by the priests at night, yet we did not dare protest; it was so much in the order of things. We barely acknowledged it to each other. It was a lonely life, amid so many people, so many demands on our time. Whether I was spending my hours in singing lessons or lying face down on a priest's bed enduring his assaults, I was still following orders. I would arise from the bed with an aching body and no feeling of pleasure while the priest lay panting and utterly satisfied. I was a favourite, with my silky hair, soft skin and feminine mouth. They all had to have me. But I never had any sense what the years ahead would bring.

An old priest shook me by the shoulder one cool spring morning several years later as I lay in bed, dreading the start of another day. "I've been told to take you to her Ladyship," he mumbled. As the priests got older, I found, they lost their air of power and became rather pathetic and sad. I got up obediently and dressed before his bleary eyes, wondering what would happen with the Lady Elisabetta. I was fifteen years old but still looked like a young boy – slim, girlish and androgynous. It was hard to imagine that she had much changed. The only thing I had heard about her in the intervening years was that she was betrothed to Prince Michele of the house of Savoy, whose father the Duke ruled a state far to the west of us Venetians.

I trotted along behind my escort as he took me through corridor after corridor in the rabbit warren that was the Palace. One particular area looked like a brothel (or so I imagined) with voluptuous women lying around bare-breasted on beds and couches. They seemed to be waiting for lovers. I slowed my steps, fascinated. In one room, whose door was half-open, I was shocked to see a man mounting a woman, taking her from behind like a beast. His body covered hers and we could not see her face. I stopped and stared. The priest stopped too. We watched together. I felt myself trembling and suddenly aroused. Women were a mystery to me and there was something about this woman's passionate moans that made me thrill in sympathy. Did I want to be the man taking her or did I want to be her?

As I stared, mesmerised, I felt the priest's hand stroking me, slowly and almost shyly. I was embarrassed, because I knew it would take me a very long time to climax. In fact, I never really had. To my astonishment the priest got down on his knees before me. His mouth felt good and I allowed myself to thrust gently into it. I continued to watch the man and woman rutting. He had positioned her over the edge of the bed now so I was able to see her flushed face and open mouth and watch his long prick sliding in and out of her. Did they know they were being watched? Quite possibly. Voyeurism was considered natural in our city. Suddenly the man pulled out and spurted onto the woman's buttocks and back in a long stream. I stared longingly knowing I would never have that pleasure. She turned over and spread her legs and I was stunned to see him lower himself between them. I had never realized that a woman could be pleasured orally and watched in amazement as she moaned, her eyes rolling back in her head in ecstasy, her hands clutching his hair. As she screamed with pleasure I found myself going limp and wobbling at the knees. The priest stood up and I leaned into him, trembling. He stroked my hair and told me I was a good boy.

"One day you'll have a woman like that, my lad," he said as we wandered dazedly away from that strange place.

"But ... that's impossible, Father," I whispered.

He chuckled. "Well, you can get stiff, can't you? Your kind can give women great pleasure, you know. You stay hard for a long time and you can caress them like another woman can. It's the best of both worlds."

To meet Elisabetta as if nothing had happened was the most difficult thing I had yet to do. We wandered through the courtyard and stopped before a large and beautiful fountain, which we sat beside. We spoke in low tones and became immediately confidential. She asked me how I had reached her quarters and I told her that I had passed through an area of the Palace where people were making love. Her eyes were round and she clapped her hand to her mouth. It was three years since she had given me a sweetmeat and she had grown taller and more womanly, with a wayward look that surprised me. Yet beneath her sophistication there was still a childlike sweetness. She held and caressed my hand as I described the woman being pleasured. She confided that she had dreams about making love to a man and could not wait to do it, that sometimes she felt like she was going to explode. It occurred to me that she was treating me like an intimate friend of her own sex and I felt slightly confused. She took a locket from around her neck and showed me the portrait of the man she was going to marry, Prince Michele. The picture showed a handsome young man with longish dark hair and a sensitive face. "He's beautiful," she said proudly. I nodded. I thought so too.

"When will it happen?" I asked. My face must have looked sad because she burst into laughter.

"But, Piero, I have plans for you! I've asked for you to accompany me. You shall represent one of our more exotic Venetian specialities – boy-girls who sing like angels. My father has agreed." I looked at her in wonder and she leaned over and kissed me on the cheek. For a moment I thought she was going to kiss me on the mouth. I flushed.

"Why me?" I asked.

"To keep me from being bored," she answered promptly. "Do you know what it's like being a prince's wife? I assure you, the little freedom I have here I won't even have there. My husband will be away at his amusements and I shall have to sit in my rooms and wait for his return. Surrounded by my women, of course, and no men. With you by my side, life will never be dull ..."

I could see the old priest far in the distance, but I clasped her hand and brought it to my lips.

"You've never had a woman, have you?" she murmured.

"No," I admitted. "Only some of the priests ..." I wasn't sure how much I wanted to tell her and fell silent, not meeting her eyes. She squeezed my hand as if she understood.

"You know the pleasure you described to me, Piero?" she whispered suddenly. "The one where the man used his mouth between the woman's legs?"

I nodded. "I'd like to try that with you, Piero," she blurted out.

I stared at her. I was literally speechless. She's used to getting what she wants, a little voice in my head repeated over and over. And you're used to obeying orders. If she wants this ...

"But of course, I'd have to let my beloved possess me first," she said playfully, touching the locket at her neck. "And then you, Piero. We could have hours of pleasure during the day, don't you think?"

"And if they caught us?" I said in a low voice.

She shook her head. "No, you don't understand. I talked to Michele when he visited here – he's only been here once, you know. He told me about his own sexual appetites and how important it was for him to have a bride who liked the pleasures of the body. His great fear is having to lie with a woman who's frigid."

Her face lit up when she talked about him. I felt an odd pang of jealousy.

"I asked him if he would permit me to share caresses with others, if he was the only one to ... spill seed inside me," Elisabetta continued, blushing slightly. "I said it would help me please him if I could have other experiences. He said he wouldn't mind my taking pleasure with a girl. I mentioned you, and I said you were beautiful and mostly like a girl. He seemed quite intrigued and said that he liked the idea of me being aroused when he got home, so aroused that he could have me instantly." Her eyes shone.

"If you desire him so much, Elisabetta, why do you need me at all?"

"Because, my love," she said caressingly, "I know it will excite him even more to think that I've been lying in your arms all day. He would soon tire of me if all I offered was adoration and a pretty body."

She stroked my face. "We're not children anymore, you and I," she said quietly. "I wish I had been able to have you as my playfellow when I was a child. They wouldn't allow it. I asked and asked. But now you can be my companion. In a different way."

"And when you tire of me?" I asked. Her face was close to mine and I could feel her warm breath. Suddenly she kissed me, pushing her tongue inside my mouth. She kissed me for a long time and I found myself unbearably stirred. She placed my hand on her breast and slipped it inside her bodice. For the first time I felt a woman's nipple stiffening under my touch. She gasped and her expression became even more sultry.

"This was what I did with Michele," she whispered. "Now I've done it with you."

Suddenly the priest loomed up on us, coughing officiously and looking a little frightened. I was frightened too, of my own desire and of Elisabetta's seductive words. I feared she was toying with me, building a fantasy that would never come to pass. I stood up, shaken, and bowed to her. She smiled demurely.

"We shall travel within half a year, Piero," she told me.

Now all my dreams were of Elisabetta, and Michele too. I imagined them making love the way I had seen the couple in the Palace doing. But I would lie under Elisabetta and touch her breasts and her hair would brush my face, her perspiration raining down on me. Then, after he had finished, she would lower her body onto mine and kiss me, stroking me intimately. She would roll off me and he would spread my legs and take me the way some of the priests had done, except this time I would welcome it. Yet as I imagined this I did not really think it would ever happen. Surely Michele – a handsome young man, not a perverted priest – would never want me, especially when he had a beautiful and willing young wife. I dreamed of Elisabetta too, of kissing her for hours until our bodies ached. To feel her naked flesh on mine would be the most wonderful thing in the world.

At last we took our leave of Venice. The priests were far more sorry to see me leave than I was to go. I had to conceal my joy and anticipation. In truth, I felt nothing as our carriages rolled out of the city. We travelled to Michele's kingdom in a long convoy. The journey took a month and we were put up at some of the great castles along the way. One night I awoke in my cold little chamber to find Elisabetta on top of me, clad in a simple white shift which she soon discarded. I was sure it was just a dream. I ran my hands over her salty, moist flesh, nibbling her breasts as she brushed them over my face deliciously. She whispered, I want you, I want you, over and over again.

I did not know what to do, for I knew I could not penetrate her. She had to be a virgin on her wedding night. Lying on top of her, I sucked her small hard nipples, slipping a finger inside her and caressing her until she seemed about to climax. Then I lowered myself between her legs. I tried to imitate what I had seen the man in the Palace do and to my delight I found Elisabetta's wetness and scent intoxicating. I pushed my tongue inside her and used sharp flicking movements to bring her off. She gave a muffled scream.

We lay together silently for a while. I was trembling. She kept kissing me and stroking my cock. She said she had never touched a man like this. When she said the word "man" I thrilled and my cock hardened. She told me that she would let me take her in the future, that she knew it was unfair to excite me like this. Then she whispered, "but there's another way." I looked at her in astonishment. She moved her mouth over my cock so that it was wet and then turned over, guiding me between her buttocks and up inside her.

"I want you to fuck me," she said, using a coarse peasant term, "the way the priests fucked you."

I obeyed. I knew that if I was caught I would be killed instantly (and no one would ever know what had happened to me, it would be said that I had died of a fever en route), yet the risk seemed worth it. I moved very gently at first, remembering how painful my own first time had been. We were both breathing in gasps and moans. Yet I felt she wanted me to be rough. Her need to experience was like a man's, I thought, and I was almost more aroused by her desire than by my own. When I sensed her exhaustion I began to stroke her between her legs from behind, and I felt her convulsing around my cock. I went limp myself and we collapsed together onto the tangled sheets. I buried my face between her soft breasts.

"And the funny thing is ... I'm still a virgin!" she whispered breathlessly in my ear. We shook with laughter. Then she said, "I love you."

I gazed at her. "I thought you loved Michele," I said at last.

"I hardly know him. I'm sure I can love him, but I know that I love you now."

She bent and kissed me. She had put her shift back on and looked strangely innocent. I did not want her to leave me. I put my hand on her breast. The warmth burned through the fabric. "I don't think my husband-to-be could give me more pleasure than you have," she said thoughtfully.

I wanted to tell her that I loved her, but did not dare.

I was riding in a coach with Elisabetta's ladies-in-waiting. They were naive girls. They chattered and laughed about Prince Michele, about whether they would find husbands themselves. They talked about how beautiful their mistress had seemed lately. "It's almost as if she had a lover!" one of them exclaimed, and then they all burst into giggles, casting coy looks at me. I felt my face grow hot and pretended to be embarrassed because I had been brought up among the priests. They saw me as a virginal figure, I thought, like themselves, completely inexperienced and ignorant. I was not predatory. If I had been, I was sure I could have seduced them one by one on the long and tedious journey westward. Instead we passed our time singing and playing cards. They treated me like a girlish younger brother – no doubt they all had brothers like this.

I was content to view the landscapes we passed through as if in a dream. Elisabetta had not come to me again. I knew that it was better that she didn't, but I wondered if she had experimented with me in order to please Michele with her skills. Perhaps I had served my purpose. I tried not to dwell on these thoughts but I had always been used before and I could not see that being a noblewoman's plaything was really any different, except that the pleasure, for once, was mutual. My body was awakening to lust, perhaps slower than Elisabetta's, for she had never been scarred with a knife and forced to endure unwanted intimacies. Yet when I looked back on my life in Venice I did not hate the priests. They had taken much from me but I could give and receive pleasure, and I could feel love.

And so, the second stage of my life began. At first I did not realize how different things would be, that I had little to fear now. The people of Michele's kingdom were unlike us Venetians. They seemed a sober lot, not religious in the fanatical yet hypocritical way our people were. The men were manly and the women prim, but it was obvious that Michele's father was a just ruler and that the royal family was loved.

Elisabetta was made much of. The wedding was a huge and gaudy affair. I scarcely saw her before it, and I did not see her for weeks afterwards. She was being taken on a tour of the kingdom. Reports reached us of how deeply the young couple were in love, how radiant the young princess was, and so on. Selfishly, though, I dreamed of a future where she was separated from Michele and living quietly with an entourage that mainly consisted of me – at least in her bed.

I became friends with a young German theologian who was studying at the court. Shocked at my lack of formal education, Johan began tutoring me in his spare time. He could not believe it when I told him how the priests had altered me.

"They did that to you! That's barbaric," he kept repeating, secretly fascinated, of course. Because I was lonely I allowed Johan to share my bed once or twice. I had never made love with a man my own age, and enjoyed it. My only previous good experience, sad to say, had been the old priest ministering to me in that Palace corridor. Johan was tender and I think he fell in love with me, but I kept on telling him that my heart was already taken.

"Who?" he asked, and continued to press me until I finally admitted that it was a woman.

"A woman!" He snorted and then laughed at my look of shock. "You'll never get a woman with child, so what woman would ever love you?"

"A married woman, perhaps," I suggested hesitantly.

"A married woman! Nonsense. Married women only take lovers if their husbands are old or impotent. You wouldn't exactly be virile enough to take a woman's fancy!"

He laughed again, throwing on his clothes. I lay in bed and watched him dress. I knew he was being cruel because I didn't love him, but at that moment

I never wanted to see him again. I was just a freak to him, wasn't I? A Venetian freak.

He paused at the door. "I hope you'll accept your true nature one day," he said earnestly. "I have. I'm quite happy to be with men for the rest of my life."

"I have accepted my true nature," I told him wearily. "It's just different from yours."

Some days passed. I lay in my bedchamber, hands behind my head. I was willing Elisabetta to come to me. She had arrived last night with the Prince and one of her ladies-in-waiting had knocked on my door, handing me a sealed slip of paper and disappearing. The paper simply said "I will come to you tomorrow after he goes to the hunt." Royal hunts were all-day affairs.

I closed my eyes. I felt weak, fragile. I was frightened she would no longer desire me after being loved by her lusty young husband. What was I? Just a boy, after all, less than a boy, really, and as Johan had said, not virile.

There was a quiet knocking. I looked around. It did not seem to come from the door of my chamber. But there was another door, one that had always been bolted. I had not even bothered to ever look behind it, the bolt was so rusty.

I stood by the door, fiddling with the bolt, wondering if she was on the other side. When the ancient door creaked open there stood my love, dressed in a flimsy robe. For a moment we just stared at each other. She looked ravishing, her breasts and lips fuller, her eyes bright. Slowly she smiled at me.

She took my hand, leading me along a dank, musty tunnel. When we emerged it was into a lavishly decorated chamber. The walls were covered with hangings and in the corner was a red velvet couch. She led me to the couch, lay down, and cast off her robe.

I gazed at her body. I ached for her, but she was the Prince's now. I could not believe that I could have her, that it could be this simple.

"Michele says yes," she said in a husky voice. "He wants me to be happy."

"But aren't you happy ... just with him?" I asked.

She shook her head. "No, my love. My father chose my husband for me and I chose you. I need you both."

I lowered myself down on top of her. Our bodies seemed to melt together, and as I kissed her lips and her nipples I felt I would die with lust.

We spent hours in amorous play. I held back from the one thing I most wanted. Finally, as the room grew dim around us she guided me inside her.

I knew I could last a very long time, and I watched her face change as she reacted to my strokes. As we fucked, she looked like a beautiful wanton saint in a state of transcendence. I was mesmerised by her ecstatic expression and continued to gaze down at her. She clasped her legs tighter around me and murmured "harder, Piero ... harder." I increased the speed and intensity of my thrusts and as I did this I began a slow swoon of pleasure myself. I heard myself saying "I love you ... I love you," and she breathed in my ear, "yes ... oh yes, my love."

We lay together in a daze afterwards. I noticed our faces were both burning.

I touched her face, then my own. She looked at me with eyes that were still unfocused.

"My God, I've missed you," she said with a sigh. Nestling in her breasts, happy and safe, I was shocked to feel a slap on my buttocks. I looked around, heart jumping, to find Michele by the bed. The picture had not misrepresented him. In person he seemed gentle, appealing, quite un-Venetian, about five years older than us. He looked as if he had just sprung from his horse: his hair tousled, clothes dampened with sweat.

"Get up, beautiful boy," the Prince said. To Elisabetta he remarked, "yes, he is quite stunning."

I climbed off the couch in a great state of confusion. "He made love to me so deliciously, Michele," Elisabetta said hoarsely. I felt ready to sink through the floor.

"Did he now?" the Prince enquired. He seemed amused by my fumbling attempts to put on my clothes.

"I nearly died from pleasure," Elisabetta continued, running her hands over her swollen breasts.

The Prince looked from one of us to the other. His face was flushed, but I did not think it was from anger.

"Come here, Piero," he said gently. I walked over to him and he caressed my face, running his hands through my damp hair.

"She tells me you're very skilled at pleasing men," he said.

"I've been told so, my Lord."

"I'm sure you've already discovered that such vices are not common in this kingdom."

I lowered my eyes. He continued to touch me lightly, running his hands over my chest.

"Yet I've certainly been intrigued by them. Do you think you could show me some of your tricks?"

I looked directly at him. I wanted to see if he was mocking me, taunting me. What I saw instead was a young man who was drunk with desire for me and for Elisabetta. Perhaps he could smell Elisabetta on me.

She was lying very still, watching us. I knew suddenly that she was responsible for this: that she had made it happen through sheer force of will and desire.

"I'll do whatever you ask, my Lord," I said. He nodded. I could see he did not want to ask; he just wanted it to happen. I knelt before him, unfastening his garment so that his stiff member rose into my hand. As I slipped my mouth over it I could hear him moan slightly. His hands grasped my hair.

Suddenly, he pushed me gently away. He gestured towards the couch and I watched as he languidly settled himself against the red velvet. His skin, paler than hers and mine, looked particularly fine against the cloth. Elisabetta crouched down, kissing his mouth, and he fondled her breasts as I resumed my task between his legs.

As I look back, I see that this was the time when my life began to bloom. I had everything – two people I loved who loved and needed me. We spent almost every evening dallying on the couch in Elisabetta's bedchamber. I knew there would be a time when they would tire of me, yet I did not fear it would be soon. Michele gave me as much pleasure as Elisabetta did, and he allowed me my own trysts with her, just as I knew they often enjoyed each other without me. But when we were all together we became childlike and insatiable, making love for hours in delicious combinations. The Court was puzzled – it was strange for a Prince to spend so much time in amorous play with his own wife. In that provincial court our unlikely secret was never discovered. Nobody ever knew what a paradise of eroticism was flowering in their midst. We Venetians keep our own council.

Morning Surprises

Clint Jefferies

I felt so strange. I was waking up, but so slowly. My whole mind was fogged. Boy, but I must have tied one on last night. In fact, I couldn't even remember last night. The last thing my poor befuddled brain could fix on was dancing with this pretty, petite blonde girl at the Cowboy Lounge.

I'd gone there, like I do every Saturday night, to find me a little nookie. There's usually plenty of girls out there by themselves, and after a week out in the fields, (I work as a roughneck out on the oil rigs), I'm ready for a little companion ship, if you know what I mean. Awake now, or at least a little closer, I struggled to open my eyes. Bad idea. The light in the room was so bright it was blinding. I quickly closed the old lids again. Definitely, a class-A hangover was on the way.

But in the short time the peepers were open, I had been able to tell that this wasn't my room. There was also the weight of an arm across my chest. Hmmmm. Must have gotten lucky last night after all. In fact, I could feel the press of a whole body against my side. It felt good. But what had happened? Shit, I hoped I hadn't been so drunk I hadn't been able to get it up or something. That had been happening to me a lot lately; and if last night had been one of those nights, morning could be pretty embarrassing. If I could only remember ... Just lying next to somebody felt good though. Real slow, and being careful to keep my eyes closed this time, I reached across with an arm and touched my bedmate's side. Warm. Smooth. Maybe I'd just go back to sleep. I ran the hand down her back. She shifted a little and nuzzled in closer. I let my fingers wander a little lower, onto her butt. Yeah. It felt so good, solid, smooth. But there was something ... What was it? Something wasn't quite right. Her ass felt – furry?

My eyes popped open again, my head shot around, and I jerked my arm away like I'd been burned. Shit! It was a guy! What the fuck ... I was laying in a strange bed, and some big, muscular dude was cuddled up to me with an arm wrapped around my chest! What in hell had I done?

I felt like I was going to panic. Why couldn't I remember? My eyes looked around real quick, like the answer was going to be written on the ceiling or something. My brain felt like some crazy roller-coaster gone out of control. This couldn't be real. I mean, I'd thought about it once or twice. When I was

73

a teenager, I'd even jerked off with a friend once, but I'd never ... I looked over at the stranger again. What was I going to do? Hell, I was afraid to move even. What if some dude had just seen I was too drunk to get home and been nice enough to let me crash at his place. What would he think when he woke up and I was all wrapped up against him? I'd just leave. I'd just get out of the bed real slow and easy so he wouldn't wake up, and leave. I started to move, but it was too late. His eyes were opening. I froze.

But he just looked at me. He gave me this wide, sleepy grin, and stretched. I could feel his muscles flexing against my side. Then, he just lay his arm across me again and pulled me up tighter against him with this pleased little grunt. "Mornin'" His voice was low, but friendly enough. Jesus, had I really ...

"Uh ... Morning." My voice was a little hoarse.

"Sandy already had to go to work – down at the diner. We didn't want to wake you up." He was grinning and stretching again.

"You want some coffee?"

"Coffee?" He was offering me coffee. Yeah. Sure. "Yeah, I'd take some coffee." This was all out of the Twilight Zone. "Uh ... Sandy?"

"Yeah, Sandy and me keep the Mister Coffee right here by the bed. Neither of us like to get up to make it in the morning." He rolled over to the other side of the bed. I could hear the sound of coffee pouring into a cup. I could see his broad back and ass. Definitely naked. I looked down. Shit, I was too. Bare assed naked. And with my usual morning hard-on. Feeling kind of silly, I reached down to pull a sheet up to my waist. I turned back. He was handing me a steaming mug. What the hell had happened at the Cowboy lounge last night – and after. I mean, he didn't look like a fag. And I wouldn't have ... But here we both were ...

I took a sip. "Uh ... Who's Sandy?"

He looked over at me again, real surprised. "Sandy. You know. My wife. Sandy."

"Oh sure, Sandy." I tried to play it off. "I ... Uh ... don't remember much about last night." I felt my face turning red, and I went for the coffee again. Had I slept with this guy's wife? Then why wasn't he beating the shit out of me instead of settling down beside me again?

"Man, you must have been drunker than I thought." He pointed to a picture on the night stand. "That's Sandy. Remember now?"

"Sort of." It was her alright. I mean, I didn't remember her name, but it was definitely the little blonde woman I'd been dancing with at the Cowboy.

He reached over and sort of ruffled up my hair with that big, friendly grin again. "Sandy really liked you. She loves to watch two guys get it on, and usually, when we pick up a third, he won't do it. But you were great."

"You mean, we all three ... well ... made it?"

"Yeah. Well, mostly you and me, while Sandy watched." He stretched again, then ran a big hand down my chest. Every muscle in my body froze. "Damn, it's good to find somebody else that's really bi like me. Most guys got so many hangups."

"Yeah?" It was all I could manage. I couldn't quite take it all in. I'd actually ... done what exactly ...

"Sure," he was going right on, "I mean sometimes a guy will get off on letting me suck him or something, but all he's really interested in is fucking my wife. But you're really wild." He stopped, and smiled big again. "You know, you got one hot ass, man." My hand shot to my butt. Between my ass-cheeks I was slick – and sticky. And now, I noticed there was this burning feeling around my butt-hole. This guy had fucked me! And I must have let him. I mean, he was big and everything, but I am too. He couldn't have done anything that I hadn't gone along with. I started stammering like a kid.

"I haven't ever ... I mean ... I'm not really ..."

"Aw, don't worry. I was going to return the favour, but you sorta passed out."

Return the favour? This butch slab of muscle was going to offer me his ass? Well, shit, I must have done it. And I was still lying here wasn't I? I mean, I hadn't punched him, or even shoved his arm off me or anything. It was just so hard to believe – ME ... But I had to believe it. Somehow, even the way he was talking about it was getting me going. And my rod wasn't hard just from needing to piss anymore.

I looked over at him. He had a really good body, lean, muscular and hairy. And he didn't look nervous like me, either, just real relaxed, lying back, naked, with his dick about half hard, sort of laying across his thigh. Maybe now and then I'd had a fantasy like this, but now, lying close with another guy like this ... Well, I'd already done it, right? There wasn't any way to undo it. And maybe I'd even feel better about it if I knew it had gone both ways ...

I was kind of scared, though. I mean, I'd never tried to do anything with a guy – not sober anyway – and not before last night. But just laying there, watching him sip his coffee, I knew I wanted it. I wanted to fuck his butt. And somehow, the thought of his cock being up my ass last night didn't bother me that much anymore. Real slowly, holding my breath, I reached out and put a hand on his stomach.

"You were saying something about returning the favour?"

"Man, you never get enough, do you?" He sounded like he was kidding me, but his hand slid down my arm and closed over mine. Real easy, he picked up my hand and moved it down lower. Then, he set it down, right on his dick. I'd never touched another guy's cock before, except maybe his – last night – and I didn't remember that. It didn't feel half bad either, smooth. I could even feel it starting to get hard. I gave it a squeeze, then another one. Shit, he was getting stiff as a board, and just from knowing I wanted to fuck him. I couldn't help wondering if I'd been hard while he'd been giving it to me.

Damn, his cock was getting huge. No wonder my butt was sore. But it was tingling too. I wondered what it had felt like. He reached across me to set down his coffee, then, he took my cup and got rid of it too.

"So what are we waiting for?" With that, he rolled over on top of me. Damn, his body felt great, hard and strong. He humped his cock against my belly, ran his hands up and down my sides, real relaxed and natural like we'd done this a hundred times. Well, maybe *he* had. But even if I didn't know what to do, my body seemed to. My dick ground against his. My hands reached for his hairy butt. I spread his ass-cheeks, going for his hole with my fingers. He gave me this sort of wicked grin, and edged his body up a little higher on mine, so I could get to his butt easier. It felt so different from a woman's ass, high and round and hard, covered with soft, sweat-dampened fur. As our bodies rubbed together, I fingered his ass, actually working one a little ways inside him. But he had other ideas – for now.

With a sort of breathless, "Damn, you're good", he twisted around on top of me, straddling my shoulders and leaning down over my groin. Then, he started to suck me off. I nearly jumped out of my skin. He was pretty good at it, too. My dick was throbbing, jerking as it slid in and out of his mouth. He licked at the tip, stroked it with his lips, then, took my whole thick rod down his throat. All the time, his own stiff cock was lying against my face. Then I got it. He was wanting to sixty-nine. Well, I figured, what the hell. I've had cock up my ass, nothing else is likely to matter much. And anyway, it felt sort of good, thick and hard against my cheek. Still a little bit unsure, I pushed my face up into his crotch, smelling his strong, musky man-smells. His balls fell against my mouth. Without even knowing I was going to, I started to lick them. That seemed to really send him off. He started working my dick even harder and faster in and out of his throat. I sucked at that hairy ball-sack in my face. I bit at it, tugged it with my lips as he gave me head like I'd never had before. Then, I took a deep breath. What the hell. I opened my mouth. At just the same time, he raised up his hips and brought them down again, stuffing his dick deep into my throat. I choked, and he pulled right back up.

"You OK, man? You just took it so easy last night I didn't even think about going slow." His cock was still poised over my mouth.

I nodded. "I'm all right. Just let me catch my breath." He grinned and nodded, but went back to licking my nuts, the end of his dick just an inch above my lips. This time, I raised up my head and licked at his piss slit. His sweat tasted good, salty, warm. I pulled back, and watched as a clear bead of pre-cum oozed from the opening. I was ready for another go now. More than ready. I slid my lips up over his meat, and started sucking cock.

We rolled over on our sides, mashing our fronts together, sucking dick like there was no tomorrow. And even though I never would have believed it, it felt goddamned good. I don't know, maybe I'd been wanting something like this for a long time. But it didn't matter now. I'd been fucked, and now I was a cocksucker, and all because I'd been drunk enough to get involved in some weird bi three-way. Whatever, I was loving it. But I wanted more.

When we finally pulled apart, breathing hard, and wiping the spit from our faces, I looked him right in the eye.

"How about that return favour you promised me?" My hands were running over his body, his thick pecs, the hard, furry ridges of his belly, his thighs.

He grinned wide. "I guess I can take it. You got quite a piece there, though." He was holding my stiff meat in his hand.

But he was ready alright. He gave me this little wink and flopped over on his stomach. He spread his legs, then reached up for a pillow. I watched as he doubled it up, and slid it under his pelvis, making his ass stick up in the air.

"Lick it first a little, would you, man? Gotta get it relaxed some."

"Lick it ... your ass?"

He craned his neck back to look at me. "Yeah. Stick your tongue in my butt good and deep – just like you did last night. I've never met anybody who could suck butt as good as you."

Well, when you find out you have a talent, why waste it, right? Not exactly sure what I was going to do, I got down on my knees between his legs, and bent over. But my mouth seemed to know. My lips ran up and down over the furry mounds of his ass. Tongue traced down the crack of his butt. Then, my hands were spreading his ass open. I could see the pink pucker of his hole, tightening, then relaxing, just waiting for me to do whatever I wanted. Then, I licked it – licked his hot, wet, sweaty hole.

One taste was all it took. Then I remembered: remembered the way I'd tongued his butt, remembered the smell of his macho ass, remembered him flipping me over, remembered the incredible feeling as his cock slammed inside my open butt-hole, remembered even how I'd bucked underneath him and begged for more. But this time, it'd be him begging. It was my turn now.

I licked his hole alright, licked it good, ran my tongue up in him again, spit in his crack, rubbed the spit around his butt with my face, forced a big wad of saliva up his ass with my lips. I was going to fuck this guy, and I wanted him good and slick. I had him moaning by now. I wondered if all bi guys liked ass-work as much as he did – hell – as much as both of us seemed to.

But my body was already moving on top of his back, my cock sliding in the spit between his spread butt-cheeks. He reached back to grab my dick, to guide it against his hole. And I could hear his voice, low and sexy:

"Yeah, man. Yeah. Give it to me now. Shove that big dick up my butt. Yeah. Come on. Gimme that fat cock. Give it to me like a man ..."

I didn't wait, or go slow and easy like I would have with a chick. No, this guy knew what he was asking for, and I gave it to him. I drove my hips forward, plowing my throbbing cock inside his tight butt-hole. And he didn't act like a pansy about it. No, he just raised his ass higher, and slammed back to push it in deeper.

He craned his head back again. He was gasping, and his smile was tight, but he was nodding, loving it. I looked down at his broad back, at the place where his hairy buns were speared by my shaft.

"Alright man, do it now, hard and fast. Just like I gave it to you."

He grinned again and gave another playful twitch of his ass, sending shivers up my back. Another invitation I didn't need. I pulled out, and rammed him again. Then again. And again. All the way out every time, then, slamming all the way back in. His deep moans were my only answer. He spread his legs further, pushing all the way up onto his hands and knees. He rested his body on one shoulder, taking the pounding, and begging for more as he jerked himself off and pinched at his own hairy tits.

"Yeah, man. Harder. Harder. Fuck my butt, dude. Fuck it deeper." He was grinning from ear to ear. "Fuck me raw, man. I can take it as good as you did."

I locked my hands around his waist and, grinning as wide as he was, I gave him everything he was begging for – and maybe a little more. I fucked him up, down and sideways. We fell off the bed, and rolled onto the floor, my cock pounding inside him all the time. Without pulling out, we stood up, and he leaned over the bureau. In the mirror above it, we could both watch me giving it to him – watch him beating furiously at his meat. I turned us sideways and went slow for a minute so we could both watch the way my dick slid in and out of his hole – watch the way our big bodies moved together – watch me grab handfuls of the muscles of his chest, twist his tits – watch the look on his face every time I rammed my cock home deep inside him. Then, suddenly: "Oh ... oh ... OH ... OOOHHH .... I'm gonna shoot, man. NOW GIVE IT TO ME! NOW! GIMME THAT HOT CUM! Yeah! YEAH!"

And I did. With one last huge slam into his ass, I unloaded my spunk up his butt. He howled, arching his back to get as much of my shaft inside him as possible, laughing and gasping as I pumped my hot cum into his body. And then I saw that thick, white wads were shooting out of his shaft, splashing the mirror, the bureau, the carpet. Still engaged, we fell back on the bed, panting and playing grab-ass. Finally, when we'd calmed down, he kissed me. On the lips.

"What's your name?"

He told me. He already seemed to know mine from last night. We took an hour break, naked, watching football on TV and guzzling beer. At half-time, he got behind me and slid up my butt again. We fucked through the whole third quarter. We were still naked on the bed when his wife came home. She watched as we sucked each other off and then joined in herself.

The three of us get together all the time now – they've even asked me to move in with them. And I love the three-ways. But you know, I think I like it even better when it's just him and me. Shit, if I'd known being bi was this good, I'd never have held off so long.

Starfish

Dan Wolff

When Martin and Peta couldn't keep their hands off each other any longer, they made love on the bed. At last. It was too late and I was too tired and drunk to really see what was happening. I was sitting on the doorstep to the roof and my eyes were sore. That's love, I told myself. That animal is love. Peta had shed his cotton shirt and trousers and was beneath Martin. She wore a bedsheet around her shoulders like a cape. She stroked herself as she moved slowly and dreamily on top of him. They kept a slow rhythm like dance partners and looked yearningly, intently into each other's faces.

Surprised I was still in the room, I left. I washed my face in the little bathroom with yellow walls. I thought about Peta's red hair and mobile face. I went into the other room and lay down on the other bed, the creaking-sprung bed with the cream coverlet. Gaish had fallen asleep in her plaid shirt but had managed to take her boots off. I fell asleep next to her. Sometime later I imagined Peta had come into the room and was sleeping next to me so I put my arm around him and buried my face in his neck.

But it was Gaish, asleep on the same bed. I was embarrassed and tried to let go, but in her own sleep she held my hand where it was.

We were renting an apartment. It was on the third floor at the top of an iron staircase in an airy well; two rooms for the four of us, plus a bathroom. It cost 200 pesos a week. The apartment was in a working neighbourhood near the Periferico highway, just below the hill with the amphitheatre which looked out over all Oaxaca in its valley.

Life was very simple. We rose late, did our laundry at the concrete sink, and went down the street for lunch. Lunch was the 'Menu de Dia', whatever that happened to be, something like quesadillas and chilli, roasted prickly pear, croquettes of spinach and tapioca, and coffee. We all got sick; Peta from eating a taco which had been sitting in oil for a day; Gaish from bad fish; Martin and I from sharing a glass of juice with ice which was not *agua purificada*. The illness brought us closer. It was hard not to be intimately aware of each other's bodily functions and the voiding that took place, when our bathroom was five feet square with a curtain for a door. We ate acidophilus, peptol bisbol, massaged each other's calves to cure nausea. I knew Martin was after Peta from the moment they met, and he was after her. I knew Martin like

79

family. Sometimes I even did her makeup for her. When she met Peta she was able to forget her heartbreak over her last girlfriend, the one who sold vegetables in St Kilda market.

"I'm not a dyke," she said. "I'm a sensitive being who has relationships with men and women in different proportions."

"Hey, not-a-dyke," I teased her when she cut her bleached hair into a two-tone and put away her leather jacket.

"Hey, androgyne," she replied, or sometimes, "hey, ambiguous." "Hey, neutral." "Hey, starfish." She told me about Peta. "He's from Shanghai. He's unbelievably beautiful, very small, and so intensely vivid he makes me gasp with exhaustion. The first moment I saw him, Sweeney, I wanted him under me. I couldn't help but think that. Am I damned?"

We were a strange bunch together; impeccable Peta, flamboyant Martin, myself who was doing my best to remove all my sexual characteristics, and Gaish who was once chased out of the women's toilet at the bus station by an old woman with a stick broom. "*soy mujer!*" shouted Gaish – "I'm a woman!" She didn't know how jealous I was.

Gaish was the explorer of our group. She followed every cobbled alley she come to, walked under every bridge and aqueduct, and later told us stories about Triki women making tortillas, or men repairing shoes with car tyre rubber, or buying water from a woman who told her Christ was whipped and beaten for her. Two nights after Martin and Peta finally broke down and fell on each other, Gaish found a tequila stand and bought a 40 peso bottle of mescal and a lime. That evening we played 'I never'. Gaish began it with "I never made love to a boy."

"Cheap shot," said Peta, who then had to drink.

I said, "I never really was a boy." That made Peta drink as well.

He said "I never know what you're thinking, Sweeney," and Martin raised her glass to her mouth and drank. "I know what Sweeney's thinking," she said with a daring grin.

So I was in love with Peta.

When we ran out of things we'd never done and started issuing dares. Peta dared Gaish to show us her nipple rings; she grabbed her t-shirt hem and gave us a momentary flash of silver. Martin dared me to kiss Peta and I did. My heart was racing but I kept my face calm and cool. I was unprepared and my scalp itched after I kissed him.

Gaish went to bed at about four a.m. and we kept drinking in our little room. Some time after that, when Peta was in the bathroom, Martin put her drunken head against mine.

"Sweeney," she said, "I'm in love."

"With Peta?"

"Yes, Peta. Isn't Peta wonderful?"

"Yes." Peta was wonderful, all right.

"Sweeney," she said, placing a hand decisively on my thigh, "let's drink more."

Because Martin and Peta were sharing a bed, Gaish and I slept in the same bed once more, the one with the coverlet covered in little pobbles of thread. Again she put her arm around me and then later our fingers were entwined. I rolled over and looked at her, surprised. She reached out and ran her fingers over my face.

She whispered to me, "I love you."

I felt the size of her, the strength of her arms and her hands. I didn't know what to do. I was out of the habit of attraction. Being attracted to Peta took all my energy; I was practising on him, slowly allowing attraction back into my life, building it up.

The room was full of grey light.

"Do you want to go for a walk?" I asked.

"All right."

We went through the room where Martin and Peta were asleep and down the iron stairway. We walked for a long time. At the market, which was already open, Gaish wanted horchata. We had completely different attitudes towards food. I wouldn't touch anything which might have been washed in impure water, but Gaish was derisive of my fear and helped herself to salads, fried meat, ice drinks. I bought tangerines while the vendor ladelled up two scoops of horchata into a paper cup and as we walked she sipped from it. I took one taste of the sweet, yeasty liquid.

We climbed the hill to the amphitheatre where the statue of Benito Juarez looked down on the city. We ate the tangerines while below us in Oaxaca the street lights shut off and the smog rose. Venus was high and strong. Clouds gathered over the range, and then rays shot through, and colour came into everything. I asked, "how long have you been in love with me?"

"I don't know."

"I didn't think you even liked me, that much?"

"I was just hanging out with you, you mean?"

"What do you want to happen?" I asked.

"I don't want anything to happen," she said. "I just wanted to tell you. I don't like to keep secrets about these things."

I said, "I'm not sexual at the moment."

"What do you mean?"

"I'm androgynous inside. I can't be a man. I don't want to be a woman either. I'm just in between, in a third space."

"Why can't you be a man?"

I was bitter. "Because not one thing about men is beautiful – not one thing. Everything is tainted by the absurd urge to dominate. I assumed you'd know what I meant, being gay."

"I'm not a lesbian because I hate men," she said. "I'm a lesbian because I love women."

"Well, what do you want?"

"I don't want," she said. "I hate possession. I hate jealousy. I love all my friends. How can I tell the moment when that love means something else? Especially when that feeling isn't always physical."

"Do you feel sexually towards me?"

"Sometimes," said Gaish.

So there we were in a city in a valley in a desert full of deep gorges, and I wasn't in love with Gaish, who frightened me with her flat scrutiny, but with Peta, who was in love with my best friend Martin, but Martin didn't mind because she thought it was cute and Peta goes both ways. Martin goes both ways. I go both ways, or I imagine I would if I ever broke this androgyny, and in fact the only one of us who doesn't go both ways is Gaish, and it was Gaish who was in love with me.

Most of the mornings that followed I had vivid, monstrous dreams and woke with a hangover at eleven. By that time Martin and Peta had gone somewhere and I wrote by myself in the library or the zocalo. Sometimes, to give Martin and Peta time alone, I followed Gaish on her eternal explorations of Oaxaca. We didn't talk much. She wasn't what you'd call a chatty person, and I couldn't think of anything appropriate to ask. We walked in a kind of brooding silence. Things seemed to have halted and I was relieved.

I've never been comfortable with sex. There it is. I like the details, the articles of sex: the way it affects daily things, even apples or eyeglasses; the way it makes phone calls into a pleasure that runs for hours. I like the way it fills your thoughts more than sex itself. I found a kind of replacement of physical sex when Martin began to take me into her confidence, and I learned all about her partners, their most vulnerable moments. Martin loved to talk about it and I loved to delve. In fact, most of my stories became things Martin had done. I told Gaish about Martin's girlfriend, the one who sold vegetables, and how we had to sneak into her house to steal back Martin's clothes when they broke it off.

"You talk about Martin all the time," said Gaish.

"I love her," I said.

"Have you two ever been a couple?"

"Nope. And we never will. We're too good as friends. Besides," I said. "I might never have sex again."

"Why is that?"

"What I was telling you, about being a man, being a sex."

"Would you sleep with Peta?"

"He's not available," I said.

One night Gaish and I left them and went walking in the hills behind the apartment. A pick-up truck load of young men invited us on board for drinks, but we left when a couple of them began to say threatening things in Spanish which they thought we didn't understand. We left them to it and walked down the hill and through the city. It was completely empty, no other drunks, no crowds, no music. I followed her all the way through the city, across the dry river, and up the hills on the other side. We walked through village streets just before dawn, streets which became stairways, streets which were the roofs of the houses below, streets which were half garden. The women who sold tortillas in the mercado were coming down the stairs in the dark, acting as though we were not there. "I don't think this place exists," said Gaish.

Everything was interesting to her. After the houses and a barbed-wire fence and a hill forested with cacti we made it to the barren summit just as day was about to break. At that point the strange energy which had kept us going through the night ran out and we lay down on our backs.

There was no sound except for the chill wind in the grass. If we lay right back all we could see was grass forever then sky. It was so cold we even put our arms around each other. She told me my eyes matched the grass below me. Hers matched the sky; pale, washed out hot morning eyes. She spread her coat over us both. An eagle, banking over the peak, passed by our heads and I saw its sharp face cock around to look at us. When the sun rose the clouds were so far off they might have been over Africa.

We walked to a road and hitched a ride with two Germans back to the zocalo. Sleepless and hungover we drank morning coffee in the Cafe Bar del Jardin, which was full of early rising white people. I looked at the marble top of our table, fourteen black tiles around sixteen rose tiles, and at the low sun shining though the laurels in the square. The trunks of the laurels were painted white with lime. I told Gaish how I thought about Peta. How Martin didn't mind because I was her confidant.

She said, "Martin expects way too much of you if she thinks that's good for you."

"How would you know?"

"I think you're being manipulated."

"No, I'm not."

We walked back to the apartment in silence. We slept in separate beds.

One night Peta danced with me. I was drinking mescal with one hand and had the other on his shoulder, feeling the skin through the thin cotton of his shirt.

I thought, I wish I had skin like his. I was looking at the triangle of his chest at the neck of his shirt. Then Martin and Peta danced. She bit Peta on the neck. She drew him over to me, holding his shirt open to show me a glimpse of his smooth chest, and said "Isn't he beautiful? Sweeney, isn't Peta beautiful?"

"Yes," I said.

Gaish and I sat and watched Martin and Peta dance. I noticed the way the black singlet Martin wore stuck to her belly, and the way the roundness of her belly balanced out the tight muscles of her back, her graceful posture. She was beautiful. Peta was shorter and moved from square hips. They were good together. That made me think I enjoyed walking about with Gaish. But we never had much to say to each other.

"I think Martin's in love."

"Again."

"Yeah, again."

I thought about what Gaish had said in the zocalo. We often came in to find Martin in only a bedsheet, which I was used to, and Peta as well, which I wasn't. I suppose I imagined one night we'd be drinking as usual and as Martin and Peta headed for bed Peta would take my hand. It was a childish thought, boyish, and I was embarrassed.

Martin wasn't manipulating me. Martin was just getting on with her own life. She was doing it for herself, not me. She was spending her days with Peta because she wanted to. As I was with Gaish.

"Do you want to go out on the roof and look around?" I asked Gaish.

"All right."

We left them dancing and went out onto the roof. Orion was right overhead; below us the yellow light of the street lit up the bottom halves of the buildings. I heard cheers and music from the zocalo. We stood on the edge of the roof for some time, watching the people in the street below. They never looked up and saw us.

"You never answered me when I told you I loved you," said Gaish.

"Have you lost all respect for me?"

"I thought you were more straightforward. I thought you knew what you wanted."

We sat together by the clothesline that ran over the rooftops, a wall of ill-feeling between us.

"Do you like Peta?" she asked.

I sighed. "I've been telling myself I do."

"Well, what about me?" she asked.

"I like you."

"Would you have said anything, if I hadn't?"

"I'd never thought about you in that way before. You're gay."

"Why does being a dyke mean I couldn't love a boy?"

I told her in my experience lesbians didn't like men to assume that. It was an arrogant thing to assume. That was one of the things I didn't like about men, the way they thought they were always wanted.

"What about now?"

"I like walking about with you."

"That's a start."

"I like spending time with you."

"But you don't feel attracted to me."

"No, that's not true. It's been so long since I acted on attraction I've forgotten what it means. I'm attracted to you. But I've just realised it's more important that I like to spend time with you. That's the most important thing there is."

We lay out there all night. I put my arm around Gaish, and I did it deliberately. Orion traversed the entire sky and vanished in the night haze which erases the mountains as if they never were. We saw the Southern Cross, and, finally, just at the edge of the night, Scorpio.

Just before dawn we went inside, and we were holding hands. We sat down on the other bed. We looked at each other in the grey light. We lay back. Then we kissed. She leaned over me.

"Do you want to make love?"

"I don't know how to have sex without being a man," I said.

"I don't know how to have sex with a man," she said.

I was shy. Practically virginal. It was dusky in the room with the curtain drawn. I wanted it to be dark. I didn't want my eyes open anymore.

Now everything was close up, like being twins in a womb. Across the bed was too far away. Now that we were touching, I wanted to feel as much of her as possible, I wanted to feel the differences in skin. Her sides, under her arms, where the skin was suddenly as smooth as ice water.

She pinned me to the bed by my shirt, tried to take it off, but I refused.

"I'm not sure," I said.

She was much stronger than me though my hands were bigger. She could pin me easily. Sometimes our embraces got more intense until we were wrestling, and she held me down. She kissed my stomach, then bit, hard and protracted, and I lay there stunned by the pleasure-pain like my blood was being sucked. My flesh rose and she licked it better. But it wasn't that she was violent, only concentrated, laser-like, fierce. "I want you," she said. She bit me again and again on the stomach while I curled and twisted.

"I guess you don't like that."

"No, I like it."

"Tell me if it's too painful."

Then everything stopped. We lay there. Looking at each other. We were still dressed.

I couldn't get over how strong her body was, how thick and strong. Her muscles were smooth under her skin, you almost didn't know they were there until you fell back exhausted. She held me hard, raised her thigh into my crotch, and I forced myself against her thigh, desperate suddenly, wanting that pleasure-pain, wanting to rip and tear or be ripped and torn, so much needing to touch her, then falling back again in exhaustion and lying there.

She took my hand and directed it over her belly and thigh, over the mound in the front of her pants, under her shirt, over her skin. She made such soft noises, rising notes, like the songbirds the men carry about in the zocalo in a tall stack of cages. Just like that.

"You're good with your hands."

"My hands are my favourite part of me."

Suddenly desperate, I had to grab her again, be grabbed equally hard, lock against her body. Hold me. I took off her shirt. Her shoulders naked twins, her head of hair startlingly black above the bare skin.

"I wonder what you'd look like in a dress," she said.

"I wonder what *you'd* look like in a dress."

She tried to undress me, murmuring entreaties in my ear. The jeans went. She was bold; she inspired boldness in me.

When we played 'I never' I saw a glimpse of her piercings; now I took one of those rings into my mouth. I felt the rough surface of her nipple, the cold metal running through it, clicking against my teeth like change. "Gently," she gasped. The rings were sensitive; tugging them hurt like a bite.

"Do you want to be inside me?" she whispered.

"I don't know."

"I don't know either."

We lay there in each other's arms. We wouldn't rush things.

On the bus to Puerto Escandido Gaish and I had the rear seats to ourselves. Martin and Peta had decided to stay in Oaxaca a while longer. We were interrupted when the soldiers at the toll came on board and asked for our passports. We went through our bags, sweaty and wondering if it was obvious what we had been doing with our hands moments before.

They looked at my passport photo and asked me how long I was going to stay in Mexico. A few more weeks, I told them.

"And your amigo?"

"No," I said, smiling. "Mi amiga."

They looked at Gaish. I suppose it wasn't obvious.

I'm Sorry

Marilyn Jaye Lewis

My mother was thirteen years old that Friday when I was born – back in the summer of 1960, in a county home for unwed mothers – and in keeping with the pathos of the situation, Brenda Lee's I'm Sorry was a No. 1 Billboard smash hit on Top 40 radio stations nationwide. I was unceremoniously dragged – by the use of forceps clamped over my eyes – out of my young mother's vagina, while teenaged girls all over America commiserated:

> "I'm sorry, so sorry, I was such a fool,
> I didn't know love could be so cruel;
> You tell me
> mistakes
> are part of being young
> Oh, but that don't right
> the wrong that's been done ..."

(I'm Sorry ©Seif-Albritton)

My mother was unrealistic about a lot of things, I guess, especially regarding her plans for me – her newborn, her little treasure. She was packing my meager belongings, which consisted of some cloth diapers and a cotton blanket, in preparation for our leaving the county home at last and returning to her real bed, in her little room in a small house in a small southern Ohio town, when my grandpa came in and gave her the news: The folks from the private adoption agency he'd called behind her back had come to collect the baby.

My mother had been under the naive impression, for nine long months, that the baby growing in her ever-expanding womb – the same fetus that had incited other kids at MacLean Junior High School to call her whore and which was now a squalling, beet-red, warm-blooded infant gift from God, needing her nipple – was hers. The forced adoption devastated her and she embarked almost immediately on a new illegitimate pregnancy that brought first a hasty marriage, and then a life-long cocktail hour in one hillbilly bar after another, because she learned the hard way that no number of pregnancies could replace the baby they'd taken away. Even though I was barely cognizant back then,

I don't think I was too wild about the separation, either. I spent the next twenty-five years wishing achingly on a lot of stars, with a huge gaping void in my soul. My nightly prayers were filled with pleas, like: God, can I please have my real mother back?

She was thirty-eight years old when I finally found her. She normally worked as a barmaid and lived off the Appalachian Highway in some holler with a truck driver. But the day my letter arrived in her mailbox she was just getting out of a brief stint in jail.

I wasn't the person she most wanted to think about right then. She tossed my letter, with the enclosed baby pictures that had been taken twenty-five years earlier by a somewhat affluent married couple up north, onto the kitchen counter and lit a cigarette.

. . . .

It was Decoration Day when she finally agreed to meet me. Decoration Day is what northerners call Memorial Day – when you go out to the graveyard and place flowers on the tombstones of soldiers you knew who died in a war, and then placed flowers on the tombstones of your other deceased loved ones, as long as you were going out to the graveyard anyway.

So she agreed to meet me on Decoration Day, in neutral territory: My great-aunt Dot's tiny, spotless kitchen.

My mother came in the kitchen door that afternoon, after twenty-five years of being separated from her baby, followed by one of the most magnetically-attractive girls I'd ever seen. She was almost as tall as I was, but she was much more solidly built. She had large, muscular arms, thick sturdy legs. She was fairly dark-complected, with dark brown hair, coal black eyes and wide high cheekbones – the result of being born half-Cherokee. I was smitten with her, instantly in-love. Here's my dream lover, I thought, what is she doing hanging out with my mom?

I had a predilection back then for getting spanked by large women. I took one look at that dark-haired girl's massive arms and thought, This is going to be great. Somehow I have to get my fanny over that girl's considerable knee ...

I was already deep into a fantasy that didn't involve much detail beyond having my jeans and underpants around my thighs and being across this girl's lap, when I was introduced by my great-aunt Dot to my younger half-sister, Rae Anne. She'd been eighteen for three whole weeks already, I was told, and was due to graduate high school the following weekend. I'd come back into my mother's fold just in time to witness an unusual family occurrence: a high school graduation – most of them had dropped-out. My newfound mother was emotionally distant, offering me no more than a quick hug when she said hello, but spirits in general were running high; Now my mother could state she had two daughters who had graduated high school.

. . . .

Rae Anne and I sat alone together out on our aunt's driveway in a couple of folding aluminium patio chairs. Conversation between us was stilted and awkward. I stared at her a lot – in awe, I'd say, having always wanted a sister. But she made very little eye contact with me in return, her eyes darting away nervously whenever she'd try to steal a glance at me and then find I was still staring.

"So what kinds of things do you like to do?" I asked, in a feeble attempt to get her talking as quickly as possible about her sexual experiences.

"Oh, I like to play basketball, fix cars, motorcycles, that kind of thing."

Thank you god, I thought, she's a dyke – but I wonder if she knows it yet ...

"Mom says you're a singer in New York City."

"Yeah," I replied. "I sing country music in these little bars and I wait tables during the day. I was married to a Chinese man for a little while, but we're separated now because he'd rather be gay and I'm fooling around with a woman."

There, I thought, direct, to the point, check out that astonished expression on her face.

"Really," she asked, in a very hushed voice – the back screen door was open and the rest of my newfound family was still sitting in the kitchen, chatting over coffee and my great-aunt Dot's cherry pie – "you sleep with girls?"

"Uh-huh," I nodded, studying her expression. Come to me baby, tell me things.

"Really? For real?"

"Yes."

She was fidgeting uneasily in her aluminium patio chair. She leaned closer to me and confided, "I'm gay. But I haven't told mom."

Hallelujah, I thought, she knows. "Are you planning on telling her?"

"No, man, I couldn't tell her that – she'd freak."

I scooted my chair closer to hers on the driveway and said, "She didn't freak when I told her about me."

"You told mom you sleep with girls?"

"Uh-huh."

"And she didn't freak?"

"No. I told her all kinds of things, she knows all about me."

....

Later that night, when everyone had gone home, I laid alone in a king-sized bed. My great-aunt Dot and my great-uncle Jim had graciously moved into the tiny guest room so that I could have their sizable bed and feel like a treasured guest who had come a long way in a treacherous night. I'd quickly discovered that most of my relations carried the guilt of my grandfather's decision to cast out my mother's baby to perfect strangers, they all bent over backwards to make me feel comfortable, in a genuine display of joy over the fact that I was finally back with my mother and maybe now all the guilty feelings could be buried.

But as I lay in the big bed alone in the dark, and thought about the day's occurrences, rather than focus on finally having met my long-sought mother, or the distant emotional stance she'd taken towards me, my thoughts centered instead on my sister.

"Is there anything you want for your graduation that you wouldn't want to ask mom to get you?" I'd asked confidentially, before she got in the car to go home.

She'd smiled. "Gin?"

"Gin it is," I'd promised her. "Just don't drink and drive."

What an amazing turn my life had taken. I was going to be present at my sister's graduation with a secret bottle of gin, my mother was going to bake a cake and the trucker she lived with was pulling out the stops and planning to buy beer and whiskey and have food brought in for everybody. I was even going to get to meet my half-brother, who'd be coming in from the neighbouring town where he lived in a trailer with his drunk old man.

He was the black sheep of the family – my half-brother. A high school drop-out with a volatile temper, a half-Cherokee alcoholic who was always in jail. It felt great to finally be in a family dynamic where I was perceived to be the golden child who had done great things – I was a singer in New York City, I'd married a man from China. The family who had raised me held a decidedly different opinion of me. After all, I'd married a known faggot – he was Chinese, of all things – and I slept around with girls; junkies some of them, musicians most of them, and I wasted my life singing in bars.

Suddenly I was very pleased with my exotic lifestyle and I couldn't wait to spend more time with my sister, regaling her with tales of what it was like to hang out in queer bars and openly bring girls home to fuck.

"I've only been with a couple women," she'd said quietly, "my gym teacher and then her daughter and one other girl. But I know that's what I want, I want to be with women. I don't care what people think."

But she was still having to be extremely careful, doing it in her car at night, after pulling off some back road and parking under the cover of trees. I remembered what that was like – being young and having to hide it. Fucking boys was one thing, you didn't want your parents to catch you doing that. But fucking a girl? It would have been the end of the world.

I laid in that bed and began to wonder what kinds of things my sister was doing to girls in her car. I wondered if she was anything like me – if she hungered for the things I hungered for, and had a taste for doing the things I liked to do. Then I started to wonder what her body looked like when she got completely aroused, stripped out of her clothes and spread her legs in the back seat. What did her pussy look like to some girl whose face was coming up close to it? What would the lips look like when some girl's fingers were spreading her open, when some girl's mouth was finding her swelling clit – did my sister's pussy look anything like mine? And if so, did that mean I looked like my mom; did I finally belong somewhere?

I had my fingers between my legs by then, I was masturbating as quietly as possible in my aunt and uncle's bed while the pictures filled my mind easily –

they were blossoming with remarkable clarity and my entire body succumbed to the sensitivity of my clit. I could see my sister perfectly in the back seat of that car because I was in there with her, it was my face disappearing between her legs as my tongue found her swelling clitoris and made her moan. I just wanted to make her happy; it was pleasing me to hear her guttural groans and cries. It would be like playing together, I imagined – only now we were grown and had special secret games to play in the back seat of her car. We'd missed those years of being little together, of being confidants and pals, of jumping around in our pjs on a Saturday morning until our mother lost her patience – listening to all that noise – and came in to spank somebody, but which little naughty girl would it be?

This time I was hoping it would be Rae Anne, I'd like to see my little sister get spanked by my mom. There she goes, I thought, over my mother's knee; down come her little pyjama bottoms and then spank spank spank, until her tiny naked tushy is fiery-red. Besides, I'd spent too many years wearing out my own spanking fantasies, I didn't need to see them anymore. I'd summoned them so many times over the years that they'd worn a smooth path through my mind's eye and couldn't ignite my clitoris anymore; Fantasies of being alone with my secret mother, my special gift-from-god mother, who hadn't left me behind, who hadn't given me up; who, in fact, loved me so much she had to do what was best for me, take me over her knee, spank spank spank – until the fantasies progressed to real life and real women who I met in bars; women who agreed to take me over their knees but who didn't stop there; who made me put on those frilly white socks and who insisted my pussy be shaved smooth; the ones who gagged me with red bandannas, threw me onto the bed – my own bed – and tied my wrists too tightly, who went too far, who took me all the way out to the edge and made me come as they inserted the douche nozzle in my ass when my ankles were tied somewhere up over my head, and then the warm water streamed steadily into my rectum, filled me up, while a hand slapped me harder harder harder and a kind but firm voice warned me to hold the water in ...

....

The night before my sister graduated from high school, my mother and her trucker boyfriend took us out to a hillbilly bar for a seemingly endless parade of malt liquor. My sister was still too young to drink in a bar, but she wasn't disappointed, she had a brand new bottle of gin waiting for her in the back seat of her car. I, on the other hand, never drank malt liquor and the sheer number of drinks being placed in front of me that night was making me queasy. But my mother was on a roll.

"She's the baby that mattered, you know," she drunkenly informed my little sister. "She was more important than the rest of you." (I had yet another half-sister who'd preferred to be raised on an aunt's farm – my mother's drinking and that sister's father's constant beatings with a leather belt had driven her off at an early age. I would meet her, too, the next day at the graduation, along with my grandpa, the man who had sealed my fate that summer day in 1960.)

When the malt liquor had gotten to be too much, my mother and her boyfriend took off for home in his truck, while my sister and I got into her car and went for a drive along the back roads.

"You can't imagine what it was like, Rae Anne," I began drunkenly, "growing up alone, to never feel like you fit in with the people around you because they all look like each other and you don't look like any of them. It was lonely. I didn't know you even existed, but I sure missed mom, every day of my life."

"It's good you came home," she replied soberly. "It's been good for mom, I can see a difference in her already. You're her victory over grandpa, you know."

We were driving into total darkness, no houses, no carry-outs, no lights. But my sister knew her way around those back roads. We came to a railroad crossing and she veered off to a clearing and parked the car.

I was drunk enough on malt liquor to feel unabashedly aroused. We were in total darkness, my sister and I, miles away from anyone we knew. Maybe now would be a good time to tell her about my theory, about how incest couldn't be wrong between two consenting adults who couldn't possibly conceive an inbred accident, another hungry mouth for the welfare state. Maybe now would be a good time to regale her with the stories of how liberating it feels to bring a girl home and fuck, to not have to hide in your car while trying to cram your eager face between a girl's spread legs. That's it, I thought, start talking dirty, that's how the juices start churning – from the pictures you plant in someone's head.

So I started with the dirty talk and I was making Rae Anne laugh, uneasily at first, but then she joined in with her own dirty stories, stories about eating pussy and how turned on she got looking between a girl's legs.

Then I unbuttoned my shirt, a faded cotton denim work shirt, and I wasn't wearing a bra.

"Do you think your tits look like mine?" I asked quietly, pinching my nipples a little so they'd perk up and get stiff. "Huh, do your tits look like these?"

Even though it was dark in the car I could feel her staring hard at me, trying to see.

"Do you think we're alike on the outside? We seem to like the same things on the inside, Rae Anne."

My sister didn't say anything. I scooted as close to her as I could get, but we were still in the front seat and there was a stick shift between us. I wanted to get her into the back seat, I wanted to make love to her so bad. Somehow she seemed more like my mother to me than my mother did; I could get close with Rae Anne, tell her things, where my mother put up that emotional distance unless she was drunk.

"It sounds like you must have had a really hard life," Rae Anne said, "not fitting in and being treated like you were crazy because you were different. I know mom didn't want to give you up, but I know grandpa did it because he thought it was going to be best for you, give you a chance at a better life."

"How could being taken from my mother give me anything but a hole inside?" I demanded.

Rae Anne stopped talking for quite awhile. I didn't know what had happened. I couldn't figure out how to get the conversation back to pussies and fooling around without being obtrusively blunt.

Then she reached around in back of her and lifted out the bottle of gin. She opened it and drank a little of it straight.

"I want to talk to you about something. I've been trying to say it since that first day we met."

I leaned in close to her, my shirt hanging wide open, and I ran my hand lightly over her thigh. "What is it? You can talk to me. You can tell me anything, you're my sister."

"I had a baby last year, a girl. And I put her up for adoption. It was my choice, mom begged me to keep her, but I thought I was doing what was best for the baby. I wanted to finish high school so bad, you know? I wanted to be more than just a drop-out on welfare."

I wish I could tell you that Brenda Lee came over the radio at that moment, wailing sorrowfully about how sorry she was – it would have been so achingly poetic – but we were in Van Halen territory, the region of the country that worshipped heavy metal. Frankly, the radio wasn't even on and the stars in the sky and the quiet night-murmuring of insects you can always count on but can never see, was bittersweet enough in that dark car on that back road. We didn't need Brenda Lee.

I buttoned up my shirt and tried to control my sudden anger.

"I came so far," I scolded Rae Anne. "It took me so long to find my way back home and now it's like it doesn't even matter, because it's started all over again for that baby girl of yours."

I had pictures in my head of smacking Rae Anne, of spanking her, like a real mommy spanks her kid because the kid did something really wrong – a mistake, sure, but a mistake that hurts a lot of people and can never be undone.

"I fucked up," Rae Anne apologised. "I'm sorry."

A Rising Son

Dean Durber

I was sixteen and stepping off a plane alone. Sixteen and listening to an attempt at "thank you" – she said 'sank you' – as Mariko accepted the small gift I gave her and gently brushed at my hand. I wasn't much into girls. Never not into them. Just never had the chances. A few kisses at parties. One quick roll on the grassy bank nearby my home. But nothing like the achievements of my best mate Shawn, who at sixteen had already fucked seven, plus one teacher. Whenever I watched him undress, I saw the reason behind his early successes. But Mariko looked like a nice girl, to me.

The mother, Mrs. Matsumoto, showed me to my room. I was the fortunate one, she told me. In a household of three kids and three bedrooms, I got to sleep alone. I figured Mariko must have been sleeping with her mother and her baby sister, the brother in another one and the father, well, I never got to meet the father. The Matsumoto family was something of a Japanese rarity. A delicacy. They were divorced. They took a foreigner into their home. And they helped me to lose my virginity at a time when I wasn't really thinking about it, not that much anyway. Not bad for a sixteen year old boy on a trip paid for by his father, encouraged by his mother, and suddenly sporting a hard-on that Mariko's gentle touch had caused. She led me on from the very start, that girl.

On my first evening, she played footsie with me under the dinner table. I don't think it could have started off in any way as an accident, because the table was too big for her feet to be dangling so innocently right there in front of mine. She had to be straining and stretching them out, teasing me now with the tickle of her toes, rubbing the white nylon of her schoolgirl socks up and down. She slipped a toe inside the left leg of my trousers and attempted to raise it up past my shin, perhaps seeking to sneak a glimpse of some dark, manly hair. I hoped she wouldn't be too disappointed when she discovered I didn't have that much. My best friend Shawn had hair. Not me. And what little I had was fair. Fair hair on me, black hair on her. Blue eyes versus brown eyes. White teeth versus crooked teeth. I didn't mind her teeth.

Mrs. Matsumoto was busy. She noticed nothing. She prepared food, took away dirty dishes and brought clean ones in rapid succession to the table, piling plates of odd-looking, odd-tasting stuff right under my nose. I guess it

95

must have been doubly impossible for her to have ever imagined what childish mischief was building beneath her field of vision. This was her own daughter, a sexless being for sure at the tender age of sixteen; and a Japanese image of purity. I too had expected chopsticks, sushi, sumo and dark green tea. Not frolics in the park and open-mouthed kissing. I was gaining a whole new insight into this land of raw, fresh sashimi. And I liked it from day one.

Mariko excused herself as the food kept on coming and motioned for me to follow. I rose from the table to an awareness of the hard-on poking out at the front of my baggy tracksuit bottoms. I casually tried to push it down with a hand inside my pocket and noticed Mishima smile. We bonded then. I winked, just to let him know I was okay about sharing my secret with him. We were boys together. He laughed. He ducked his head to shovel a heap of noodles into his mouth and I listened to him slurp and swallow. Nice sounds that my mother would have been ashamed of, disgusted by. I was thinking about him a lot as I stepped out of the house, with Mariko, his sister, into the chill of the night.

Instantly, she took hold of my hand and made me run beside her to a nearby park, where it was too dark to see a thing except cherry blossoms. They were everywhere, in full bloom, too bright to hide. I suspected that had I been able to see or read, I might have noticed a sign, something telling us not to venture in after dusk. Possibly people had been murdered or raped in the very spot where I now stood, but what did I care. In nervous hands, I was holding my first pair of tits. They had been eagerly exposed from the protection of their bra by Mariko who was nothing like the girls back home. They let Shawn go this far, never me. But now I played with nipples, not really knowing why, and listened to Mariko's moaning. Each time I flicked them or squeezed them between my fingers, I felt a small pant of her breath push its way towards the back of my throat. I squeezed them harder. A deeper breath filled my lungs. I swallowed and filled my mouth with Mariko as my cock poked at the restrictive cotton of my pants.

Lying on the ground, semi-wet grass penetrated our clothes. This must have been far more of an irritation to Mariko with me the one on top. That's the way I had seen it done in so many dirty movies shared around class. That's the way I wanted to do it first. I'd heard this was how it worked best, for boys. And Mariko never seemed to mind. She never spoke much. She just screamed, and thrust her hips towards me, mumbling words that I found confusing. "Iku! Iku! Iku!"

From memory, and a few basic lessons, this verb meant "to go". What was she asking? Did she want me to stop? Did she want me to wait? There was no holding back. I was too far gone. So I just collapsed on top of her and floated as she wrapped her arms around me as if to say 'sank you', and we lay there for a while, breathless, until one of us started to giggle. It was Mariko. Then we both giggled. Though I never once thought of that moment as funny. I lay there and wondered what Shawn would think when I told him.

When we got home, it was late, but nobody asked us where we had been. Mrs. Matsumoto was still in the kitchen, making noises with pots and pans, shouting from time to time to kids who paid her no attention. We were all too preoccupied with the pictures of fighting on the programme on the box.

"Anime," said Mishima, pointing at the screen.

"Cartoon," I replied.

We all liked them. Mariko, Mishima and me, sitting close on the sofa. A little sister kneeling on the floor in front. We stared at that television as if there was nothing else worth looking at in the world. I kept my eyes fixed and thought of the people around me. I was so glad to be part of the family.

Soon Mrs. Matsumoto poked her flustered head through the split curtain that separated her space from ours, and spoke. Mishima stamped his foot hard on the ground and kicked at a book which went flying across the floor to where his mother was standing. She bent down, picked it up and placed it on the table without uttering a word. Mishima must have been driven by guilt to get up and leave, but tried to keep his eyes on the screen for as long as he could as he backed out of the room and closed the door reluctantly behind him. I guessed it was time for homework. Poor bugger. And Mariko? Would she have to go too? At least my mother never hassled me about things like that. She was always too busy talking on the phone to her friends about forthcoming weddings or concerts, bridge nights and luncheons every day of the week. My father would ask sporadically, but would never wait long enough for an answer before reciting his overused speech about the need for a good education, my pathway to a successful life, like him, sixteen hours a day in an office with a suit that choked at his neck. They didn't know what subjects I studied. They never asked. I didn't miss them. Not one bit. Hardly even knew them.

I planned to shuffle secretly and swiftly along the sofa to fill Mishima's space and get myself closer to Mariko, without getting too obviously close. But Mishima put a stop to my plans on his sister by opening the door and sticking his head back in. "o-furo?"

He said it many times and then finally I understood. I looked at Mariko, who smiled and motioned for me to go. She upset me. I really liked what we had done and I was hoping we could do it again sometime, soon perhaps. But now I had to follow Mishima to a tiny room with a sink and a washing machine, everything inside a sickly bright green. Plastic everything.

"What do you want me to do?"

"o-furo."

He slid open a glass door to reveal a steamy room, half of which was a bath, filled to the top with clear, clean water.

"Ah, arigato!"

It had been one hard, dirty day. All that sweating with Mariko. Plus the sitting on a plane for more than fifteen hours, nodding off on the person next to me, drooling on their shoulder, breathing in stale air and risking my life to get here. Yes, a bath was a good idea. To relax and think about what I had achieved. And what I would say to Shawn. About a girl called Mariko. And now her brother Mishima, who was almost fully undressed in a second, tossing his clothes into a pile on top of the washing machine, and finally removing his underpants to show me a small, brown cock surrounded by wiry black pubes.

His skin was much darker than mine, or Shawn's. It looked more healthy, more appealing. I had this sudden urge to reach out and touch his arm, just to test how it felt. It had been almost six years since I had last bathed with a boy. In the past with my brother, a cousin, often with Shawn. But we had grown out of that when we started sprouting hair beneath our arms and made demands for the door to be locked. I felt lonely alone in the bath. And now I felt ugly, standing beside the brownness of Mishima.

I was about to jump straight into the tub to hide my naked shame when Mishima grabbed me by the arm and held me back. He placed two small plastic stools side by side on the tiled floor and motioned for me to sit on the one next to his. It was so low that I worried about the shit from my arse that might have been rubbing off as I squatted uncomfortably on it. In the corner sat a heap of shampoos and conditioners that Mishima chose from, opening them up to pour way too much over his head. As he raised his arms, I noticed black wiry hair poking out from the crevices of his pits. I stared at that for a long while. Water poured down from a shower nozzle that hung just above our heads, and washed over his face. When he had finished lathering up, he handed me the bottle and I copied exactly what he had just done, raising my arms in the same way, wondering if he was looking at me. I closed my eyes tightly and imagined he was. When he stood up to soap his entire body from head to toe, I stood too and copied. When I couldn't quite reach to the small of my back, he took the soap from my hand and did it for me. He turned and I did his, wondering how far my fingers were permitted to go. Finally we washed it all away, watching the suds disappear down into the ground, knowing without shame that both of our cocks were a little bit larger than they had been when we had first undressed. Mishima smiled and pointed to the tub. I hurriedly agreed.

There was barely enough room inside for one, not two. It was much deeper than the baths I was used to, which made it possible for me to sit in it with my back straight, leaning against the side, the water coming right up to my chin. But I couldn't stretch out my legs. Not without having them run along the side of Mishima, which he didn't seem to mind me doing considering he was already doing the same with his. His skin was as smooth as it looked. I could not remember if Mariko's had felt the same way. It had all happened too quickly with her. But here I was again, slowly building up to something, with his hand tickling across my leg, further up, to the thigh, on the inside and softly touching the bottom of my fully erect cock. Mishima took it shyly in his hand and leaned forward. I responded. I grasped hold of his and we kissed. He tasted so clean. A picture in my mind of Shawn. The touch of his tongue against mine forced a sudden rush of blood, which I thought would explode at any moment from the head of a cock that he toyed with, and fondled, until suddenly two lots of discharge were floating about and sticking to our skin. Mishima splashed and started to laugh. I laughed too, and stepped out after him to help pick off bits from the side of the tub as the water disappeared down the hole. Mariko was still waiting when I entered the living room, my face all flushed and warm.

My trip lasted three weeks. Every day with Mariko and Mishima. We never talked together about the things we did, but I think they both knew what went on. They shared their time amongst me with too perfect precision for there not to have been any prearranged plan worked out between them.

"How was it?" asked Shawn, keen to see me on my return. I told him it had not been as I'd expected and I left it at that. Our friendship had already begun to fade. I never showed him the letters I received from Mariko and Mishima, in separate envelopes. Nor read to him the many replies I sent back. I came top of the class in Japanese that year. My teacher said I had a natural gift for the language. I always maintained my Japanese family had been particularly helpful.

Rough Boy

(Inspired by the song by Pete Townshend)

Deborah Block-Schwenk

Jane and I are walking hand-in-hand exploring our new neighbourhood. Suburbia has a quiet aura of security and permanence that's attractive, a pervasive freshness like the aroma of newly mown grass.

But we know, having both grown up in the 'burbs, having escaped and now, coming full circle, returned, that the scent is also chlorine gas, a vapour that can suffocate. It scars you invisibly and leaves you shaking. The night comes when you wake up, shell-shocked, in a strange man's bed and realize that despite all you were taught, you never learned anything truly important.

When I first came out, I thought I was gay. Why shouldn't I be? There were men everywhere: at the gym, flirtatiously showing off their smooth, well-muscled chests; in the bars, in tight jeans and T-shirts, blood propelled by the thundering beat. Even on the city streets there were men with a certain look in their eyes, a subtle way of walking like a dance to a secret song. Our eyes would meet, then a quick flash to the body, then as we passed, a quick look back. If we caught each other in that tiny second of reexamination, one of us would break his path, turn around ...

The man I settled down with was not a man I'd met in the gym or the bars. He was a big man, furry and affectionate. It seemed the essence of masculinity to curl up against his warm body, smell his earthiness and strength. I'd lay my face against the curls at his chest, nose and lick my way to a nipple which I'd tongue for a while. Then I'd nuzzle my way down his abdomen, pausing to lap the sweat from his navel. I'd tease his thick cock for a few minutes before sucking heartily on his heavy balls. Once I had him groaning and cursing me with wild, exaggerated oaths ("Damn you, Scott, and damn the bitch that birthed you under an evil star."), his fingers twitching in my hair, only then would I take his dick back in my mouth and finish the job. Joe loved it; loved me, even.

Then there was a woman at work with dirty blonde hair, forest green eyes, and lips like a promise. She filled my fantasies; more than that, she made me remember going to the prom with my first girlfriend. I'd been happy that night. I began to ponder getting married, having kids – all the worlds I'd been shut out of.

When I told Joe I had a crush on a woman, he laughed.

"Fuck her if you want to," he said, and kissed me, his beard inscribing our bond onto my skin with every scratch. Then he rolled me over and fucked me, sweet and deep, until I was the one swearing.

When I told Allison I was bisexual, she ran away from me like we were teammates in a post-modern relay race. After three years Joe and I broke up, and I went back to the bars, to the streets.

I met Jane coming out of a gay porn theatre. Voluptuous, with a smile that tugged at me the way the moon pulls the tides, she asked me to coffee. She would try anything once, she explained, and had a thing for queer men. Before a month had passed, I had a thing for her. Our courtship consisted of cuddling on her couch watching old movies and getting smashed in gay bars, ogling the men together. Soon we were combining households. I was enthralled by her sexiness and sense of humour, her fearless laugh, her conviction that the world was ours to conquer. And if my conquests included men, that was fine. If I picked up an open-minded guy, she liked to watch. If he was bi, sometimes she joined in.

My job moved to the suburbs and we decided to move with it. Maybe it would be different now that we were grown-ups, less susceptible to isolation's icy paws.

Our walk takes us to the neighbourhood mini-shopping-strip – convenience store, drug store, video store – with a gang of kids hanging out in front. Goth kids, all in black leather or lace, trying desperately with their thrift store clothes and makeup and angst to overcome the banality of their existence. I envy them their precognisance; it wasn't until college that I began to understand how hollow my upbringing had been. I pity them, too; they're too young, most of them, to escape. They're reduced to being misunderstood, ridiculed as freaks.

Meanwhile we're walking by hand-in-hand like any straight middle-class suburban couple.

The kids tense up, put on their tough/exotic/aloof faces. They don't want to know us or be like us. Except I catch one of the boys' eyes for a moment and that wordless something gets exchanged as fast as dope on a street corner. He's a little older than the others, thin but not stringy in a battered leather jacket. A pretty guy, and he's wearing dark lipstick to blur the line into androgyny even further.

The expression in his face draws me. There's more than just attitude in his slouch and jacket and the way he worries his full lower lip. He's been around a couple of blocks, this kid. At the very least, he knows what it means that I'm looking at him like a hungry cat eyeing a pigeon, wishing there were better light, wondering how he's built under that bulky jacket and those dirty blue-grey jeans that have seen many better days. His face is a little in shadow; I can't tell if the smudges I think I see are stubble or dirt or bruises.

He's not smoking so I can't ask him for a cigarette and then we've breezed past, heading back into another cookie-cutter subdivision.

I mention him to Jane and she giggles, breasts bobbing.

"Yeah, I thought he was cute. Kinda young, though. You want a boy toy, Scott?"

"I get the feeling he's older than he looks."

"That sounds like wishful thinking to me," she teases, her blue eyes sparkling unnaturally in the intensity of the streetlights.

"It is wishful thinking," I agree, pulling her close. Her breasts pillow up against my chest, and my cock stirs. Jane has amazing breasts, supple and sensitive. I'll play with them tonight, suckling her pink rosebud nipples. Maybe I'll jack off between them.

I'm thinking this as she kisses me. I'm also wondering about the boy, imagining the firm plane of his chest against mine, imagining catching his tongue between my lips.

A couple weeks later I run into him in the grocery store. His face is clean and pale in the light of the dairy aisle. No bruises, just a hint of stubble. A long, thin, faint scar along his jaw. No lipstick today. He has a nose ring, multiple earrings, blue eyes. His short hair is dark and thick; I wonder if his body hair is as luxuriant. I still can't see too much of his frame under that thick jacket.

The boy looks deliberately away from me as I come up, down to the paper in his hands. How incongruous, a goth kid with a shopping list. He's waiting for me to make the first move.

There's a notebook from a community college in his cart. Good, he's not too young.

"Hey, do you go to Bunker Hill?"

He looks up at me now. Beautiful dark blue eyes framed by lush dark lashes. Lips you'd have to be blind not to want to kiss.

"Yeah, I'm taking a couple of classes there."

"Cool. What kind of classes?"

"Journalism. Design." He shrugs. "I put out this 'zine. Here." He fishes inside his jacket and pulls out a slim magazine. "A present for you." He grins at me. "I'm Simon."

"Scott."

"New in town, huh?" Does he size up every local guy for potential tricks?

"How'd you know?"

"Just a lucky guess. I gotta get going. I'm working today." He pushes past me without a "nice meeting you" or a "see ya around." I watch him go; he has nice long legs and a trim, fuckable ass. Damn tease.

Before he turns the corner, though, he looks back at me. He sees me leering and grins. "My number's in the 'zine," he says. Then he's gone.

The little sneak, I can't get him out of my head now. The vision of those eyes flashing like sapphires, those full lips grinning at me before he turned away, knowing exactly what I was thinking, leaves me hard and weak-kneed at the same time. I want to tear that bulky jacket off his body, throw him down, take him. Make him swear – or scream.

Jane laughs at me. She loves it when I'm obsessed. I call his name out during sex once just to tease her, and she cracks up, tossing a pillow over my face.

So I read his 'zine. It's about bands I've never heard of, and body piercing, and loose networks of anarchist queers trying to build an anti-authoritarian society. He's not a bad editor, and the design flows nicely. His name and number are on the masthead.

Jane dials the number for me and puts the phone in my hand. He's home. Before I'm really sure what I'm saying, we've set up a dinner date for Friday. He says he's glad I called.

He lives in a nice newish split-level a ten minute drive from the not-quite-renovated Victorian Jane and I are renting. She's wished me luck with a kiss before going into Boston with some friends.

Simon's gothed himself up for me. His black hair is slicked back off his forehead, making his eyes seem even darker and wider. He's wearing dangling silver-gilt earrings in one ear, two tiny pearls and an onyx in the other. He has eyeliner on, and dark red lipstick slicker and glossier than dried blood.

Under his omnipresent black leather jacket he's got on a black T-shirt with the collar ripped out. A sliver ankh on a black silk cord hangs around his neck. His jeans, faded black and worn along the crotch and knees, are tight.

Simon gives me a one-armed hug as he gets into the car and I want to drive him to my house, push him down on the bed, explore the bulge at his crotch with my already sweating hands. But we're in the suburbs, and I made a reservation at an Italian restaurant.

Everyone in the restaurant stares at Simon while trying not to stare. He knows it, wears his attitude like a cuirass even as he hangs his leather jacket over his chair. They're staring at me, too, trying to figure out our relationship. I don't look gay – I'm too average-looking, with dark blond hair in no particular style, brown eyes, clean-shaven, not even an earring.

As we eat I learn a little more about him. He's not quite twenty-one and lives with his father. He works in a used record store four days a week, plays bass in a band called Spit Blood, puts out the 'zine, takes classes at Bunker Hill Community College. He might transfer to a university one day, but he's not too worried about it.

With an entire dining room as an audience, we haven't done as much flirting as we might have. Just some eye contact, and our knees touching under the table, and he has a way of biting his lip and looking at me through his dark lashes that's somehow coy and fierce at once. The draw of his practised, illusory innocence is potent. I feel like I've drunk more than the single beer, wonder if there's a liqueur as seductively blue as his eyes.

"This place sucks," he says after the waitress brings us coffee. The way he draws out each "s" sends smoky dark snakes crawling down my spine. It sounds like he wants my cock in his mouth and I want it, too. My dick's throbbing, half-hard.

"Let's get out of here, then." My voice is gravely with lust.

"There's a place I want to show you," he says as we leave.

He directs me to a club in a failed industrial park in a town I've never been in before. The music's loud enough to rattle the old factory windows. The lights are strobe and neon, sweeping the room with dizzying pulses as we enter. Everyone's wearing black besides me.

Nobody stares, but we get a few curious glances as we thread our way through the crowd. Simon knows the way and I sense he's known here, too.

We arrive at a back lounge, its entrance shrouded in cigarette smoke. This is queer territory: two long-haired boys in poet's shirts have their lips locked together. A girl all in lace is sitting on another's lap, playing with her hair.

Simon touches my arm and draws me further into the room. Silhouetted by the strobes into a wraithlike incarnation of desire, he slides out of his jacket. Then he leans against the wall and reaches for me. He pulls me close and we're kissing.

I can taste his waxy lipstick; I can taste the black coffee he drank at the restaurant that's thirty minutes and a million worlds away. I plunge my tongue inside his mouth and he meets me with his own, tangling and caressing.

I slide my arms around him. His shoulders are thin but muscular. I trace down the sensuous curve of his spine with my fingers. His ass cheeks yield invitingly under my hands.

His hands are on my belt, pulling me closer to him, grinding our crotches together. He's hard; I'm hard.

We break the kiss for breath and I put a hand in his hair, pulling his head back. The light scent of the gel in his hair tickles my nostrils as I nibble down his ear, tugging at his earrings with my teeth. I lick slowly down behind his ear, his thin body shivering in my arms. I kiss along his jaw, trying to feel his scar with my tongue. I catch his lower lip between my teeth and pull gently.

He manages a gasp, then my mouth's on his again. If I knew him better I'd bite, taste blood from those lips he's coloured like blood to tempt me. But I don't know him at all and I'm not willing to take risks with a rough boy who might just be a one night stand.

I pull his head back again, kiss below his jaw, his neck, the hollow of his throat. His pulse is pounding faster than the music's frenzied beat.

I slide my arms over his shoulders and push him back against the wall, shoving our bodies together. I roll my hips against his, pressing in on his erection. Pressing harder.

He moans in my ear, his hands on my shoulders gripping like a vise. He's mine. I wonder if it's safe to do him in the bathroom. Instead I pull back a little, and wait for him to open his eyes. I'm panting with hunger, ready to howl like a cat in heat.

"Come home with me," I tell him. "My girlfriend's out. And if she gets back, it's cool. She knows all about you."

Those intoxicating blue eyes narrow. "She knows all about me, huh? I've heard that one before."

Sure this is all a game as old as civilisation, but it annoys me that he doesn't believe me. "We have an open relationship."

I start to pull away; I want a little space suddenly, but he doesn't let me go. His grip is strong as he pulls me back toward him.

"It's cool, Scott." It's the first time he's said my name, and I warm at the tone. There are embers in his voice that could ignite into flame with just a touch of fuel.

But the expression in his eyes is sober, and older than his twenty years. "When my dad found out I was bisexual," he goes on, "he said, 'That's good, so when I beat the queer out of you there'll be something left.'" One of his hands brushes the scar on his face. He doesn't have to say it's a memento of that occasion.

Over a drink he tells me the rest of the story. Barely sixteen, he ran away after that last of many beatings. He lived from day-to-day: crashing with friends when he could, shoplifting, working odd jobs, hopping through shelters, selling himself on the street when he was desperate for cash.

"Three weeks before my eighteenth birthday, I got arrested." He laughs; it's funny now. The kind of amusement you get from remembered terror. "I'd solicited an undercover cop. I was underage and it was a first offence, so I got probation. But despite all my begging, they called my dad.

"And you know what? Dad felt guilty – my mom had left and then I'd left. He was convinced I was dead, and it was his fault. He'd even gotten some help to deal with it – 'anger management' they call it, very clinical – so the cops and social workers eventually convinced me to go back home. We got a family counsellor and my probation officer kept an eye on things.

"We don't get along great, but it sure as hell beats living on the streets, and the rent's free. He doesn't hit me anymore, but he still screams at his girlfriend once in a while."

It's a sobering story. These are the things that aren't supposed to happen in the suburbs behind the veneers of the pretty houses. Yet they do. There's nothing I can say to fix that.

"Yeah, and I'm lucky. I got out of it alive, and not addicted to crack or infected with HIV." He gestures with a lifted hand and flick of his wrist, as if it were possible to banish the memories like tossing away a cigarette butt.

I catch his hand between mine. His fingers are a little cold. I can't protect him, but at least I can give him a little pleasure.

He looks at me with those eyes that have seen too much. "Hey, does your girlfriend really know you're out with me tonight?"

I nod, trying to warm his fingers between my palms.

"Then what are we doing sitting here listening to my fuckin' soap opera? Take me home, man."

It's hard to drive straight when a boy you really want's got his hands in your lap and his tongue in your ear. But we make it.

Jane's not home yet, I note as I pull him into the bedroom and shut the door. Then we're embracing, hungry mouths devouring each other.

Simon pulls my shirt off, sliding hands and mouth across my chest. He leans into a nipple and sucks, biting a little. My breath catches, pain and pleasure dancing like whirling dervishes under my skin.

"That's great," I murmur. His hand wanders to my other nipple; he tweaks it and I groan. He's found one of my weaknesses.

My cock's straining against my pants and my brain's buzzing with desire like a hive of bees have all decided to take flight at once. I want this boy bad.

I hear the front door creak open. She won't come into the bedroom unless we ask.

I get a hand in Simon's hair and drag his mouth off my body.

"Jane's back," I tell him. "What do you think about letting her watch?"

He bites his lower lip in that unconsciously seductive gesture. His eyes are hooded.

"Simon, I want you either way, baby," I continue. "I want whatever you want. No pressure, okay?" I take his face in my hands and kiss him gently on the mouth.

We can't keep the kiss under control, though, as his lips and tongue match mine. The intensity escalates like a chain reaction in a nuclear plant. We're melting down together.

Simon pulls away a moment later to call out, "Hey, Jane, come on in! Might as well share the wealth."

She trounces in, filling out the yellow flowered dress she bought after I got my job. Jane doesn't say anything, just sits in the cozy old chair at the side of the bed and smiles sweetly.

I let Simon look her over. He hasn't told me if he's still bi, if he cuddles up with some of the adorable goth girls sometimes. But he's mine tonight, anyway. Jane knows that.

And when I pull Simon a little toward me, he turns to devour my mouth with his sweet lips. The impending reaction picks up its pace again.

I get Simon's shirt off finally, splay my hands across his skin while our mouths are still engaged with each other. He has soft sparse curls across his chest. I run my fingers through their sensuousness and he giggles against my mouth.

My mouth leaves his to slide slowly down his body. His skin tastes fresh and hot, like summer, with just a hint of sweat. But he's too thin; I can feel his ribs against my tongue. His navel's pierced; I grip the ring and pull very gently. His moan vibrates through his stomach.

I peel his pants down; they're button-fly. He's not wearing any underwear. He grunts as I strip him. His cock's thick and a solid average six inches, cut. I flick my tongue against it, then again, quick wet motions. I keep on, slower now, licking my way around his dick like it's an ice cream cone. He doesn't taste like ice cream, but I shiver with anticipation as his saltiness leaks into my mouth.

Simon writhes, groaning a little, and it's an opportunity to slide a hand under him, tickle the sensitive spot behind his balls – he gasps and twitches – then slide a finger between his cheeks to the entrance to his hole. I circle it a couple of times, then begin to inch my finger into his tightness.

Simon relaxes, letting me in easily even without any lubricant. He's done this many times before. My finger slides in deeper and he sighs in the back of his throat. He reaches out a hand and lifts my chin away from where I'd been nibbling at his balls.

Our eyes meet. His pupils are a little dilated, his expression distant with desire, his face changed the way a bank of fog transforms a familiar street into a mysterious landscape.

"So that's what you have in mind, huh?" he murmurs.

I can't tell if he's teasing me or chiding.

"Simon, I want to fuck you like you wouldn't believe."

He smiles. "How do you know what I'd believe? You've got some rubbers?"

"In the night table."

He pulls the drawer open by feel, tosses the condom box and lubricant tube at me. While he's fumbling I'm sliding my finger in and out of his body slowly. Drops of pre-cum roll down the swollen shaft of his cock, gleaming like pearls.

I pull my finger out slowly, and caress his inner thigh. He shivers.

"Roll over," I bark.

He grins at me. "Not until I see what caliber weapon you're packing, pardner."

I scoot up so his searching hands can undo my pants and strip off my briefs. My rod's an inch and a half longer than his, and a little thinner. A good size for fucking men (except the most notorious size queens) and women both. I guess I'm just blessed.

Simon licks his lips in anticipation. He's playing with me – stroking my balls, running his hand up and down my cock. I hadn't thought it possible for me to get any harder, but his fingers are working magic.

"Roll over," I command him again.

His grip tightens. "You sure?"

I didn't have half his self-control when I was his age. I didn't even have it now.

"On your stomach, impudent boy." I roll him over, tickling him between his ribs. He curls away from me, giggling.

"Stop it, Scott!" He's choking with laughter. "All right, I deserved it, just fuck me. Please."

The "please" melts me. Everything he's been through, and right now he's offering himself to me. He wants me. His pale buttocks are firm but resilient as I stroke his ass, their curves enticing me toward further intimacy with him.

I use a little lube this time to get two fingers inside, thrusting and stretching. His body yields easily to my intrusion; he pushes back against my fingers with an eager moan. There is no questioning the pleasure that's shivering off his thin, lithe body. I pull back to put on the condom, shift until my sheathed cock is just at his entrance, and push.

Jane echoes Simon's gasp as I enter him. I don't look over, but I know she's got a hand fingering her clit, the other probably rolling a hard nipple between her fingers through the yellow dress.

I'm concentrating on the boy, though. I slide in slow and easy, giving him a chance to learn my body just as I'm learning his. He sighs when I've pushed in my furthest and hold still for a minute, savouring the intimacy, the tension, the solidity of his body under mine. I kiss his cheek and he smiles. His breathing is slow and shallow.

It speeds up fast once I start moving again. I thrust into him and he pushes back against me. We're united in our passion, two boulders poised to be swept away by the same avalanche. Ready to tumble through a canyon that's hot and tight.

I pick up the pace, shifting to go a little deeper, and he moans. The muscles of his ass clench around me and I push into the tightness again. Again. We're both panting now and I'm slamming into him like a piston into a cylinder. I'm breathing into the tiny dark hairs on the back of his neck. His fingers are interwoven with mine, clenching hard. His fingernails are digging into my skin, but I don't care. The world has narrowed to the tension in my cock and his tightness and the rumbling of my blood in my ears as the avalanche gains momentum.

Simon comes with a series of short, breathless moans. The pulses in his body tighten around me and he bucks up against me, pushing me in to the root.

The motion surprises a sound out of me and rolls a splatter of stones against my wilting self-control. I push him back down flush with the bed and hurl myself into him.

I'm a little rough; I know he doesn't care. Dimly, I hear Jane's little moans, almost yips – she's coming and trying not to make too much noise. I don't think a volcano erupting would have shaken my concentration as I push into his welcoming body, pressure building, boulders rolling.

With a cry, I pour myself into him and over him. My teeth sink into his shoulder. My orgasm rolls over me and through me, its manic rhythm set to the roar of rock splitting, to the resounding clatter of tons of gravel settling. His ass tightens around my cock, prolonging the pleasure.

Slowly, it fades. My cheek's against his nipped shoulder. The air hangs heavy with the dense scents of sex drifting through the room.

Simon sighs as my cock begins to soften inside him. The sigh fills me with more gratitude than a dozen screaming orgasms; he doesn't want this moment to end, either.

I pull out slowly, slip off the condom and dump it in the trash, looking over at Jane. She's got her dress hiked up to her waist; her cunt's gleaming and dripping with her juices. She grins at me, licking her fingers.

Simon giggles. "I forgot she was here," he says as I lay back down to gather him into my arms. "That was great."

"You're great," I tell him, then kiss him hard. His thin body is almost bonelessly relaxed in my embrace. I pull him close, ignoring the sweatiness of the curls on his chest and the drying cum smeared on his stomach. I'm not tired of him yet. It might be weeks or months – or years, even – but I want to keep seeing this boy. I hope he feels the same.

Eventually, I loosen my grip. He squirms free of me, gets up to trot to the bathroom. I hear him piss, then water running as he cleans up.

He swings the door open but stops before he reaches the bed. "I can go if you want," he offers.

I shake my head. "I'd rather you stay. The bed's big enough for three."

"OK," he grins and gets back in next to me. I pull him close again, nuzzling his neck.

Jane grins, trips off the light, moves to the bathroom. I'm half-asleep by the time she lays down on my other side, her lips tickling along my spine. I turn to give her a good-night kiss before snuggling up against Simon again.

I wake up last. Simon's kissing Jane and playing with her pale, voluminous breasts. I'm already hard, and I can tell from Jane's flushed skin that she's well on her way, too.

Simon sees that I'm conscious at last and grins at me. His hair is tousled and his face stubbled but youthful in the morning sunlight. His sapphire eyes are gorgeous.

"I'm glad to see you and Jane getting acquainted," I say, smiling. "Go on."

"Well, I – I never really got into fucking girls," he says, embarrassed. I'm not sure if he doesn't like how it feels or if he's insecure about his lack of experience. But I don't want to dig it all up now.

"May I?"

He moves away from Jane and I slide in toward her. I kiss her. She rubs her cunt against my cock eagerly. She's wet, all right.

I slide into her joyfully. Familiar, softer, wetter – it's different from a man.

As I start with her, I reach for Simon, too. Jane's gotten to him first; she's jacking him off as we fuck. I put an arm around him, anyway, so he knows he's included, so my sweet rough boy from the suburbs knows that we're both glad he's here.

Who Says ...

Lani Ka'ahumanu

for now
my attention moves away
from mouth, neck, shoulders
inner arms, erect nipples
and the heat of your crotch

turn over I say
get on your knees
my hands, fingers, nails
glide down your back
firmly grab your cheeks
lightly scratch skin
my strong tongue slides
over clear soft shield
exploring secret places
banned in Boston

the pleasure is found
just below, just above
just beyond the limit
set years before

the pleasure though
is all mine
to give
and I do
relishing the excitement
of your ass
pushing against my face
primal animal sounds
calling out to me
yes, oh yes
you stroke your cock

I lick your balls
and pull away
just long enough
to lube my glove
you move to meet my hand
inviting entry
inviting possibilities
promising us
as much as we can imagine
I slip easily in
to the warmth
my fingers thrill
to the muscle holding me
on the edge

- 2 -

you play with my desire
to fuck you, to take you
the growing hardness
throbbing inside you
brings me to a tension point
I gasp, biting your ass
you rock
moving out
and pushing in

I want you
I say I want to fuck you
I want to fuck you
with more than my tongue, my fingers, my hand
I want your legs in the air
my breast in your mouth
my dildo up your ass

turn over I say
pinching your nipples
I take you in my mouth
sliding a condom down the shaft
lingering to savour the movement
we play with the power of our passion
you finger my throbbing clit
slowing just before I cum
you open another condom
breathlessly I watch
you roll the skin
over my dildo

drip and massage lube
with the warmth of your hand
I am wild, I am in heat
you fill my dripping cunt
with slippery latex fingers
I scream and fall on all fours
beneath me you smile
we laugh out loud
I find your mouth
so sweet, so sweet we kiss
sucking darting tongues
I want to devour you
I want to fuck you

-3-

I put your legs in the air
feet on my shoulders
dildo up your ass
there are no words

there are no words
we are transported
to another place and time
our bodies in tune, playing
like fine instruments
a symphony of sound
we are transformed
by the music
of a language
beyond any label
female/male
it is pure energy
a communion of spirit
shameless and powerful

there are no words
we roar like lions
howl like wolves
trumpet like elephants
building to a crescendo
the grand finale
an epiphany
takes our breath away

crying like babies
we deserve a standing ovation

but can't get up
our bodies will not be moved
we laugh, we laugh out loud
a tangle of latex, lube, sweat and saliva
exhausted and exhilarated
who says safer sex isn't hot
oh baby, who says ...

Lani Ka'ahumanu 9/92

A Tale of Two Tops

Alex Quinlan

"She's expecting you, right?" We stood outside her patio door, as my nerves finally won and started delaying.

"Yes," he said. "I told her I would be late, and she should go to sleep." He grinned evilly. "She knows I like to wake her up."

His smugness vaguely annoyed me, and did nothing to alleviate my tension. "And where are the toys? Where are we leaving them? How can we get them into the room without waking her too soon?" The toys were in a bag at my feet, and I grumbled to myself at the state of my nerves. Before I could take myself in hand, he acted.

After a searching look, he reached up to my chin, tilting my face into the moonlight. His bangs shadowed his face into silver-toned planes and angles, delightful to see as I looked everywhere but back at him. "We have gone over this five times already. What is the problem?" The pressure of his gaze finally drew mine, and after a moment more I met his eyes.

The grey of them was lost in shadow, my memory supplying the colour. His look was one of concern, not the smug haughtiness he had shown a moment before, and with a sigh I finally let him see in past my attempt to deflect his notice. "You are nervous." He sounded startled, and brushed my hair away from my face. "You weren't this way last time I saw you top."

"Yes I was, you just didn't see it; I was working on someone I had lots of experience with. Also, by the time you saw me I was working on controlling it, on using the energy, and on *not* showing it." I took a deep breath, continuing, "And of course I am nervous. I don't *care* if she and I have been baaaaahing at each other for months – this is the real thing." That sounded so cheesy I nearly blushed, but was interrupted in my own reaction by his questioning tone.

"Baahing?"

"Yeah. You know. The joke about lesbian sheep?" He still looked confused, so I took a deep breath and, after a nervous look around the area, continued in a soft voice. "There was a study done, ages ago. I can find the cites if you want. Someone was studying the sexuality of, of all things, sheep.

"Well, it seems that male sheep will fuck anything that doesn't move fast enough – signalling desire by simply mounting the object of their desire, male

115

or female. If a female sheep is receptive, she stands still – does absolutely nothing. So, the researchers concluded all sorts of things about male homosexuality amongst sheep, but reported that they couldn't come to any conclusions about female homosexuality."

I grinned into the darkness, anticipating his reaction. "No one could figure out if the females that were standing still were desperately, forlornly, yearning for the gentle touch of the equally motionless female sheep next to them. A lesbian friend of mine, upon seeing that report, commented 'Sounds like every lesbian bar *I* ever went to.'"

He grinned. "I see. Does it help you to know that I've been hearing about each of you, from each of you?"

I blinked, and my stomach turned over. Again. "Great," I muttered.

"What?"

"Oh, now I just have 'She *likes* me?' on top of my usual stage fright."

He dropped his hand from my shoulder with a sigh of exasperation. "Look," he said, "This was your idea. You are the one who wanted to surprise her with being in the area. We can walk away right now, and she'll be ok – she knows that sometimes something comes up with my wife and I can't get away."

I shook my head vehemently. "No. It's just the old 'what do I do with a woman' nervousness. I'll get over it someday. Or I won't." I grabbed up his hand and kissed the palm once, resting my face in it for a moment. Then I pulled away and stepped back into the shadows again. I took a deep breath. "But not if I never try. Let's go, I will be fine once we start."

He opened the door and stepped through, carrying the bags – he was enough stronger than I that he could do so far more quietly than I would have been able to. We stopped next to the jacuzzi and unzipped the bags, taking advantage of the space to make a little noise. I emptied the pockets of my close-fitting clothing so I wouldn't clink the car keys and other pocket debris when we moved closer to her room.

As he locked the door behind us, I stretched my arms back and rolled my head to loosen my arms and shoulders. My breasts shifted as my bra did, and I could feel my nipples come up, from friction, from excitement, from anticipation. 'Great' I thought, 'she's been talking to him about me? Just what I need, performance anxiety.'

I knew that wasn't the issue, that I was distracting myself, but I also knew that the only way to get through the issue – and tonight – was to just go forward. Now was *not* the time to introspect into a spiral, especially about my shyness around women.

I took a deep breath and started to calm myself down with a pep talk – c'mon, you *know* she likes the whips, you've watched her play often enough with other people – when I felt his hands on me, his body behind me as he cupped my breasts. I strangled a squeak, and a flinch, and made myself relax back into his embrace.

"I could take you right now," he breathed against my ear.

"You could," I agreed. "But you won't." My body wanted to melt, wanted to just release into his control. It would be so much easier to let him direct all the action tonight than to do this under my own control, to show this clearly how I wanted her, too.

"Why not?" he murmured. I could feel him thrusting softly against my ass. "We've done it before in this room, don't you remember?"

I shook my head, not in denial, but to shake off the memory of kneeling at his feet as he jerked off into my face. That powerful encounter – energy and power shared, given and taken – had culminated in his marking me with his seed, spraying over my face and tits as I had joyfully orgasmed to his control.

That weekend, that night, had compelled us to persevere in our desires, those carnal and those for more depth, through months of unavoidable and unchangeable geographical distance. The trust we had now, to share this woman, had grown from that time spent learning each other, however far apart we were. But submitting to him was not how I wanted to come to her – I needed to be here in my own space, my own right, my own desire.

"That memory won't help me get into topspace." I murmured, even as my body rubbed back against his cock in the crease of my ass, the clothing between us frustrating in its own right. "Besides, I am too noisy – you know how I scream when I come."

I breathed deeply and fought my own desire for him with words. I needed to regain some control – over myself, over the situation, over who was doing what to whom, tonight. He hadn't been able to deal with me in my Top mode before, and this didn't seem to be getting any better. But I couldn't let his insecurities pull me off center.

He chuckled breathlessly as he let me go. "You're right. You are noisy." He picked up the bags and then looked back at me with a wicked grin. "But you do know how to be quiet. We proved that then, also."

I managed to keep the comment of "Smartass" only in my mind as I followed him past the clutter of everyday living and into the dressing room that connected to her bedroom. We stopped for a moment, and worked on slowing our breathing. I found our heads leaning together for last minute words, and realized we both had more need to be quiet with only one door between us and our prey.

My heart was pounding, and I could feel it in all of my body – my chest, my breath, my vagina as it fluttered in residual reaction from his touch, pumped by the renewed adrenaline. I was all-over with nerves again, caught up in the need for stealth. I breathed a question, voiced just enough to be quieter than a whisper. "Where's the knife?" He patted a pocket. "And the blindfold?" He nodded. I opened my mouth again and he put his finger over it.

"Enough." I subsided, closing my eyes and tilting my head back to pull the air deeply into my lungs. As I shook my arms and shoulders out again, the soft noises of his undressing caused me to open my eyes automatically. My attempt to calm down was cut short by the sight of his skin gleaming in the light reflecting from the hallway onto the mirrors in this narrow room.

In the near darkness, his skin's paleness caught the light, broken only by the shadow of the asymmetric thatch of chest hair, looking like a baldric across his chest. His body fur was surprisingly thick for what was visible on his arms and legs, and the unfamiliar sight of him filled me with the need to store up his image in my mind.

His cock was half hard, and just that was enough to catch my breath in my throat. The lean, compact lines of him made my groin go tight. I shivered as I could feel my muscles pulse once in desire for him, and I finally had to turn from the sight, shaking my head to clear it. This wasn't the time for this. Later, maybe. Depending on how things went.

He gathered his tools, and opened the final door. Leaving it ajar, he padded silently into the room, obviously familiar with its arrangements. His way was made easier by the dozen or so lit candles she had left scattered over the room. I picked up the toy-bag and eased it past me gingerly as I stepped into the opening. I needed to just stand for a bit and let my eyesight adjust before I risked putting the bag down on something noisy.

Her red-gold hair across the pillows gleamed in the candleglow; one of her hands lay cuddled under her breasts, the other unseen. She had kicked the covers mostly down, they were just over her feet. Her softly curved body glowed in the light, and I gazed my fill in the time he took to move into position.

She'd had her hands on me before, and I had been incredibly startled that she wanted me – more so than my usual disbelief in a woman's interest. All I had to do was describe her to people, and they would start drooling – red hair, slender toned body, eager and playful sexuality. She wasn't my type, being neither tom-boyish enough to trigger my response to maleness, nor lush enough to trigger my longing for the balls to come on to a female – but her interest in me was no longer deniable, even to my denseness. The last time we'd been together, she'd made the moves. Now it would be my turn.

Easing his weight gently onto the bed, he set the blade down silently on the headboard, and cradled her head gently, enough to lift it and put on the blindfold. She gave a soft moan, but otherwise didn't move.

Something about her response caused something inside me to click, so strongly I could almost hear it with my ears. I grinned, laughing soundlessly with just an outrush of air, suddenly completely confident in the knowledge that this would work. My nerves drained away in the rush of what can only be called Topspace. I must have made some sound, because he looked up at me, and grinned widely, nodding, seeing that I was finally *there*. I rocked on the balls of my feet, the building sense of focus sharpening all the visual contrast around me.

He stroked his fingers over her throat. "Wake up, little one," he murmured, "Wake up before I hurt you to wake you." I laughed soundlessly at the hunger in his voice. She shifted, a sudden cry escaping from her as her hand reached up to her face. He intercepted it, his fingers tight on her wrist, and I saw her nipples crinkle in reaction.

"Hello," he said more strongly, deeper, rougher. "You *did* remember that I was coming over tonight, didn't you?" She made a small noise, and nodded slowly. "Oh good." He grinned at me then, sharing the delight in her reaction to the blindfold. "Don't touch the blindfold, little one." She nodded again, and he let go of her wrist.

His fingers stroked over her throat again, and I could see her swallow from across the room, watch her shiver in soft fear. "I brought something special with me tonight," he murmured. Her head tilted quizzically against his grip in her hair, her hips squirming with the tug. He grinned, watching her, as he reached up to the headboard and picked up the knife.

He opened it one handed, the deliberate *SNICK* of the lock loud in the silence, and I heard her gasp. Laying the cold steel across her throat, he laughed, deep in his register, and she squeaked very loudly. It was a delicious sound.

I watched as he stroked her with the blade, blazing the tip down her throat and turning it so the serrations dragged over her breast, white scratch lines catching the flickering candlelight. "Don't. Move," he ordered, and she froze, no longer trying to rub against him. In a more conversational tone he added, "I haven't blooded her yet – she is hungry. I can't guarantee how deep she would cut."

She squealed again, softly, her body almost quivering with tension as she suppressed the shudders that I saw wanting to come through. He marked her whole upper chest that way, slowly dragging the blade over her collarbones and breasts, across her nipples as she tried not to move. Her own well-known craving for blood-play warred against her fear of the unknown blade, and her need to obey just inflamed the conflict.

I stood there, watching, waiting for my agreed-on entrance, and had trouble keeping my own breathing soft enough for her not to hear. My dominance heated me, tunnelling my vision down to the players in the game. It is always a different sort of arousal from the more simply sexual; it is less involved with my body, or perhaps only using the body as a tool for manipulation. It is a need to move, to hurt, to take what is offered, to take *all* of it and give back attention, focus, energy, heart.

He took the flat of the blade and slapped her erect nipples, and then squeezed one with his thumb against the metal. "Maybe that is near the edge," I heard him murmur to her, his voice barely reaching me. "Maybe not. What would you do if I cut your nipple, little one? Would you squeal?" I saw her start to nod. "Would it hurt?" She nodded again. "Would you cum?"

I saw her writhe and blush, and heard a voice just barely audible say "Probably." He grinned, and pulled his thumb and the blade off, stretching her nipple out, causing her to cry out loudly for the first time. Quickly he pinched the other one, trapping it against the unyielding metal, and curled it over his thumb, stretching it upward, holding it tight.

"Do you want me to?" he asked, voice harsh suddenly. "Do you want me to cut your pretty nipples, do you want to bleed for me?" Her mouth worked but no sound came out. He pinched harder, and she screamed "YES YES," her voice raw with need and fear. His cock leapt to full erection, not even moving against his body with his motions, and my own sadism reared as well, heat filling me from her surrender.

He yanked his finger and the blade off, suddenly, dropping the knife on the pillow next to him. He flipped her over, using his legs to shift her hips, and shoved her mouth against his erect cock. "Suck, now." He growled it out, feral voice. "Open that mouth and SUCK ME!"

This was my cue. At some point as I had watched him toying with her pain and fear my subconscious had decided which tools would be in my hands that night. I reached into the bag and they almost magically came to me, without need to search for them. As always, when deep in this mental space, I worked without thought, the flow taking me through.

The soft satin cord, unravelled at the end into a mass of fluff, most often described as a thuddy cloud; the stingier suede flat and nasty; the pvc strands, so like a koosh that hasn't been cut; the nasty wicked monofilament; and the tool known by those who had felt it as The ThudBeast(tm), 45 long tails of heavy black suede were what I found in my hands when I was done, and I grinned. It would be a delicious range of sensation for her, and for me.

I found I could almost feel her reactions already in my head as I planned out my moves, which toys to use first and how to shift between them. I picked them up leisurely, shaking them out quietly, giving her time to get involved in what she was doing. Yeah, so I am a toy slut, sue me.

Standing again, I stepped quickly and as quietly as possible over to the bed. I was careful as I laid the floggers lightly out over the end of the bed; I didn't want to give her any clues to my presence. Not yet. She wriggled and thrashed a bit as she sucked him, his hand lightly in her hair but not forcing any motion.

His face was that odd not-quite-slack that most men get when a good cocksucker is working on them but they are not giving in. I grinned at him and mimicked his face, mock-holding her head in front of my crotch and thrusting at it. He stuck his tongue out at me, but couldn't manage to smile through the effects of her talent. She still hadn't noticed my presence. Life was good.

I took the satin thudcloud in my hand, feeling the familiar weight of it settle into place. I stroked the tails, once, lightly across her back, and she froze. He laughed, that dark chuckle again, and shoved on her head with his hand in her hair. "Did I tell you to stop, wench?" She squeaked around the mouthful of cock, shaking her head. "Then keep sucking."

He punctuated the command with a downward thrust of his hands and she choked as she moaned and resumed her work. I stroked again with the tails, and nearly laughed out loud with sheer delight at her reactions. She pulled her knees under her and lifted her lower body to the touch, begging for it.

A shiver ran through me, my own dominant and sadistic desire and arousal meeting her masochistic need, and I felt my focus narrow down again, losing the periphery of my vision, even losing him till all I saw was her, and her reactions, and her body to play with.

I brought the tails down against her, and started working into a pattern, swatting her back and down to her ass in cross rhythms and strokes. This was just a warmup, this flogger not able to do much more than bring a soft pink blush up on her skin. When I had that much, I suddenly itched to do more.

I grabbed up the suede with my off hand and just suddenly worked it in, seeing her twist and surge as the different tails hit, dropping the satin cloud to the floor. I shifted around so I could swing differently, wanting to keep missing his legs, and to where I could see both of them and still whip her back and ass.

His face was tense, his body tight as her head bobbed manically on his cock, moving in time to my strikes. I heard his noises, the soft growls and snarls of his arousal making my insides tight in memory. I grinned a question at him, and he nodded, barely, and I kept going.

"Don't cum, slut," he murmured. "You haven't earned my cum yet." She moaned and obviously increased her efforts by the way he gasped. I laughed soundlessly again, and he growled at me, which she fortunately took as being aimed at her activities, and he writhed as she redoubled her efforts.

I swapped the pvc strand flogger in, seamlessly matching the rhythms, riding the liquid flow of the energy welling up between us all. I struck harder, deeper, using two hands now and more than just gravity, swinging my upper body into it. I brought the tails down on her shoulders, her ass, her thighs, and up again, a smooth rhythm of pain delivered to the willing bottom.

He waved at me a moment before he got my attention, and motioned his one hand down her body. I quizzically moved back to the foot of the bed, striking only on her ass and thighs. He picked up the blade again, and started stroking the serrations over her back, over the reddened flesh that I had whipped into sensitivity. I grinned and dropped the pvc strand whip, and kneewalked onto the end of the bed, straddling her lower legs.

I found the nasty monofilament whip in my hand, and suppressed an equally nasty chuckle. The monofilament strands were blue, vivid in the golden flickering light, and I could not suppress the grin as I remembered that she had dubbed that the 'My Little Pony' whip. He grinned back at me, and said to her, "Hold still." in a voice dark and low with his own heat.

He moved slowly, carefully, sliding the knife-edge along her reddened, scratched back, as if he were going to slice her flesh. As he did, I struck her ass with the monofilament, and she bucked, a half squeal of fear mingling with the pain – but he had lifted the blade.

"That's one cut," he murmured, and I felt her shake under us, unable to tell if he lied. Again he stroked the edge along her skin, and again I struck her ass. She screamed, the noise muffled around his cock. He bucked and nearly dropped the knife at the sensations of her mouth on him. I just grinned.

I swung the whip in a circle, the whifft-sound of monofilament line filling the air as the nasty stinging terror of the monofilament drove her uncontrollably to writhe between his legs despite her orders and the grip he had on her. We teased her for a timeless time with blade and whip and never actually cut her.

Suddenly he pulled off the blade, dropping it down next to him, nearly dropping it off the bed. I had lost track of his state, and was wickedly delighted to find him gasping, trembling with his own effort not to cum. He motioned to me, one hand around his own neck, and after a moment I figured out what he wanted.

Dropping the whip, I scooted up so I was sitting on her ass, and leaned forward, sliding my hands around her throat. He pulled up on her hair, pulling her mouth off his cock, and I tightened my grip so that her body's pressure pushed her throat against my hands. I held her off his cock, but only barely, her eager needy mouth seeking his cock still.

"I'm gonna cum on your face, slut." She nodded, unformed noises, whimpers and incoherent begging falling from her lips. I held her up, my hands pressing against the arteries, careful pressure on her windpipe to make her feel like she couldn't breathe, make her think she was being choked.

I felt myself humping on her ass, and realized that my own pants were drenched with arousal. With an audible laugh, low in my voice range and hopefully unrecognisable, I let myself use her for that. With a soft cry she started squirming under me, rubbing up against me, and I laughed again in sheer delight at the power she gave with the need she was showing.

"gonna cum ... face ... slut" I looked up at him, his guttural voice drawing my attention as he jerked himself off, watching the face that went with the noises I had heard so often on the phone. He suddenly cried out and I ducked my head, burying my face into her hair, and taking the opportunity to bite her on the shoulder.

She screamed and bucked as he came on her face, spurting in gasps over the blindfold, onto her cheeks, onto my hands. I found myself crying out also as I orgasmed, surfing the energy, the sadism and power and fear. I let my hands go, let her head down as I dropped my hands to the bed on either side of her. I shuddered over her, panting for air, slowly coming down. She continued to squirm under me, whimpering in her own continued need.

He recovered first – as men often do – and chuckled softly. "She isn't done yet, is she?"

I raised my head and slowly grinned at him, the world swimming back into focus as my own glow faded deliciously. "No, she isn't." I sat up, slowly, and moved all the way back off her legs, watching her for some reaction to my voice.

She lifted her head and started to turn, one hand coming up to the blindfold. She started to squeak what might have been my name, but he grabbed her hair and her hand. "I said, Don't Touch The Blindfold," he said, and gripped her hand in the web between thumb and index finger, pulling it away from her face.

I chuckled and moved off the bed, and took off my own clothes, as I watched him hurt her and make her writhe with just his hands, gripping and pinching with strength I hadn't suspected. The air was both cool and hot, in waves, as I peeled the sweat-damp fabric off, ending up with everything inside out in disarray on the floor. I was shaking, possessively wanting her now, wanting a proper release for me, wanting to have her mouth on me as it had been on him.

When I was naked I got back onto the bed next to him, panting as if I had run around the house. "I want her mouth. Now." I demanded. "You can have her ass." I twined my fingers into her hair where his had been, locking gazes with him, tugging on her head. He glared at me, as if he were the only one running the show and how *dare* I give him orders. I could almost see his hackles rising.

We locked gazes, and I could feel my own growl rising to meet his yet unvoiced one. As he opened his mouth to speak I realized this was *not* something she should know. I suppressed my growl and simply shook my head quickly, and nodded down to her blindfolded face. He blinked, and with a final glare, backed off – off the bed, out of the confrontation – saying, in a voice completely at odds with his facial expression, "Oh yes, her ass. So deliciously tender, now ..."

I sat down where he had been, taking his place, taking control. Splaying my legs to either side of her, I pulled her messy face to me, her beautiful face, bearing the marks of her efforts. I knew she could do more. Stroking my fingers across her cheeks, gently, I murmured "At least *I* won't use the knife on you. Tonight."

As she gasped I pulled her face to my breast, feeding her a nipple. "You *know* how to suckle on that," I growled, and she proved that she did. I groaned, loudly, arching into her mouth, and heard a SMACK! as she bucked, surging against me.

Opening my eyes I saw him pull back for another blow and SMACK! as he started spanking her, slow, hard, single strikes that drove her whole body against me. I moved her mouth from nipple to nipple, both of us writhing on the bed, and restrained her against me.

My arousal shifted back and forth; intense sexheat flooded me as I watched his one hand get wetter and wetter, glistening with her juices as he slowly worked it deeper into her. Her growing desire drove her to attack my nipples in frenzied bouts of nipping and suckling.

Then the tunnel-visioned heat of dominance would take me again as I watched him spanking her, feeling the impact of his blows in the surge of her body against the hold I had on her. I reached over to her bedside table and tossed him the tube of lube and then simply sunk into the sensations, arching against her as I surfed the waves of her pain and need again.

She suddenly started grunting and I looked up and out from where I had gotten lost in my own body. He had gotten his fist almost into her, his face gone as feral as when she was sucking him. The look on his face made me growl, and as suddenly I needed her mouth elsewhere. Working with his thrusting, I pushed her face down to my crotch, sliding down and spreading my legs wide so she could get her face into my cunt.

She and I cried out together, mutual shock of intensity, when his hand finally pushing all the way into her pushed her hard against my clit, and she started manically licking. I held her face there, growling and panting, her mouth showing more experience than I had credited her with. He thrust and twisted, fisting her drenched cunt, fucking her into me, and started talking at her.

"Do you want to cum, slut? Do you want to cum as you get fucked again with my fist?" She nodded and I bucked, gasping and squirming, both hands in her hair now, using it as reins, as control, placing her mouth where I wanted it.

He laughed, nastily. "Can she cum yet?" and it took me a moment to realize he was asking me, and to find my voice, panting for breath between each word. "Not. Until. I. Do." She arched and squealed as he did something, and so did I, her tongue frenziedly working on my clit.

"Get ready" he said, and I didn't know who he was talking to. "You had better be ready to cum when she does, slut, or you won't get to cum at all." She squealed and started sucking harder, her hands coming up between my legs and plunging into my cunt.

I fucked her mouth, fucked her fingers, as he fucked her cunt with his fist. She writhed between us tenser and tenser, her begging noises driving me higher, hotter, further into that heated Dominance that has little to do with my body's orgasm and all to do with the staticy white heat I get from power.

But her tongue was winning, as was his fist, her need drawing my own into being till I screamed out "YES" and came, clenching her head tightly in my legs, screaming out my orgasm as he thrust hard into her cunt and said "CUM bitch!" and she screamed into me and came, still licking and sucking and fingering me. I rocked and bucked and rode my orgasm for what seemed like forever, giving her back all the power and energy she had let me feed on.

I came out of that no-where place, that mind-blank space where orgasms send me, to find my legs still wrapped around her and my hand petting her red-gold hair, tangled in sweaty strings over my thighs. He was laying beside me, one hand on her head, the other propping his head up. This shit-eating grin was on his face, and I just started laughing, softly, unable to stop. She lifted her head, and started to pull off the blindfold, stopping mid-motion. Her face turned, seeking him, seeking permission.

He reached over and pulled it off her, and she blinked, owlishly, turning her face from one of us to the other. Suddenly she grinned, and cried out "You BITCH why didn't you tell me you were in town?" and leapt up onto me, her body full length on mine now, our breasts rubbing and sliding with our mingling sweat. She kissed me, hard, her arms around my neck, locking me to her.

I wrapped my arms around her and hugged, tight, kissing back, opening her mouth with my own and kissing her deeper as I shook suddenly all over in release of a different kind, relief that the surprise was welcome ... that I was welcome. When I could, I pulled back my head and grinned at her. "Baaaaah," I said, drawing the sound out.

He nearly fell off the bed, he was laughing so hard.

Last Call

Jamie Joy Gatto

"I have loved strangers, and after them I will go." (Jer. 2:25)

I would've never worn my bathing suit to a bar, especially at night, especially to that bar where I seem to know everyone, unless I was in "a mood", as my husband calls it. The suit was a fabulous, fine jersey knit, a flirty little one-piece 1940s glamour girl number. It was sleek and black with an oh-so-low halter neck and a peek-a-boo skirt that fell just over my ripe, smooth ass. Classic, dangerous, perfect. I simply couldn't resist. But, I put on the suit, and only the suit, with no change of clothing, to go to a pool party where rumour had it an ex would be with his new wife. Actually, not just my ex, but also the ex of my husband and I both. And, the new wife: Baptist to the bone. I couldn't wait to ignore both of them. I wanted to sashay past them with my pride intact, even after he had lied about our past to woo her, lied and said that our entire relationship had consisted of a drunken one-night fling, lied and never once told her that my husband had been his lover on and off since they were both fifteen.

Although the pool party was a bust due to a typical temperamental New Orleans downpour, that last lingering stare from Mr. Ex at my husband's crotch, and that one haunting whisper, "You look hot," that way he said it to me with his particularly disturbed brand of yearning, just as we passed in the hall, was all I needed to accelerate "the mood", to boost my pride and to take my fine little ass in a suit with my sexy husband elsewhere. I loved the fact that he still wanted us both, but that he had locked his deceitful soul into a lifetime of unfulfilled longing. Something about his pain gave me pleasure, even a bit of closure. Oh, Paul and I were not going home yet, and furthermore, we were walking in the night sparkle of drizzling rain. I practically skipped to St. Joe's bar, shiny sling-back pumps clacking on the pavement, leaving Mr. Ex to his abysmal life and Baptist bride.

The bar glowed dimly with the promise of a perfect martini in a V-shaped glass, crystalline chilled and tasting of baby tears, wet with olives and whispers of vermouth. But, the bartender made my mouth water. I knew him by name and little else, and I was thirsty.

Figuring that my bare feet couldn't stand in Bette Davis pumps forever, I angled and vied for the only available seat at the bar. Paul kissed me as he slipped away to say his "hello's" and probably grab a game of pool in back. The moist crowd pressed around me as I slid onto a leather-covered stool.

Crosses dangled and danced overhead in the breeze of antique ceiling fans, some handmade, some seemingly from churches, others jewelled and sparkling in the glow of a Victorian gothic chandelier. St. Joseph stood vigil over the oak altar crowded with whiskey, wine and import beer, his aureole outshone by a row of fat Christmas bulbs while Ren, the barkeep took my order, "Dirty, up and dripping wet."

"How salty do you want it?" he asked.

"Filthy," I said smiling, believing fully in transubstantiation.

I wiggled on the sweaty stool to keep my rump from sticking to it, then lifted the glass with two hands, savouring each heady sip. A multitude of possibilities surrounded me. The long, smooth neck of a leggy woman invited me, her head tossed back in laughter. The wink of an older man glistened with seedy desire. The biceps of a college boy rumpled boastfully as he lifted a pool cue, pocketing the bright red three-ball.

Faces hummed, laughter tinkled, something shimmered inside me just below the surface, at first a pale weakening, then a rush. My seat dampened, not only from sweat. I bit my lip and tasted the curve of my lacquered nail. My pinky barely parted my mouth, touched the wet inner surface with tiny traces along my lips.

In my head, armies of men lined up for miles, filled me with cocks of every size. They pushed in and out and left their mark on and in me as come flowed out of my open cunt like sweet milk. Rows of round luscious milkmaids followed, each one licking the cream from inside me, their breasts full, brushing my thighs, my face, stuffing pink nipples into my mouth, filling my mouth with rows and rows of their succulent flesh, some breasts small and pert and others meaty and full, each one satisfying a tiny craving, yet never filling me completely. I sighed aloud and the sound of it pulled my attention back to my physical surroundings.

I swirled the tiny sword stacked with olives in my drink. My eyes searched the room for Paul, but he was not in sight. Ren bustled about serving drinks. There was really no one else I knew well enough to talk to, much less share the goddess that stirred within. From behind me, a familiar pair of broad palms brushed my hair aside, squeezed my shoulders.

"There you are, Paul," I said.

"I love it when you do that," he said, "I had to come see the look on your face."

"Do what? What look?"

"You were biting your finger."

"I'm not biting my finger."

"You were, and I love it," he said, "It means you're in a mood." He pointed to a small group at a table drinking beer, "I'm with some school friends in back, if you want to come meet them."

I really wasn't in the mood to remember names, smile and nod, be polite, not tonight. Play the straight-wife role in my Betty Grable bathing suit, what was he thinking?

"No, I think I'll keep my chair," I said eyeing Ren.

"Well, behave," he winked.

"Never," I said smiling, looking up at the painting. "My Painting", I named it, hung in an elaborate gold frame high above the service area. Painted in Roman-style text across the top of it were the Latin words, "Porten Se Bien", loosely translated, "Behave Well".

It was done by the same interior designer that had hand-sponged the walls a rich hue of terre verte, having had the sense and taste to leave the ceiling untouched, blotched and burned, aged in a shell-shocked patina that no faux finish artist could ever hope to reproduce.

In the painting, a robed, bearded sage floated in a blue sky of clouds, along with a great human eye, a large pair of smiling lips and a single human ear. All seemed to watch over, perhaps even protect, the earthly scene below. On mortal ground, a man whose back was to my gaze, stood nude. Before him a nude woman, arms opened, offered herself to him. On his left, a nude man leaned over, buttocks raised in invitation. Their vulnerable naked flesh was surrounded by thorny blooming cacti, a paradox of potential pain and fleeting beauty. Below the figures, three open roses blossomed under cracked human skulls.

Life is short; why should anyone have to choose? Pick both, I urged the faceless man, go for it. Take the risk before your perfect flesh turns to dry dust. Besides, I laughed to myself, they probably both like to watch.

That's when I noticed her. She didn't seem like much at first, just a college girl, especially because she had been seated. When she stood she was at least as tall as Paul, even wearing flats, with caramel legs for days in those little brown shorts. I could not have seen her face because of the way she stood, talking to Paul, with that pony-tail cascading down her back, barely brushing the smooth curve of her spine.

When she angled to the left, I caught the warmth of her high cheekbones, her smooth skin. She laughed, shook her head. I glimpsed a taste of her full lips, white teeth contrasted with tan skin. I could not see her eyes, but nearly got up from my seat to do so. When I realized I was staring, I ordered another drink from Ren. "Do you know her?" I pointed casually, pulled my stool closer to the bar.

"Who, Alana?" he said, "Sure. She comes in all the time. She works over at PJ's. Why?"

"Just wondering," I smiled, tried not to look at her. I waited a beat, took a sip of my martini, looked over at the table. Paul and Alana were sitting alone, their chairs pulled close, as if they were whispering to one another. She tugged on her long pony-tail, twisting it around her hand. Finally, I could see her eyes; I could not discern their colour, but she looked at him like she meant what she was saying. Paul put his hand on her shoulder, she nodded. He got up from the table and walked toward me. I chewed on an olive, pretended not to see him as he approached.

"Having fun?" I asked.

"Yes, as a matter of fact," he said, "there is someone who would very much like to talk to you."

"Who?" I asked, taking a huge slug of vodka.

"My classmate, Alana. You met her before, don't you remember?"

"I met her before?" I said, taking another gulp, nearly choking on an olive, "When?"

"New Year's Eve, don't you remember? At the Columns."

"New Year's Eve at the Columns ... after I drank how many bottles of champagne?"

"Oh, I see," he laughed, "You really don't remember her."

"Was it before or after I danced on the table with Duncan?"

"Uh, I think after. But, don't tell her you can't remember her. She recalls you well."

"Me?" I said. I finished my drink in the third gulp.

He pushed my hair aside and leaned into my ear, "She wants to talk to you," he whispered, "about sex."

I spun around in my seat, "What about sex?"

"Ask her," he said, "She likes you," he smiled.

"She likes me?"

"Yes," he said, "go talk to her."

I tugged at my bathing suit straps, "Ok," I said, standing up in time to see her go into the ladies room. As I sat alone at the table, I turned to look for Paul, but he was already chatting with Ren. I watched the door of the ladies room, wished I could go in and fix my hair. I found my compact, then began to touch-up my lipstick.

"Your lips are beautiful," Alana said sitting down right next to me.

I nearly jumped. I was afraid to move, thinking I'd draw the lipstick line halfway up my nose.

"So red next to your pale skin." There was a hint of something foreign peppering her voice. It was a gentle voice, although it cracked when she spoke, I found it soothing. She moved in a little closer, turned to face me. She was close, right there.

"Thank you," I sounded strange to myself, "Where are you from?" I said, feeling rude, "I mean, you have a lovely accent."

"Brazil," she said, "My family is from Brazil." She still wore her mono-grammed uniform shirt that smelled strongly of the coffee she must have been serving all evening at PJ's. At last, I could see that her eyes were a pale jade green. She leaned closer, "I remember the first time I saw you," she said, "at the Columns. You were dressed in that beautiful gown, those gloves. I remember your smile," she said looking a little frightened at her own boldness, "Your lips, they haunt me."

I couldn't speak; and if I could've, what on earth could I have said? I couldn't decide whether or not to kiss her right on the spot or to bolt. Instead, I just froze.

"Your husband tells me you are like me," she said, "That you love other women, too. I have loved other women, but I have never shown it. I have waited all my life for the time when I could say all these many things that have haunted my heart since I was a young girl. I have waited to find a beautiful woman who could understand the way I feel for both men and women, to teach me, to let me try. I have always loved boys, too, and I have even been very happy with men. Even so, I have never had the courage to speak about my desires for women to another person, not until I came to this country and found that there is a way to be accepted here, that it is okay to love a woman and not to be disowned by your family, disowned by your husband or friends. Of course, I could never, never tell my family, but, at least here, I have found some courage, some courage to try."

I reached out to her, squeezed her hand. She took it to her lips and brushed my fingers across her mouth. "I want you to show me how it's done, to teach me," she said, almost begging me, "I think it would be beautiful."

I tried mentally to form a word, but couldn't, so I nodded.

She touched my knee lightly, with her fingertips. I could smell her breath, so human, so sweet. "Imagine," she said, "how it will look, you and me. Your ivory skin, and mine, so dark. The way your mouth will feel on my body." She opened my trembling hand with both of hers and rubbed a tiny circle on my palm, "How will my breasts feel being touched by your breasts as we kiss, how will they feel being touched by your hands, by your mouth? Will you put your fingers, these small, white fingers," she said, "into me? Inside of me? Will you let me touch you, too?"

She searched my eyes, "Will you teach me how to please you," she said, "Will you teach me how to love a woman? I want to learn what it takes to make you, to make a woman come." I opened my mouth to speak, but she said, "Don't answer, not yet. There is something I must ask of you first," she looked worried, "Do you find me beautiful? Because if you don't, I could not bear to be with you. I want to please you so much."

"Oh, yes," I whispered, "Oh, yes." I took her hand and kissed it. I kissed it over and over again, wanting to take her right there, to go anywhere where we could be alone.

She looked relieved. "There is something else ... I," she looked deeply into her glass, turned it slowly, "I would really like it if my boyfriend could be there, too. You do not have to touch him if you do not like him, or even to let him touch you, only for him to watch. You see, I told him that I would do it for him," she said, "but, what he does not know, is that I am doing it to please me, that I have always wanted to do this, and, of course, to please you, if you will only let me."

For the life of me, I could not speak. No syllable would pass my lips. All I could think was, She's so gorgeous. All I could do was nod and stare.

She said, "Do not answer me now," and placed a business card in my hand. I held it up as if to read it, but my eyes would not focus. I could only see her. "Please, call me in two weeks," she said, "after my final exams. If you want to show me, I will learn. I will promise I will try to please you." She leaned into me, whispered in my ear, "Two weeks," she kissed my ear softly, "Only in two weeks."

I sat in my seat holding the business card until I could read what it said, "Alana Zocchio, Assistant Manager, PJ's Coffee." I tucked it in my purse.

"Last call," Ren said.

Northbound Train

Wayne M. Bryant

Just a year ago a business contract brought me to Malaysia. My proximity to Thailand led me fulfil a childhood fantasy of visiting the ancient kingdom of Siam. While in Bangkok I met Raywat, a Buddhist monk trainee who befriended English-speaking men to enhance his vocabulary. The ones he liked, he offered to sleep with. Raywat became my first Asian sexual encounter. His vows may have made him a virgin with women, but he certainly knew his way around a man's body.

Western concepts of sexuality amused him. By his early teens, Raywat knew that all the adult men in his life, including his father, had sex with other men. There was no sexual identity – no homo, hetero, or bi – this was just what men did.

Remembering this, I returned to explore a different part of the country. A taxi took me from Don Muang airport to Hualampong Railway Station in Bangkok. Here I could stow my bags and buy a ticket for the night train to Chiang Mai, in the north of Thailand. The train fare would be cheaper than a hotel room in Bangkok and the city would be a perfect home base for hikes and elephant treks into the hill country, where the Lisu, Meo, and Karen people live.

My chief concern was realized when the ticket agent said there were no sleepers left for that evening's train. Since my time was limited, I opted for a regular seat rather than waste a day waiting. Luckily, seats in all three classes were available. To my surprise, first class, which would give me more room to stretch my legs, was only 100 bhat (about three pounds) more than the second class car.

Keeping an eye out for cute, young men in saffron robes, I spent the remainder of the day at the royal museum exploring the history of the only Asian country never to be colonised by a European power. Late in the afternoon, walking back to the train station, the sidewalk was an endless, bustling flea market. The aroma of fish curry caught my attention and, despite the street vendor's protest that it would be too hot for my western palate, it was delicious served over rice. Other tables yielded fresh fruit and drinks for the long ride ahead.

The station itself was cavernous, nondescript, and teeming with people. As

131

the train boarded, I was pleased to find my assigned seat in a European style car with cabins. Two comfortable bench seats, enough room for three people on a side. There's something sensual about the feel of a rail compartment fitted with real wood, leather upholstery, and windows that you can open. The fact that it was old and worn did not matter. This would make a cozy home for the next eleven hours.

My compartment was empty and stayed that way as the rest of the car began to fill. Shortly before we were scheduled to leave, a large group of people burst into the cabin in noisy celebration, carrying various household belongings. I couldn't understand a word they said, but my hopes for sleep were fading. As the conductor announced our imminent departure, all but two of the party scrambled out the door, leaving a young man and woman.

The three of us stowed our luggage, settling into our roomy compartment. Shy smiles, but no words passed between us. The couple cuddled and dozed at one end of the opposite bench. Snacking on some fresh and tangy jackfruit, I stretched out to read a chapter of Somerset Maugham. The motion of the train made my eyes weary from refocusing. Sleep came quickly and held me close until I felt something bump my elbow. Too comfortable to worry, I was just drifting off when it happened again. With caution, my eyes opened and looked around. The compartment was nearly dark except for a small sliver of light seeping in from the corridor between the thick, drawn curtains. Something flashed briefly through the light. I followed it and realized that it was the leg of the young man.

Now I could make out that he was kneeling on the floor facing the other bench. Looking higher, a slender leg was draped over his shoulder. Through the dim light, a look of ecstatic anticipation was visible on the woman's face. Licking his way up her inner thigh, he was softly blowing on her skin. Squirming now, she let out a soft moan. The closer to his goal, the slower he went and the more agitated she became. Willing to wait no more, she grabbed him by the hair with both hands and forced him hard between her legs.

Clearly enjoying this, he hungrily threw himself into his pleasure. She thrust her hips forward, still holding his head and making soft, growling noises deep in the back of her throat. These turned to whimpers and finally stifled screams as orgasm swept her away. For the next several minutes, her body was wracked by one wave of pleasure after another until breathless, she gasped out something in Thai and he stopped. This was having a profound effect on the voyeur in me.

Slowly he reached down and began massaging her feet, paying careful attention to each toe. After several minutes, she opened her soft brown eyes for the first time since I had awakened, and looked directly into mine. A shock of adrenaline pulsed through my body as I shut my eyes, reopening them only to acknowledge that she must have known I was watching. Her eyes caressed me, and she smiled broadly, surveying the bulge in my jeans.

Still holding me in her gaze, she asked, "Did you enjoy to watch us?" All I could manage was, "Yes ... yes, I did." Moving to a sitting position, I added, "You are very good together." This seemed to please her. She said her name was Ali, they were newly married. They had been lovers for two years in Phuket, where they both worked. With typical Thai candor and lack of shame, she explained that she had worked in one of the sex clubs for which the resort island was famous. He had been a cook in a large hotel there. Now they were using their earnings to open a small restaurant in Chiang Mai.

A serious expression crossed her face as she introduced her husband as Surin and asked if I liked him. I glanced at his gentle face, smooth back, and narrow hips and said that I thought he was very nice. But she leaned forward, rested her hand above my knee and said, "What I mean ... my husband like men ... you like him?" Here was a question that would just be too dangerous to ask a stranger back home. It had never occurred to me to ask Raywat if Thai women knew about their husbands' male partners. Ali obviously did ... and appeared to take pleasure in it. Surin had been watching the whole conversation expectantly, but did not seem to understand English. When I nodded and said, "yes", she leaned over and kissed my cheek and a smile broke out on his face.

She stood and began unbuttoning my shirt as he slid his black cotton pants past his beautifully shaped butt. Once naked, my body relaxed under Ali's strong hands as she gave me a traditional Thai massage. Part way through, Surin began stroking my foot, rubbing the arch and toes with wonderfully scented oil. Each firm caress aroused my entire body, the sexual energy mounting. Ali finished up with my fingers as he was massaging his way up the back of my thighs. The two moved in concert, he standing behind me, she seated in front.

The veins stood out thick on his erect, uncut penis as it disappeared into the condom she supplied. Ali gave a playful tug on his sparse, black pubic hair as he applied lubricant to fingers, opening me. When she covered my throbbing cock in latex as well, I was almost too distracted to notice. It was only when she lowered her head and swallowed my entire length that she regained my full attention. Her experienced tongue and mouth were like velvet – as good as the best man I'd ever had. I nearly came when he slid his finger into me.

Fully in control, she backed me down gently as he added a second finger. Ali took my hand and placed it on her breast. The already erect nipple grazed my palm as my fingers cupped her warm, firm flesh. Gradually moving my fingertips together, I squeezed her nipple a bit. She moaned. Squeezing more caused her to wince. As I eased off, she looked me straight in the eye. "Harder" was all she said, and gave my left nipple a pinch to make sure the message was clear. It was, and before long her shaking torso and facial expression matched those I had secretly observed earlier.

It was at that moment that her husband chose to enter me ... hard, hot, and filling me to capacity. Long, firm strokes that made me groan with pleasure. The heat being generated inside me was intense. Ali concentrated on licking my balls and applying pressure at the right times and places to keep me from going over the edge. "Bliss", I thought, as he continued to fuck me, now more tenderly, pacing himself.

Reaching for my backpack, I located the bag of fruit and felt around for a mangosteen. Successful, I pulled one out, cracking open its leathery skin with my one free hand. The dripping fruit slipped easily from its skin and traced a smooth path around her breasts on its own natural lubrication. The stark white of the pulp contrasted beautifully with her smooth, dark skin. As I began to lick the sweet juice off her breasts, she grabbed my hand and brought it to her mouth, swallowing the fruit and two of my fingers. Ali ran her tongue the full length of my fingers as Surin pushed his own length deep inside and held me tight.

As her breathing again became more ragged, Ali stood, turned around, and bent over the seat. She reached behind and guided me toward a hot, wet vagina that was definitely in no need of additional lubricant. Surin, having little choice, followed as I moved forward, giving me a little kiss on the back of the neck as I entered her. The three of us moved together in deep, rapid strokes as I reached around Ali and pinched both nipples. Doing her best to stifle a scream, she came so violently that the three of us almost collapsed on the seat.

Slowing to the rocking rhythm of the train our bodies moved easily against each other. This gentle motion, punctuated by the occasional rhythmic tightening of muscles, went on for several minutes. Gradually passion found the pace until we were fucking frantically, soaring past the brink, exploding into what seemed like a thousand different pieces, yet together as one whole.

Somewhere between ecstasy and the first light of dawn my senses began to return. Warm, naked bodies cuddled on either side and the smell of sex in the air drew from me an involuntary moan. They smiled when I opened my eyes and rubbed their noses together with mine in a three-way version of the traditional Thai "kiss". Outside the window steep, reddish hills rose against the lightening sky. In silence, we gathered our clothes and dressed, preparing for our arrival in Chiang Mai. At the station, I helped carry their belongings to the "tuk-tuk", a sort of Thai taxi, and watched a little sadly as they drove out of sight. It was several minutes before the small crowd of people who had gathered intent on renting me a room came into focus. I couldn't help wondering what other adventures might be in store in this magical land.

Nobody's Business

Raven Kaldera

I met Holly at a bisexual conference on a crowded college campus; among the scruffy students with their backpacks she stood out like a hawk among fluttering chickens. Tall, pale, elegant in a spandex dress that slid just off one shoulder and heels that made her even taller, she moved through the crowd as if her presence itself was a knife slicing it open. I noted the leather jacket that she swung from one slender hand, noted the handcuffs on the left shoulder. My jacket had them too, in the same place.

I cornered her later and managed to get her to talk to me. I'd taken off my cuffs and tucked them in my pocket. "She's a pro," a friend had whispered. "Won't play with you without two hundred in cash." This turned out to be a smokescreen, though; after she'd relaxed with me she confessed that it was just a rumour she'd spread to keep would-be bottoms at arm's length.

"Sometimes being a top can be difficult," she said. "There are so many unattached bottoms, so desperate, following one around." She ran her fingers through my hair.

"It must be worse for women," I said from where I sat at her feet; I'd gone into submissive mode straight away for her, curled up next to her impossibly delicate black heels. "It's not so bad for men, especially in the gay community." I shook the bangs out of my eyes and looked up at her. "I've never bottomed for a woman before," I said. "Been with plenty, sure, but I only just got into the leather scene with my last two lovers, and they were guys. I went from straight vanilla to leatherfag in one easy lesson." She chuckled.

"You aren't scared, are you?" she asked, running a razor-sharp finger along my cheek.

"Of course I am," I retorted cheerfully. "But it's the good kind of scared. Like just before you go into the haunted house at the amusement park." I kissed her exploring hand. "I hate to tell you," I said. "I switch, topping and bottoming. Fifty-fifty. Sort of like being bisexual, I guess."

She smiled her cool, amused smile. "I hate to tell you," she said. "I don't." Her hand found the nape of my neck and I shivered.

"I can live with that," I said, my voice husky with desire.

Darkness behind the blindfold she'd put on me. Those sharp nails travelled everywhere over my chained body, touching, pinching, stabbing, until I writhed

135

and made swamp-thing noises through the bandanna stuffed in my mouth. Tossing my head back and forth as she hurt me down there, putting clamps on my scrotum and the edge of my cock, the buttplug stuffed up inside me. Nothing I hadn't done before; Danny and Matt and I had been pretty heavy into painplay and I hoped against hope that she'd find my abilities as a painsink attractive, that I'd please her. I grovelled at her feet as she leaned her heel into the buttplug and whipped my buttocks raw.

Later, as we lay together in the darkness, she smeared Vitamin E cream on me and told me that she might not be able to see me again. "It won't be up to me," she said. "It'll be up to my girlfriend."

"You have a girlfriend?" I squawked, indignant. "Like, serious? Why didn't you tell me?"

"Hush." Her cool hands worked the cream into my welts and I drew my breath in with a hiss. "It was only supposed to be a one-night stand, but ... I like you. I like you a lot, and I want to bring you home. We have a deal, you see ... before either of us can take on another lover, they have to pass under the scrutiny of the primary partner. The only exception is hunting licenses." She chuckled softly into the back of my neck. "When one of us is going away for a weekend, we can apply for a hunting license from the other person. That means we're allowed one-night stands without going through the rigmarole, but if we want to see the person again, we have to start from scratch as if we hadn't boffed them."

I was silent, picturing an angry dyke with a labrys itching to do some nonconsensual painplay on my evil testosterone-ridden body. "Great. Just great. What's the likelihood of her actually letting me ever see you again?"

"If you're respectful and treat her like an equal, pretty good. Remember, I do this for her, too. But don't get any ideas about getting us both in bed together in lipstick and lingerie. She's butch. She'd probably slug you at the very idea."

I'd read my queer history while dating Matt. I knew just enough to be confused by the issue of butch-femme. "Uh, butch as in doesn't allow herself to be touched, or-"

"Oh, no, she's very sexual. Butch as in she might as well be my boyfriend except that she's got tits and a cunt." Holly fingered my sore arsehole and I gasped. "She bottoms to me, too, in the bedroom, but outside of it we're equals. Remember that."

"You're acting as if it's all decided," I said, pulling away from her exploring finger. "I don't even know if I want to go through this."

"Courage," she said, hovering over me in the dark. "Either I'm worth earning or I'm not."

When she put it like that, the choice seemed obvious.

Jake (which I learned later was butch for Jacqueline) was short and wiry, with her hair in a close quiff and a ring through her septum. She wore ripped jeans and combat boots. Her eyes were brown and suspicious, and she snapped a number of sharp questions at me where I sat nervously on Holly's couch. Did I understand that they were primary partners? Did I understand that Holly wasn't available for a full-time relationship, that their commitment came first? That we had to use safe sex? That acting jealous or possessive or otherwise interfering would get me booted out? Don't get defensive, Holly had warned, and I did my damnedest to keep my voice level and my eyes focused, although I was tense with resentment. The two of us bristled at each other, but Jake had apparently also been warned not to be a boor, because she pulled it back in and suggested we go down to the pub for a beer.

It was a gay bar, which I figured was designed to unnerve me in case I was a typical and possibly homophobic straight guy, but it failed spectacularly as I recognised two former one-night stands there and ended up describing in detail to Jake my first time with a man. He'd come after me in the men's room of such a place, thrust me up against the wall, opened my zipper, and devoured my cock so aggressively that I was half afraid I wouldn't get it back. That made her laugh, and I steered the conversation towards muscle cars, which Holly had already informed me that we both liked, and we spent the rest of the evening discussing the relative merits of Porsches versus Jags, and where one could even theoretically drive a car at 175 miles per hour.

By the end of the night, we'd each told the other one about our first queer lovers, our coming out, and most of the ones we'd had since. I realized with an odd pang that I'd told Jake far more about myself than I'd told Holly. She officially, tipsily, rubber-stamped me with a punch in the arm, gave me a surprisingly tight hug, and told me that I'd better have a high pain tolerance or her Mistress would make lunch meat out of me. We staggered back to their apartment together, and I fell asleep on the couch.

The next morning when I awoke, Jake was nowhere to be seen, but Holly was standing over me in her black satin panties and heels and nothing else, except for the riding crop in her hand. "Get up," she ordered, and the crop smacked down on the pillow mere inches from my face. "You've got work to do."

At first we played with her separately, only meeting by chance and occasionally hauling up our shirts to compare marks, like a couple of frat kids showing off our trophies, but then Holly decided she wanted us both together one night. She tied me to the foot of the bed and made Jake serve her, and then switched our positions. Jake was never made to be naked, I noticed, and she constantly wore her strap-on with the realistic cock. That wasn't a new thing; I knew she packed it in her worn jeans most of the time, but it was interesting to see her wearing nothing but that and her T-shirt. Whatever she looked like with her crew cut and muscles, it didn't look feminine to me, but it was, I had to admit, strangely interesting. Holly called her "boy", as in "Come here and eat me, boy." I got so used to seeing her with the rubber cock and balls sprouting from her groin that it was almost a shock when Holly pulled it off and fistfucked her there on the bed until she screamed.

I was untied by then, and Holly ordered me to hold Jake's wrists while she worked her hand deep inside her butch's cunt. Instead, I held her hands, letting her squeeze them as she needed to get through the pain and into the pleasure. I'd done this before; held the hand of boy bottoms while they struggled against that wall, their masters or daddies working them over. It wasn't that different. Looking at Jake's sweating face, I realized, my breath hard in my throat, that it wasn't any different at all.

"I wish I could do that to you," Holly said as she peeled off the rubber glove afterwards. Jake was curled up in a happy ball of afterglow and I was stroking her shoulder, moved as I always was by being able to witness such transformative ecstasy close up.

"You can," I said, "but you have to give me an enema first. It's safer. So if something actually tears, God forbid, I won't die of peritonitis before I get to the hospital."

She shook her head in amazement. "Ye gods. Why did I wait so long before finding a gayboy to fuck? I swear, you're so much more ... experienced ... than straight guys."

I sighed. "I'm not a gayboy, really; I sleep with too many girls for that." I grinned up at her. "Just bisexual, that's all."

"Like all of us," she said, looking speculatively at the lube supply.

"Jake's not bisexual," I said. "Jake's a dyke."

"Sure she is," said Holly. "You want that enema now, or what? I'm dying to try this."

"Holly," said Jake, struggling to a sitting position, "please. No."

I looked back and forth from one to the other. "Butches aren't bisexual," I said. "It's just not ... it just doesn't ..." I trailed off. The two of them were exchanging glances.

"Maybe the reason that no butches come out as bisexual," Holly said succinctly, talking to me but keeping her eye contact with her partner, "is because men aren't ever attracted to butches anyway, and the few that might agree to boff them just treat them like girls." Then she tore her gaze away from Jake's pained face and snapped her fingers at me, pointing toward the bathroom. "You. Get in there. And get down on your hands and knees; I want to see you crawl."

After I'd been cleaned inside and out, Holly filled my arse with lube and worked her slender hand in, slowly, the way she'd done it for Jake. Unlike some guys, I stay hard throughout the entire experience of handballing; it was all I could do not to come until she ordered me to. She had Jake hold down my wrists as I'd done for her, but we were, for some reason, very careful not to make eye contact with each other as I strained and groaned and finally shot a stream of white jism high into the air.

When I'd recovered, Holly strapped on her own cock, a big black shiny thing like an insect's ovipositor, or the organ of some science-fiction android, and she made us both kneel at her feet and take turns sucking it. She had one hand anchored on each of our scalps, and she thrust the chokingly huge black cock into first my mouth and then Jake's, and then mine again. Our hands were cuffed behind our backs, so we couldn't touch except for the warmth of our bodies pressed against each other as Holly used us, but I stayed hard the entire time in spite of the fact that I had already come.

Holly was out of town the next time I showed up; she'd taken off somewhere at the last minute without telling me that our weekly date was off. I was pissed, but Jake looked so down that I didn't want to lay my anger on her. "She's going to be gone for a whole week," the butch mumbled. "It's a business thing. Job interview in the next county. God, I hope she doesn't get it. That sounds awful but I'd have to give up my job to follow her, and it's not easy to get work when you look like me." She ran a hand over her short hair, one hand hauling up on her ripped jeans, and looked so much like a boy that I had to remind myself, sternly, that the bulge in her pants was rubber. "You might as well come on in anyway. There's leftover coq au vin from last night. I cooked her a farewell dinner, but she hardly touched it, she was so excited."

I straddled a chair and accepted the beer she handed me. "Oh well. I can always go over to the Camshaft and see what kind of action I can pick up. It'll do me good to be the top for a change." It was a testament to the power of Holly's overwhelming attraction that I hadn't been driven nuts by the urge to switch in months.

"Gay men," sighed Jake. "You're so lucky. Dykes can't do that, just go pick up a trick. They all want to get married or something, and if they're tops, they want to own you." She opened a bottle and stared at it. "Holly tends to get all the extra action in this relationship, since she's the bisexual."

I remembered what Holly had said the week before about butches and bisexuality and very deliberately didn't comment. "Well, cheer up. If you were a gay man, you wouldn't be doing it with Holly."

"You are," she pointed out, turning away and opening the fridge.

"You have me there," I admitted. "Do you really want to be a man?" I was momentarily distracted by her tight, athletic butt. Almost a boy's butt, that.

"Nah." Jake shrugged and pulled a covered dish out of the fridge. "I'm not a transsexual or something like that. I know, because one of my ex-lovers did that. I don't mind my body being female so much, having a cunt and all, but I just don't like to have sex as a girl. If I think of myself as a boy when I'm getting boffed, it's just so much more of a turn-on."

"You'd make a pretty sexy boy," I said. I don't know why I said it; I think it was meant to be a consolation, but Jake's eyes lit up and she smiled for the first time that day.

"You think so?" she asked, and there was such hope in her eyes, such longing to be seen as desirable, that it touched me. I'd been there, I remembered what that felt like.

"Yeah," I said. "I think that if you were a boy, the daddies'd be fighting to get you to suck their dicks."

Her brown eyes never left my face. "Would you want me?" she said in a small voice, and I knew, instantly, what she was asking. Several voices jostled for supremacy in my head – what would I do with a butch? How would I treat her? Like a girl? Like a boy with no dick? Jake was looking at me, though, jaw thrust forward, beer in one hand and the other jammed into her pocket, half begging me, half daring me, and I was hard as a rock in my jeans, and there was only one thing to do.

"Can you suck cock, boy?" I snapped, dropping into top mode, shifting position on the stool to make sure that she could see my erection. I grabbed it through my jeans, rubbing it, not taking my narrowed eyes from her face.

In answer she put the beer on the counter and dropped to her knees in front of me, going for the zipper of my pants, and I felt my dick engulfed by an eager mouth that took it all the way to the hilt in one thrust. A growl of pleasure escaped me, and I thrust in again. She deepthroated it a few times and then pulled back, looking up at me with an intense expression on her face that could have been lust or worry. "I've never done it before on a real one," she said.

"That's OK. You'll learn on the job." I pushed her head back down. "Lick up and down the shaft, like that, yeah. Now take my balls into your mouth – gently – there, now lick up and down again." I talked her through it until she seemed able to handle it herself; towards the end she got braver and her tongue strayed towards my arsehole, but after a blindingly pleasurable minute of that I needed to come and pulled her head back up. "Hold still, boy," I said. "I'm just gonna fuck your face till I come. Open your throat and get your gag reflex out of the way. Now."

She took it like a trooper, hanging onto my legs, snatching her breath between thrusts. At the last minute I pulled out and sprayed her with come; I wanted to come in her mouth but there was the safe sex rule. She knelt there on the floor as I caught my breath, looking up at me. I stared back at her, considering my options.

"What are you going to do, sir?" she asked, looking unsure.

I grinned and grabbed her by the collar of her T-shirt. "I'm going to hijack Holly's boy. Get your arse upstairs." I tossed her in the general vicinity of the stairway and she scrambled up almost on all fours. I followed, mentally inventorying my tool selection. Holly had a well-stocked toy chest but I really didn't want to use any of hers; it'd feel like sacrilege, and anyway using her girlfriend was bad enough. I had my belt, the handcuffs still in my jacket pocket from ages past, and my heavy leather gloves; it would do. It would have to. Jake was stripping off her pants like they were yesterday's news; her cock in its harness slipped out and bobbed at her crotch.

"Attention!" I barked at Jake, who'd obviously never done that before and looked panicked for one second before stiffening into a half-assed attention pose. I snapped my fingers, looking displeased. "Stand straight. Lock your hands behind your neck. Spread your legs. Wider." I stepped up to her and put my hand on her arse, bare except for the narrow leather strap on her harness between the taut cheeks. I squeezed them. "This is the position you're going to take your beatings in when you get them from me," I told her, slipping my hand between her legs. I didn't know if touching her breasts would ruin her boy fantasy, so I avoided them and grabbed her rubber cock, grinding it backwards into where I knew her clit was. She arched her head back and whimpered, and I shoved harder, rhythmically, like I was jerking her off. Then I stopped, and her shoulders slumped. "No, you don't get to come yet," I told her. "Gay boy bottoms have to learn to exercise some discipline.

You can hold off until I tell you, can't you, boy?"

"I can, sir!" she gasped, and I took her at her word. I pulled my gloves out of my pocket and slapped her ass with them, reddening it slightly. Not enough to hurt much; that was for later. I yanked up her T-shirt and slapped her tits with them. She made a noise of protest and made as if to take her arms down to protect them, but I slapped her across the face with the gloves as soon as she moved.

"You keep your hands where I told you, boy!" I barked. "I want to hurt those pecs of yours. Flex yourself so I can see them."

An entirely different look came over her face. I was willing to treat them as if they were pecs, and that was a whole different matter. She tightened her muscles, and I admired the curve of her delts. "Nice. You work out, don't you, boy?" I commented, slapping the gloves back and forth across her chest. She nodded, head back, biting her lip in an expression of both pleasure and endurance.

I stepped behind her and pulled my belt from its loops, folded it in half, and cracked the folds together in that noise that always makes a bottom react. It worked on Jake, too. Her breathing came harder, and she adjusted her stance. I cracked her one across the buttocks, and she cried out, but didn't flinch too much. "Thank you, sir!" she grunted out. I smiled. This boy was better behaved than some of the boys I'd been with. Holly'd trained her well. I let her have another one.

"Sir!" she gasped, almost stumbling. "Sir, I don't think I can stand for this without falling over, sir!" In her voice, I heard the need to please, to not fail through incompetence. Jake wasn't a bottom who got off on being told they were a stupid shit; she took it personally if she failed her top in any way.

"Up against the wall," I ordered, and she gratefully staggered forward and pressed herself against the wallpaper. I moved up close behind her and whispered nastily in her ear, "I haven't beaten anyone in months, boy. You know what I want most right now? I want to beat you until I can't lift my arm any more, until I'm tired of it. That'll be a long time, boy. You think you can do that for me?"

She gulped. "I'll try, sir," she said. So I stepped back and let her have it, whipping that little butch until her back and buttocks were bruised and welted, criss-crossed with virulent red and purple marks. She took it all, too, in teeth-clenched dead silence; it was her way. I must have laid over a hundred strokes on her before she finally cried out, and then I stopped, instantly. My arm was aching and I was panting, sweat pouring down my face. I'd forgotten what work it was to whip someone.

I moved forward and leaned against her and she gasped as the leather of my jacket pressed into her welts. Reaching around to where her cock hung, permanently stiff and at attention, I grabbed it and pressed it back into her crotch, rubbing it as if I was jerking it off. Her breath came in long gasps and she pressed her red-and-purple ass back against me.

"You want to be fucked, don't you, boy?" I snarled in her ear as I flattened her against the wall, and she held her breath and nodded, as if she didn't trust

142

her voice.

"Not my cunt," she said. "That's Holly's."

"Fair enough." I pushed her onto the bed, face down, and she scrambled to get to her hands and knees, waiting for me. There was a gallon dispenser of lube by the bed – Holly didn't do half measures – and I slathered it into her crack, around the strap of her harness, into her rear hole. My pants were discarded, and my boots; a condom found its way from the nightstand to my dick in record time, and then I was easing myself slowly into her tightness. The steel-belted silence she'd maintained during the beating seemed to desert her as I worked my way in; she beat the mattress with her fists and groaned, but didn't try to pull away as I thrust back and forth. I was so hard that it didn't take longer than two minutes for me to shoot off. As we tumbled to the pillow together, I was a bit worried that it hadn't been a particularly memorable fuck for her, but when she turned her head I saw that she was smiling.

"You all right, boy?" I asked, stroking the nice definition on her upper arm. She nodded, grinning, and then ducked her head as if in embarrassment.

"I've never ... with a ... I mean, I wanted to, but-" She seemed to be too far gone in an endorphin haze to speak clearly, so I shushed her and put my arms around her.

"Do you want to come?" I asked her.

"I think so, but ..." She still seemed shy and incoherent. "Could you ... play with my cock?"

"Sure." I took hold of it again, rubbing the shaft, making sure to press in into her flesh on the downstrokes. She moaned in pleasure and bucked her hips. "Can you come from fucking with this thing, boy?" I asked in surprise.

"Yeah," she said sheepishly, and I had a sudden idea. Desire for it filled my guts like a hot flash and I started to get hard all over again. Getting a handful of lube, I turned her onto her back and greased the rubber pole until it was sloppy with goop, and then I used the rest of it to carefully lubricate my own arsehole. I stood up and took off my jacket, removing the handcuffs, and then cuffed her wrists together through the bars of the bedstead.

"I don't need your hands for this, boy," I said. "All I need is for you to move those hips." Then I straddled her and lined up that rubber cock with my own hole, and eased myself down over it. One thing I'd learned about myself with my first male lover is that the idea that tops don't get fucked is a crock. In my book, anything the top orders the bottom to do to them is dominant. Slowly – Jake's dick was good-sized; I wondered if she was a size queen – I slid myself down until I was sitting right on her pelvis, that long length buried in my arse. Her eyes were so big and her expression so awestruck that I laughed. "Move it, boy," I told her, and she proceeded to give me a good ride, bracing her feet and bouncing me up and down with everything she was worth. Somewhere along the line she came, bucking and thrashing, and I had one of those sensual little arse-orgasms that don't quite reach the genitals, and I tried to come with my cock but it didn't quite happen, but it was all right because the feeling of being reamed out was just as good.

And somewhere along the line I forgot that Jake was a woman, that she was anything at all except a boy with a hard cock under me. "Good boy," I gasped during our violent gyrations, "my boy, my good boy." Somewhere along the line it completely ceased to matter.

Afterwards, we lay together quietly in Holly's bed. After beating the shit out of her, I was paradoxically afraid to touch her, hold her, but after the first few minutes of awkwardness she reached out for me. "What would have been perfect," I murmured into her ear, "would have been for Holly to walk in the door while we were screwing."

She chuckled. "Yeah, while the cat's away the mice will play. That's what she'd say."

"Well, I'd just plead an overwhelming need to switch occasionally. And you?" I bantered.

She was silent for a moment. "Bisexuality," she said finally. Then she turned her head into my shoulder, hiding her face. "Could I really be your boy?" she asked almost inaudibly. "Or was that just scene talk?"

"You belong to Holly," I said.

"I belong to myself," Jake retorted, and then amended, "Except for my cunt, that is. But ..." She was silent for a moment, and then said haltingly, "I know I don't have a real cock, and if we went into a gay bar and you called me your boy, we'd be laughed out of there, but ..." She trailed off.

I hugged her tightly. "Girlfriend, I don't see anyone else beating down my door for the job. You want it, it's yours." I felt her taut body relax in my arms. "'Course that'll mean you'll have to endure two sets of beatings. I wouldn't want to ruin you for Holly's tender mercies."

She snorted. "I'm tougher than I look," she said.

"That's a frightening thought," I told her, and kissed her.

So now I have a Mistress and a boy. Holly ended up taking the job in the next county, but she commutes back here on the weekends and puts us both right down on our knees, where we need – and long – to be. It's only a short-term contract, and she'll be back here by the fall. And during the week, I have the fascinating privilege of exploring the up-close intricacies of real bisexuality with an eager-to-please boygirl. Sometimes, while we're fucking, I watch her face as her head tosses from side to side on the pillow. On the left, it looks female; on the right, male. I'm not sure I know which one is making my dick hard, making me come, but frankly, I don't think it matters any more. We are what we are. And what we are, that's open to debate, but we certainly are having fun.

Nothing a Litre of Vodka won't Cure

diversity33

The morning after throwing up into the cat litter tray again I tore down Kay's photos from my wall once more, for about the 20th time. As Loca howled and glared reproachfully at me, unwilling to go near my drunken residue in her toilet, I read Kay's message to me on last years birthday card: "If our friendship dies then I will be black and moody for the rest of my life, ie, it would be truly foul. My tension is dispelled as soon as I see you, and things subsequently are ace!" I guess this was an apology and a sort of declaration of love, or at least the closest I was ever going to get from her.

I started to crumple the card in my hand but gave it a reprieve yet again and instead shut it away in a draw with all her letters and other mementoes of this 2-year long soap opera.

I'd first met Kay when I started work at the East London Hospital in Whitechapel. We seemed to have a lot in common, she was 25, short, blonde, slim, a very cool and calculating personality, giving nothing away. I thought she was very attractive but didn't risk any stronger feelings as she was so obviously straight, with a partner of several years, and flirting with the guys in the office. But I was wrong about this, god was I wrong.

We got on very well, going out on the piss every week. Her relationship was heading through a bad patch – indeed this bad patch seemed to consist of the last four of the five years they'd been together – and she welcomed any excuse to put off going back to his flat in Dulwich. She was looking for support and advice, but my experience of men was pretty limited in a way, and I'd never lived with a guy, so mostly all I could do for her was hold her and get her drunk.

I didn't understand how she could stay with, or say she loved, someone who was often cold and hostile towards her, who expected her to accommodate herself to his life and plans, and who had become very overweight and physically unhealthy. When I met him even his fingers were bulbous with fat, it made my skin crawl to think of her being fucked by him.

I began to realise that I did fancy her a lot, and was basically terrified of this. Despite so many years of unrequited longings for women, I still had

145

no clue how to get a relationship with one. Yet sometimes I thought she was flirting with me, I caught her staring as we waited in the lunchtime hospital cafe queue, her eyes lingering on mine as we talked crap in the office. Was I reading her signals right? Just what was going on here?

Then one night we both got totally stoned on vodka and Stella. She teased me about fancying Ajay, my extremely butch boss, and being a closet dyke but I guessed she didn't really believe it. I told her she was well out of order and she backed down: "Sorry if I rattled your tree a bit, you like meat and two veg I know, especially wrapped in a crispy uniform, but maybe you should give the other a go, just to see what it's like, eh?"

"And what about you?" I demanded, grabbing her as she laughed at my defensive reaction, "I've seen you staring at women, don't try and deny it!"

"Yeah, Louisa, you know, she was my girlfriend last year. Beautiful body but completely screwed up in the head, I couldn't take it after a while. Don't tell Dave about this, will you!"

I was stunned, it hadn't occurred to me that she would be more experienced than me, I thought at most she was 'curious' but wouldn't go though with anything if I did show an interest in her – not a game I wanted to get into, too hurtful.

Fortified by masses of alcohol, somehow I ended up in bed with her in her flat, Dave was away, and I hardly knew what to do or which bits to start with. I stroked her beautiful breasts and nipples with my hands and then licked and suckled them with my tongue. The teats were huge, like button mushrooms, they felt perfect between my lips. She lay back, arms behind her head, smiling slightly in apparent pleasure, just letting me work on her – this was to become the usual pattern of our lovemaking, alas. I closed my eyes as I went down on her, tongue sliding along the inner lips then circling the clit. She guided me as I caressed and worshipped her body until she was shuddering uncontrollably in a long climax. Then at last she gripped me and held me tight and kissed me.

Afterwards I was disappointed in a way – it hadn't been so very different from sex with a guy, not more emotionally close or anything. But her body was as beautiful as any man's – I stared fascinated at the ice-cream cones of her small boobs, caressing them with my lips until she finally passed into sleep. Beside her fragile small body I felt like some huge ungainly bloke, a kind of protective feeling that was strange but kinda sweet.

After the Stella night things went crazy and I totally thought I'd lost a good buddy and indeed things weren't right for a while. We carried on going out together but now I didn't have a clue what was going to happen at the end of the night. We slept together again a couple of weeks later – this time Dave was home, so she waited until he was asleep before slipping out of his bed and into the spare room to kip down with me. Not much happened, I was afraid of making too much noise in case he heard as he was just next door, but managed to make her cum again burying my tongue in her bits as she squatted on my mouth for what seemed like hours. 20 minutes before his alarm was due to go off she slipped back into bed with him, and he seemed none the wiser.

When we slept together I felt totally loved and accepted, every aspect of her body was beautiful to me, her soft skin, the curves of her breasts and hips, her smell ... However at other times I felt completely rejected when she rushed home to Dave at the end of the night, leaving me to wander miserably back alone to my maggot, dog shit and mad woman infested pig sty in Kilburn.

She admitted she was afraid of being seen as a dyke, the pressure of being seen as 'abnormal', but I sensed also she had no idea of how to deal with women in relationships, having been so used to manipulating men by her sexuality and beauty. Dave didn't seem to be aware of her many infidelities or that we had shagged in his bed, but was quite jealous of her time, getting nasty with her whenever she went out with me instead of him. They moved to Brighton as Kay was starting a computing course there, and Dave went too, probably to make sure she didn't stray too far.

I was also trying to escape from Kilburn – felt like I was living in the twilight zone and had to get out to preserve my sanity. Found myself a new place to live, a flat in a house owned by a bi bloke, Alan, in trendy Clapham, expensive but I was just so pissed off with sharing and people stealing my food, and didn't want to end up in some squalid bedsit again.

After New Year Kay phoned me up, Dave was away and it was like she was asking me to come and see her simply to keep her company. I was a bit pissed off and said what I'd been feeling, that she only wanted me when he wasn't around – that she wasn't willing to consider my needs and feelings. Still went down to Brighton the next day though, and had a great time boozing, sitting on the stony deserted beach with multiple cans of beer, flicking through porno mags back in her flat and then standing at the windows flashing our boobs at the builders on the house opposite, the usual stuff. Went back to the beach in the evening with a fresh 'slab' of beer cans, trying to spy on the gay guys cottaging under the West pier, but it was too cold for even these blokes to get their tackle out, alas.

Kay started to worry me, talking about how guilty she felt screwing around behind Dave's back and how devastated he'd be if he found out, how devoted he was to her really. This didn't sound like the most encouraging lead-up to the night of passion I'd been hoping for. "There's about 18 things I'll have to tell Dave if I'm going to be honest with him," she said, fearfully.

"Just make sure I'm the last on the list!" I protested, frowning at her as she huddled up on the cold sand, the grey waves reflecting lurid orange light from the promenade arcades. This contrast of nature and artifice made me very depressed for some reason, I longed to be on a Pacific reef somewhere, miles away from anyone else, just the two of us together in the wilderness.

By midnight was so pissed I was nearly paralytic, she was almost dragging me back to the flat. She undressed me and put me in the bath and washed me, cos I was basically incapable of doing anything for myself – felt very caring and nice, but no sex. Slept together in boxers and t-shirts, I reached out for her during the night and she held my hand, but I wanted her hands in more interesting places ...

By Easter we'd been 'together' for nearly a year, in our own strange fashion.

But she sounded more frightened than ever about her gay side. She claimed she still wanted to be friends but couldn't cope with all the "weird shit" between us, ie, the sex, even though, I reminded her, she'd initiated this in the first place. Very pissed off, went out with my booze-buddy Andrea and got totally plastered, trying to submerge these bad thoughts in a sea of alcohol. Spent the next day throwing up at regular intervals and couldn't remember how I'd got home at all.

Got offered the chance to move to Australia by Mak, a guy I'd met at 'Disfigurement Support', who was getting a job over there. Very keen, as I'd lived there for a year after my dad kicked me out of home at 18, and loved the way of life out there, the freedom, the endless sun and booze. Kay was very unhappy about the thought of me disappearing; without me around she would just be stuck alone in her miserable relationship with Dave.

Emotionally our relationship was like a perpetual honeymoon, we always managed to patch up an argument afterwards, but I wondered where it was going. I often felt she was happier if I didn't initiate the frustrating fumbling that was our version of lesbian sex. One time when we slept together she built a barrier of cuddly toys and spare pillows between us in bed, as a joke, she claimed, but I knew it really wasn't at some level.

Kay phoned me up a couple of days later in tears – Dave had hit her after one of their incessant arguments, she didn't know whether to leave him or not. She came round, to stay, I assumed, and I tried to console her but she was scared to let me touch her at all. When we got back from the pub at 11pm I went straight into my room as usual to change.

"What are you doing?" she asked suspiciously.

"Just changing into shorts, is that ok?"

"I guess I can trust you," she laughed doubtfully. Then she phoned Dave and made a pathetic apology to him for running away – he threatened her that he would chuck her out for good if she didn't come back immediately: "If you don't, then you'll find you can't get into the flat at all." I was silently urging her to tell him to go to hell, but he put down the phone on her and she sobbed despairingly.

I started preparing a separate bed for her when she decided she'd rather catch the last train home back to her violent and obnoxious partner, even though it was an hour-plus journey with god-knows what drunken weirdos around. Really made me feel valued.

Mak was interviewed for his job in Oz and got it, so now that option was open. Made it clear to Kay that I was seriously thinking of going, and this seemed to make her much more attentive, dropping in after work or inviting me out to lunch. She now worked near Battersea bridge as a temp, so was only a 20 minute walk away. Though she might as well have been in Inverness for all I'd seen of her before this sudden change of heart. She even reached the point of suggesting that she spend one or two nights a week with me and the rest of the time with Dave – typical bi, wanting the best of both worlds ... But I knew this wouldn't work, I'd always been very monogamous in all my relationships (even if several happened at the same time) and wanted to be her only lover, not just a secondary partner. Plus Dave would completely flip if he realised what was going on.

She stayed over again at the weekend, no sex but some nice drunken cuddles once the light was out. Long discussion in the morning – she'd clearly begun to finally think more seriously about our 'thing', prompted by my impending move to the other side of the world. She pointed out the very coy, girly way I always talked on the phone when telling dad I had a new man, as if begging for approval from him, but that I never told him about her, or acknowledged the relationship to anyone else either. "I don't want to be seen as a freak," I said, a bit defensively, "I love you cos of who you are, not cos of what gender you are, that is totally irrelevant."

"But you haven't even told your sister, it's as if you pretend it doesn't exist."

"How can I claim to anyone that we are together when a) you're not living with me but with your boyfriend, and b) even when we do plan to do things together, you keep letting me down? They would think I was totally naive or deluded, maybe I am anyway to carry on like this, in hope ..." I felt I couldn't make any assumptions about this relationship at all, I knew any I did make would be quickly disappointed by her behaviour.

She sat up and stared at me, Alan had already gone out to work and it was a bright cold winters day outside. The cat had nested on the bed between us and had just let out a fart as she slept, oblivious to the emotional discussion being conducted across her. "But you keep telling me, even forcing it on me, that you screw around all the time, with loads of men and women, whenever you get horny you basically go for it without even a thought of me!"

"But I am loyal to you, in spirit," I protested, stroking her soft blonde hair as she looked doubtfully at me, "you are the only one in my heart even when I'm going down on a knobbly monster dick or groping a 52H boob ...".

Over the next couple of months I went through the medicals and clearances necessary for the Aussie visas, just doing temping as a secretary while we waited for these to come through. I'd got in touch with a couple of girls in Oz through the internet and it sounded like Sydney was still dyke heaven. Could hardly wait for things to come through and make my escape. Helped Kay and Dave with their move back to London, Dave simply sat and watched us most of the time, not helping at all as we hauled boxes and furniture around, claiming he couldn't 'cos of a bad back. He was even heavier now – 20 stone.

The last time I saw Kay she said the relationship with him was back on track, but behind her show of confidence was a mass of fear. She broke down and begged me not to go, playing on my worries about Mak's agenda. But I'd decided I was going to abandon him anyway as soon as we got to Oz.

She promised she would change, but I knew she felt what she felt and I couldn't alter it, that'd she'd never leave Dave for me. I'd spent the last two years of my life on a continual roller-coaster of infatuation and despair, hoping, futilely, that she would change, and this had to be the end.

My genitals were surging again just from the contact of her warm soft body as we cuddled, but I was wary of putting too much faith in this automatic physical reaction anymore. Perhaps sex is just some illusion of connection, an intimacy that can never be actually attained ...

The day before the flight I wrote a final letter to her: "Kay,

I don't think this letter is a good idea yet I can't not do it – maybe I just won't send it!!

To lay the cards on the table mate is to say that I am totally in love with you. If I had just one wish it would be to spend the rest of my life with you – where we live, what we do, how rich or how poor we are are all irrelevant to me – all that matters to me is that we would be together and that you were happy!

The last thing I want to do is to add more stresses to your complicated life but I have been going crazy thinking about all of this all the time.

I wouldn't want you to see me as a straw to grasp and use and then discard when you've changed your mind or when I don't serve a purpose anymore, I don't have much self respect but I have enough to know that I don't deserve that. I would have liked to live with you as a mate, (if that was what you wanted), to share a dingy bedsit in Brixton or a flat in Brighton. To have a laugh, get drunk, run around naked, find jobs, pay the bills, whinge and cry and make cakes, just how it has been I guess.

You love Dave and you have six years of history together and he is a successful guy and I fully understand why it is very stressful to even consider leaving him. Most of me thinks that you shouldn't, most of me thinks you should stay with Dave and I should be the one who leaves, I am responsible for stirring things up in your head and making things difficult for you and him – once I go to Oz then maybe we can all get on with our lives and live happily ever after!

I have absolutely nothing to offer you Kay, no money, no security, no home, no prospects, no history, no opportunities, NO DICK! For those reasons I think you should, and see why you do stay where you are. I guess all I could offer is my love and in this world all that that carries is uncertainties and pain.

I hope we can still be friends after this, I'll stand by you no matter what mate, what ever you decide or end up doing, whether you stay with Dave, or you go it alone, or you meet someone else or run away and join the Foreign Legion – I'll always be there for you.

Maxie"

As I boarded the plane, looking out one last time at the grey chill Spring evening, at England, I knew she'd be on the phone as soon as I got to Oz, begging me to come back ...

Andie

Piglet

Early this morning we got back from the club. Loud and putting the lights on and slamming doors. Your make-up smeared and you flopped down on the sofa.

We decided in the end not to watch the video. Someone made coffee, strong, from the filter, but it couldn't keep us awake. And a few at a time our friends left till there was only us.

Beautiful boy, you were asleep long before the last of them left. Cradling yourself and hugging a cushion. Rich black curls falling over your face. "Aaww, how sweet," they said as they stood, coats on and ready to leave.

I tried going to bed. But knowing you were downstairs kept me awake. The sun was up when I made my way down to the lounge, a step at a time on the staircase.

Sound asleep. The curtains were not properly drawn and a beam of sunlight caught your bare shoulder. Soon you would be dreaming. What do 17-year old goth chick boys dream of?

I decided that I would send you to her. Cross legged on the carpet, hoping I still had the power, I closed my eyes and concentrated.

You dream of sunlight so bright that everything is bleached to grey. You dream of silence after loudness – only a ringing in your ears. Your back is up against a wire fence and you are naked.

A sea of grey grass slopes ahead of you up a hill. Someone appears at the top of the hill and runs down towards you. She is as tall as you and dark-haired, dark eyebrowed, dark lipped. She wears a summer dress and a band of silk to contain her wildly flying hair. She laughs, out of breath.

A few yards from you she stops, gathers herself a second then approaches you more slowly. There is wickedness in her glittering eyes, dark intention on the face of an angel.

She raises her hand to feel your face. Your lips stretch to caress her hand. You move forward and find you are restrained at the neck and by the arms and legs. She feels your chest and runs her fingers round your neck, holds herself close to you for a few seconds delighting in tantalizing you. She is speaking but you cannot hear what it is that she says. You tell her that you will do anything she wants. Any act you can perform or service you can give. Knowing full well that when someone said this to you it meant nothing to you and she may well feel the same. Still you tell her. You cannot hear your own words.

She is looking into your eyes. Now she has slapped your face which you will just have to deal with as she is now untying your bonds, so gently. Then she leads you away, dragging you by the ropes at your wrists. You stumble, barefoot, across the grass.

There is a glade between some trees and there she lays you down. She takes off her dress and straddles you. She puts your erect cock into her vagina. It is all very basic.

With her hand she closes your eyes firmly, another hand stops your mouth. You feel her moving on top of you to make herself aroused. Her skin is silk and warm where it touches you but cool when it meets your flesh at first. You know you cannot raise your arms to hold her — you are hers, you must only let yourself be used.

Suddenly she stops and releases the blindfold and gag she made with her hands. You can feel the presence of someone else standing by your side. You look up. It is a young lad who looks very much like her. Her brother who has come to see where she is and what she's doing.

They argue, he slips a knife from his pocket and looks down at you, lustfully. She is saying no. She puts up a hand to stop him and she smiles. He smirks also. He throws the knife aside, knowing he won't need it — you will not fight.

He rolls his checked shirt over muscled arms and looks at you with all seriousness. The family beauty seems more striking on him than her, more troubled and imperfect. He hauls you to sit on his lap and buries his face deep into your neck to nuzzle and enjoy. His hands take possession of you and feel their way clumsily around. She is watching and smiling.

They take turns to kiss and toy with you, first her supple little mouth on yours then his animal untrained passion. In front of your face she gives him a deep kiss and shows him how to use his tongue.

With her encouragement he screws you on all fours and with her foot holding your head down in the grass and dirt. His strong thighs slam his cock into you repeatedly. Then she kneels at your side to hold your cock and she starts to wank you gently. You stretch your arms ahead and hold onto the grass. You feel but do not hear your own gasp of climax.

He stops fucking you, although he hasn't come yet. She pushes him down on the grass and brings him to orgasm with her hand, inches away from where you lie.

Then you're watching their feet as they walk away.

I guess I fell asleep on the floor next to the sofa. It was you that woke me. Your curls tight and wet and dripping down on me. You'd had a shower.

You were crouching and stroking my face. You didn't mention your dream as we hugged on the sofa, watching daytime soaps on TV. But we started to nuzzle each other just that little bit more intimately than before.

Pretty boy, your lips with their perfect cupid's bow are kissing mine. Now I suck marks onto your neck between the faded ones left by some other vampire. You gasp and lean back. I place my hand on your bare chest, and I feel the heat of you.

Which Bisexuality? – O, *That* Bisexuality!

Miodrag Kojadinović

Shut went the door: *Bang!* – and the clatter of high heels echoed down the corridor. To the left turn, and further along the tiled stairway. We stand still; well, *stand* is not exactly the right word, as I am leaning over him, doggy-style, my dick planted in his arsehole. The woman who just walked in on us is his fiance – bride-to-be in a week's time, actually – and it appears Brandon has not shared with her our little secret. Ah, well ...

While I am still dismayed, he starts squeezing his sphincter lightly, a couple of times in a sequence. The moment, however, is lost, and so is most of my hard-on: the flippant and merry god of fortuity, Kairos, has flown away. Not that it is a matter of some big luck getting a piece of his arse these days; not any more. But I do admit that there was a time when I was so foolishly enamoured with his lupine predatorial gait that I would have easily walked, in steel shoes, all the way to the Moon to get it for him.

"No, boy!" I say, as I pull out of him, slip the condom off and toss it into the ashtray. Luckily none of us smokes, so it won't coagulesce into a Levy-Straussian stinking mess of archetypal waste of faeces and ashes. I am glad I have not resumed smoking after I came back to settle in Paris again, and he, actually, never did, having been born in California in the early 1970s. He looks at me with those fury-filled wolf whelp brown eyes for a few seconds and then dives for my flaccid dick, starts sucking. "Brandon, 's OK" I say, louder this time. He pays no heed, continues yet more eagerly. I relent, lay back, spread my legs wide, so he can have access to my butt to finger and rim later on, close my eyes and give in to the moment. He has developed into an expert cocksucker over the last several months, and I am damn proud of it.

When I met him first, Brandon used to think he was straight. He'd grown up in San Fran, and "had many gay friends", but "their stuff was just not him" he claimed. He was simply not interested, OK? – OK, buddy! If you say so. And I withdrew. Hardly even acknowledged him with a nod when we'd meet at the computer labs at the university. I knew that his apparent advantage – the much-flaunted full cognisance of, indeed familiarity with, gay men, and his decisiveness he was not one – was going to ease him over to my side, now that, faraway from home, in the city famous for its romance-&-sex allure, he could afford to look at things in a non-North American way.

I could see a faint desire to crossdress in his carefully manicured fingernails and neat haircut, always a tad too perfect to be butch, as well as I could sense that the mincing butt yearned to be slapped, until all his fences broke loose and his real self was divulged, herded out in the open from its tight shell, startled with the wide world of possibilities open to a pigboy as willing and devout as I wished myself to believe he was. O, man, that butt drove me mad with lust, so sexy, so inviting to the whip, so unattainable!

Every third or fourth weekend, Liz would come over from London, and he would strut around Boulmiche and the Quartier Latin with her at his hand, smiling as a Cheshire cat. Sure, she would have been considered attractive by the standards of straight tourists who flocked to the area, with her shaggy blond mane, tanned, all legs and tits; his black hair and pale complexion a perfect match for her Nordic looks, particularly as they were accentuated by his black, or black-and-white clothes – mostly plain black. It took two months from when he let me feel up his belly, ostensibly to check the abdominal muscle, to when we sixty-nined first, in an early morning, after a theme night at Le Keller Bar, in a fellow-Australian ex-patriot Adrian's garret bachelor's, just off the Pyramides metro station.

His arms with powerful muscle, his slim waist and hard bulky gluteal globes, a.k.a. "bubble butt", are his best assets; the tight T-shirt and the perfect-fit pants emphasise them tantalisingly. On the other hand, his calves and pectorals are still somewhat underdeveloped and his four-'n'-a-half-inch boycock makes him vulnerable and insecure, easy prey to guys who have taught themselves to flaunt their bigger endowment in a most overt macho manner, especially since I had specifically picked my two horse-dicked friends when, half a year into our "relationship", it was time for his submissiveness to be tested – and expanded – by lending him out to other daddies for a weekend.

Naturally, when I brought the issue up first, he snottily said he'd never do it, who did I think I was, he shouldn't have gotten himself into this fag bullshit all along. Then he mellowed, cried some and pondered on how stupid a mistake it was to do it with a man (i.e. me) even once; he elaborated on why men are pigs, but when I asked him if that included himself he went into a fit, threw his collar at the floor and started shouting. I had to snap to the armchair in which he was crouching and slap his face a couple of times until he calmed down, sobbed some, hugged my leather-clad thigh fast and cried silently for a while. Then he called me "Daddy", smiled through tears, apologised solemnly, and went on his knees and hands to pick his leash and collar in his mouth and bring it to me to fasten it in its place. He even licked my hand, something he had never done before.

Now, I am, of course, not old enough to be his father. I am thirty-six and he twenty-five. Not even in societies in which boys are initiated at the earliest imaginable age could I have possibly sired him. I would have actually liked it much better to have developed an older / younger brother type of a relationship, if only because I lack and idolise it, being an only child. However, the very first signs of surrender, after months in which he'd go baloney as soon as I playfully slapped his butt lightly, was when he let me hit away without holding back for the first time, once during a France-Italy soccer game, as he lay on the couch in his Y-fronts, his head in my lap. As I hesitantly repeated the full-blow slap and followed it with a series of moderately heavy ones, he chanted: "Yes, Daddy! Yes, give it to me harder!" Although at the time he could have easily stopped me, and would have had every right to do so, he didn't. Neither did he stop calling me "Daddy", even when I reached for my belt. And so the word stuck. I was to be an ersatz-father figure for this bisexual boy-man.

His mouth does miracles with my cock. His tongue darts to and fro to rub against the underside of the shaft, as his throat muscles finely caress the head. So that not a hint of a scratch mars the squeezing movement, his teeth are completely covered with inward-drawn lips and his gap is wide, not a small feat in itself, considering the size of my venous, thick and longish dick. (Longer ones I've seen, but not many thicker ones, not that I'm bragging.) His total devotion to the task has something beyond the desire to please me; it is a strange mixture of a starved-hungry craving and a holy rite of an officiating high priest. He seems to have completely forgotten about Liz.

I am very close now and he knows it. Yet he slurps and suctions all the harder. He will swallow it all again. Yeah, baby, that's it, do it for Daddy! Stick your manicured finger up Daddy's rectum and touch the button to cause Daddy to go crazy. Make Daddy the centre of the universe. Show Daddy what a good cocksucker you are. For him only, for Daddy alone of all men. Be a good whoremouth for Daddy, so that Daddy can – aaargh! – love you forever, fill you-urrmph – to brimming with – arh! – sweet milt, feed you etern-ah-ah-ah-lly with Daddy's secret – ah – beebread. "OK, enough!" So that you can stop sucking Daddy's dick when it is spent and turned into a mass of nerves. "I said stop it! Boy!" He does, but he looks at my cock yearningly, then throws an almost angry glance at my face.

Anyway, I do not understand this bisexuality thing, honestly. I did give it some thought, and, before Brandon, it seemed to have come down to, basically, two options, which I put away into little boxes with neat labels as either fags who would rather fit in, at least to some extent and superficially, within homophobic society, which – granted – after a century of psychoanalysis is more prone to accept "bisexuality" (whatever that is) than the fully subversive homosexuality, or, on the other hand, as guilt-ridden over-PC-ed straight boys who, so as to prove they are not biased, feel that they absolutely have to give gay sex a try before they ascertain they are not into it. Yeah, right, like you'd have to fuck a pussy to know you didn't like it. Or to have a perfectly whole tooth drilled through to know that it hurts.

After Brandon, I do not know any more. He seems to impinge upon every concept of bisexuality I had thought out. Sure, he insists that he started as a "straight" man who "let himself be seduced" into it, but aren't we all "straight" at some point, at least at the time of adolescent peer pressure?

Besides, he took to it (i.e. to "us") as a fish to water, so that I long suspected he must have done it with one or other of his Californian beach bunny pals and was only playing hard to get. But than it happened that I got a proof how much he also enjoys fucking Liz – perhaps as much as he loves our sessions. It pains me, but it is so. I know, because, unbeknownst to both of them, I have seen it.

No, I haven't actually observed them in person while at it. I wouldn't have been able to keep still when he took the male role: I would have gotten over there and turned him into a little boy by making him admit he wants my dick inside him more than she wants his inside her. *The bastard, he really got me hooked on topping him!* What I did was make this little arrangement with an amateur spy camera I got cheap at the home security shop. It fitted within a silly wooden squirrel I gave him one day. I could see he was perplexed, as the object was quite discongruent with my usual, much more eclectic taste, but, so as not to offend me, he placed it on the mantelpiece, next to the pseudo-artist shots of his paternal grandparents in heirloom frames.

The thing just stood there for two weeks. Every time he'd go shower after sex, I'd turn it round this way and that, trying to find the perfect angle. It's not easy. Anyone who thinks it is should try doing things that require extra precision right after having climaxed, with a possibility to check the outcome only a few hours later. Finally, on a Wednesday eve, it appeared I had found the perfect angle. I zoomed on him in his sleep and could almost feel tenderness about his vulnerable look of an abandoned youngling, tenderness which – of course – I would never show him when we were together. But when Liz came on Friday evening, they moved the bed about and I got a full tape of the head-plank jerking, strewn here and there with shots of their upper body, when she'd lean back and he lay eagerly atop her. It was like a porn movie poorly edited to "erotica" in order to be shown to the general populace on Channel Three at 1:30 AM.

The next month, they went on a boat trip with her second cousin and when they came back slept peacefully through the night. Then the Chunnel was open and instead of her coming over, he went to London. It was only natural that a man would be more curious about technical achievements and treading the unexplored, he explained. (It actually meant double Geminis are always in the know about latest fads.) The next time I'd forgotten to recharge the battery in the transmitter. So it took four months before I eventually got to see them. And it would have been better if I hadn't. For it hurt. Tremendously.

Here was Brandon, who I had learned to think of as the boy whom I had salvaged from heterosexual banality, and he was licking this blond babe's cunt with gusto. "My" bad boy, whom I have so often spanked to orgasm, carried Liz around, holding her in his arms, impaled on his dick – annoyingly coming in and out of the field of the squirrel's not-really-all-seeing eye – prancing around with macho self-assuredness, unbridled and brutally wild as a caveman, as she visibly moaned. (This spy-camera has the image feature only, models with both picture and sound options not only cost three times as much, but were also bulkier and thus less innocuous.)

Later, when, tired of the athletic-sexual exercise, they eventually laid down on the bed, this time positioned in perfect frame and clear focus, he fucked her with abandon, his arm muscle rippling heavily as he held her tighter, his bum twitching wildly, the way I thought it only did under the rough kiss of my belt. I saw him doing things I never have, and probably never will. It, at the same time, strangely alienated me from him and made the moments we shared yet more valuable. It makes what has just happened between us somehow special, because of the liminal place he can choose / afford to occupy, shifting with relative ease from my "shady", "aberrational" side to the societal place of "normalcy".

I never told him I had seen him in his heterosexual throws of passion – why would I? But he did sense something and was trying to extract it from me a few times, usually, cunningly enough, while orally servicing me. Only the strict self-control power of my Saturn conjunct Ascendant, a feature of my chart which otherwise kept me from experimenting sexuality with anyone until I was twenty-one-and-a-half, prevented me from blurting it out once, when during the Full Moon of Harvesters his tongue made love to my shithole in an especially tender way. But I didn't, and am glad that I did not. Daddies are not to be weak, not to have soft spots. They are to be hardened, tough guys. Even if they are only thirty-six, and their sons twenty-five. That is why Daddies have the right to beat their sons' butts whenever the sons allow even for a hint of weakness.

That is the Law of the fathers and I am a part of it. This boy has made me. This man was to marry in a week's time and now perhaps never will, which does not mean he won't have his share of pussy, perhaps father a child, even. Yet I am the Daddy and he is my boy, forever. And as for being "bisexual" – what the fuck? – if it makes him happy to say so, I can cope with it, as long as he sucks dick as well as he does. I am sure you told your ole Dad, or at least your Mum, that you too might be bisexual, when you came out to them and they persisted asking if you were sure you were a homosexual. Might it be that you were not sure that you were not bisexual, they asked, pleading for that white lie.

And you said you might be, didn't you? You said that it was not very likely at that point of your life, but, yes: perhaps, after all, you may turn out to be bisexual, didn't you? I can't hear ya! Come on, spit it up, didn't you say you might be bisexual too, boy?!

Affair of the Heart

Isabelle Lazar

My friend gave me a Melissa Ethridge tape. Her first album. She should have never given me the damned tape. There's something so seductive on this tape.

'Does she inject you? Seduce you and affect you?'

The words swirl around my head slicing through me like a hot knife. I thought I was cured. I was wrong. Where is she? Is she out there? And will she be the one I finally change my life for?

"Jessy?" I am jolted from my reverie.

"Y-Yes."

"Jessy Kramer?"

"Yes."

"You can come in." I walk into an antiseptic classroom. Seven sets of eyes look me up and down. Except one. She stands in the corner. And turns slowly. Catching my eye, I suddenly realize – I'm home.

Well, hello, I think. The dyke of my dreams. It's too crude a word. But she is F-I-N-E, Fine. Sleeveless, white turtleneck which reveals her formidable biceps. Lean jeans, lean ass, slim legs. I start to salivate. She looks tough, and soft on the inside. I wonder if I'm right.

"You'll be auditioning with Peter and Sean here."

"O.K." I say, dumbfounded. She still hasn't said a word but the whole room seems to be smiling at me. I think I'm going to get this job.

Now she smiles at me and saunters over. Actually, she walks with a purpose, I'm just seeing everything in slow motion.

"Hi. I'm Taylor Scott. I'm the director." And she shakes my hand as any Tom, Dick or Harry. She has soft, supple breasts under that turtle neck. Their largeness betrays the secret she guards with her life. It's ok, you know. It's ok to be feminine sometimes. The Femme/Butch thing doesn't fly with me. I'm too new.

The audition whizzes by leaving me in a fog of emotions as I return home. And that night, as my husband fucks me, I picture her face. What am I doing? No. What am I doing here? I want her. To take her. The way I'm being taken now. To be taken by her the way I'm being taken now. I'm falling ...

My dream that night is vulgar. I dream that it's my wedding, though it has no resemblance to my real wedding, whatsoever. And that before this wedding, immediately before, we have a bachelor/bachelorette party. Everyone sits at small cocktail tables, something akin to Rick's Place in Casablanca, and around us dance transvestites. They are obviously transvestites as they are tall with masculine features and overly effeminate.

I remember this one in particular. He (she?) was tall, black, looked like Wesley Snipes in drag, wearing a red dress with ruffles at the bottom. As the main attraction, they would lift their dresses and underneath they weren't wearing any underwear. He lifted his dress and I saw a very large vagina, or rather just the outer lips. By large, I mean close to a foot long and half a foot wide. This thing went all the way up to his belly.

In my dream, he took a hold of this thing from the top and bottom ends and stretched it even farther, pressing together the overly-thick and hairless outer labia.

And just when you thought you'd seen it all, he grabbed the lips and pulled them apart exposing underneath a penis and a set of testicles.

I woke up in a cold sweat.

.... 2 ....

"I called this meeting so all of you could get introduced. I know it's a bit unusual to have the leads and the extras all together, but this is an Indie and independent films march to the beat of a different drummer, so to speak.

"Those of you who have been in and around the Hollywood system know how impersonal it can be. I want this shoot to be different. We are a small group and, for the duration of this shoot, I want us to all be one big family. That means if you have any questions or concerns you can come up to anyone of us.

"Which brings me to another point. Jessy Kramer, as you know, will be playing one of the leads. She is also going to double as my associate producer. Thank you, Jessy, for volunteering." She finally turns to me and I beam with pride. She grins back seductively. "I hope it was volunteering and not a draft."

"It was, " I say and thank God that I now have a reason to meet with her outside work hours to discuss 'work', of course!

She invites me to stay after everyone leaves, presumably to talk about just that, business. But not a word is mentioned. Instead, we talk about our lives and I know I want to save this moment for posterity. Not because we talk about anything so earthshaking but because I know without question that my life will never be the same. It's easy enough to look back and see 'Oh, that was the turning point.' Hindsight is 20/20. But to be in the moment, totally aware, and know beyond a shadow of a doubt that this is where your life changes is almost too much to handle. I think that's why people are applauded when they 'Come Out'. It's moments like that which bring you the closest you'll ever be to the sensation of grabbing Time by the back of the neck and holding it still for just a moment. Where you – and not Time or Circumstance – have leave to make the final decision.

I knew this was such a time for me, and it both terrified and inspired me. I had lived until my 27th year abiding by all the strict rules Society, Culture and Etiquette imposed. I vowed that night that this would be my time now.

.... 3 ....

We go to Harry's Cigar Room, my husband's new designer hobby. The place is cool though, I like it. Very 60's crash pad complete with lava lamps, bean bag chairs and velvet couches. I steal a moment to sneak away while he futzes with his Monte Cristo and call Taylor for the first time at home after hours.

"Just calling to see how you are."

"This is a surprise." I hope it's a good one.

"A nice surprise, but a surprise." That's lucky.

I can't believe how excited I am to talk with her ... as if she were a lover, not a colleague. I know I'm playing with fire, but I don't care. I realize I'm married but I don't care. What good is a marriage if it's a sham – if I'm really bi or gay? I need to know what I am.

.... 4 ....

We did the mating dance of two-steps-forward-two-steps-back for about a month while rehearsals were going on. This one night in particular I came dressed up especially for her: Skin-tight boot-cut black jeans, black vest and jacket. Black boots. She noticed. When she picked me up for rehearsal, 'Rhythm is a Dancer' was playing full tilt in her Beemer. (What did you think – a truck? No. She's a professional – butch.)

Have you ever heard the song? Yea, but have you ever really listened? Really let the rhythm seep in under your skin and stroke you from the inside out? The visual began as a small eruption inside of me, stemming from my libido, allowing me to feel it before I saw it, and slowly, painfully making its way to my brain. From behind my eyes I could see us: Her and me. Her dashing me against a brick wall. The feel of rough, scratchy bricks slicing into my shoulder blades. I could picture it so vividly I felt like I was gnawing on those bricks. And her gaze, unwavering in her focus on her desire – me. She walks closer with a purpose. I can feel my heartbeat pulsing its way through my cunt, threatening to break it open and shoot out. I can see it laying there with the familiar thump-thump, thump-thump of my desire. She sees it too. I demure. What if she's cruel? What if she's just taunting me and doesn't really care? She crosses the distance between us in two strides and unceremoniously enters me – hard. I am bifurcated on her steely arm, a willing prisoner of my own lust.

She throws the tape into rewind and jars me back to reality. "You mind? I missed the song." Then, like she's reading off a laundry list, "I want to get that feeling, too." Wow!

"Was my face that obvious?"

"Yea," she grins, though we have never spoken out loud about what is really happening. Is this it? Is this the admission? Well that was easy. I may prove to be a wiz at this lesbian thing. Emboldened, I reach out and take her hand, my heart racing.

"Where are we going?"

"I want to show you this one place by my house." I'm game – for anything. And do you know where she takes me? We pull off the main road and wind around upwards. Back here, where city lights are far away, the sky stretches like a vast dark quilt punctuated by silver dots that illuminate our way. The crickets have started their nightly opera.

We reach the top, an empty parking lot with only one other car of love-struck fools visible in the distance. I wonder if they're two women, too? Or two men? Nothing so boring as a straight couple, please. Not while I'm in gay heaven with the dyke of my dreams. Ok, I'm getting melodramatic but what do you want? She took me to Inspiration Point.

So I don't hesitate. The minute she takes her foot off the clutch and pulls up the parking break I lean in. Femme etiquette doesn't allow me to kiss her first but I ignore Ms. Manners for the moment and spread her lips with mine. She reciprocates. No preamble necessary, let's just get to it.

Whew! I forgot what it was like to make out like this. My husband and I haven't done it in years. I'm not sure we've ever done it like this. The feeling of danger in tasting the forbidden fruit is intoxicating. And I know my nature well-enough by now to understand that I live for this. I once told my husband that I missed the danger in our relationship. His comment was, "So? What? You want to do it on the back of a moving truck?" No. I want to be dangerous not stupid. But I could never quite get that through to him.

I lap at her unmercifully as if she is the last oasis and I've been stranded in the Mojave for the last four years. I have rather. I see that now.

The gear shift stubbornly refuses to cooperate making contortionists out of us as we neck. Enough of this. She moves to my side and I straddle her. Her hands slide under my vest and cup my breasts. Oh, my God, we're at first base! You'd think I was a teenager pulling the baseball reference somewhere out of a junior high sensibility. Who talks this way? Guys do. Well that would account for it seeing as how this is my first woman. I wonder if lesbians call it first base, too? Somehow I doubt they need to.

She flicks and tantalises my nipples. This is a curious sensation. I'd forgotten about those. And someone once told me that women have something called a clitoris but I don't much know anything about that either. I wonder if she does.

I pull away and look at her, just to make sure she is real and I am not just having another wet dream. She makes a 'V' with both hands around her chin and says, "I want you. Right here." What does that mean? My thoughts turn perverted – and then I realize I'm right. Oh my God, this is getting serious. Home base ... I mean, uh, all the way ... Oh, Christ. I gotta grow up really fast here. She makes me feel so safe, though. Somehow I know that she won't just fuck me and leave me. Fuck me? How is she going to fuck me? We'll get to that when we get there, I think. But something stirs in the back of my head. A long-dormant, primitive instinct seems to have been awakened and, I realize, that it doesn't matter how she fucks me – or if she does. Nothing matters anymore. I think that instinct – is called love.

.... 5 ....

She picks me up for a meeting, presumably. At least that's what I tell my husband. But I dress the part differently. They say that women dress not for men but rather for other women. I've never dressed for a woman like this before. I never dressed in such a way so that a woman would want to fuck me. I know how to dress that way for a man. That's a no-brainer: Mini skirt, high heels, lingerie if he gets closer. But for a woman? And not just any woman: A dyke. I have to get used to this term. Dyke. That's what I am – I'm a dyke. I'm coming to grips with this concept.

I dress as dykey as I know how at this point and still come out looking like a femme kitten. I've got on a spandex, racer-back top and biker shorts. The socks are strictly 80's aerobics – well I can't be totally butch. I need to leave something for her. I give my husband a quick peck on the cheek before we go.

On the way there, we do the mutual read from top to bottom but say nothing. She looks cool in her black jeans, sleeveless T-shirt (she obviously cut off the sleeves herself. What is it about people that do that to a perfectly good shirt? But at this point, everything is an aphrodisiac. I think about her strong hands and muscle-bound arms tearing at the helpless little sleeves – then I think of her turning those hands loose on me ...) and Timberland boots.

We go to an unincorporated area of Chicago suburbs. It's full of greenery. The City Council here is serious about preserving the natural environment. The little village is where we're going to film in a few weeks. There is a beautiful antique gazebo situated on a green, empty acre. All around are trees, Chinese bridges, a pond. Gorgeous. All this nature makes me hungry – and horny.

We sit under a tree with our books and papers. We try to talk about business but my outfit gets in the way. She becomes mesmerised by my exposed belly button. Just the effect I wanted.

"I want you," she says.

"So take me," I counter coyly, feeling protected by the expansive, open lawn.

"Let's go," she says and I follow, full of trepidation and excitement. We wander toward the far edge of the green to a row of dense forest foliage.

I don't know what happened. At some point we started kissing. At some point all of my clothes came off to be used as a 'throw' for me to lay on while she positioned herself between my legs. I ended up with 12 mosquito bites and several bloody scratches from the twigs – but I didn't feel them.

.... 6 ....

We go to Maggiano's on Clark Street. Our waitress comes by. I order my usual, Kettle One martini, straight up, two olives and dirty. He has his Gimlet. We're becoming the quintessential 90s couple, well on their way to being alcoholics, much like his aunt and uncle who have been drinking themselves into oblivion after work each day for 40 years. Come to think of it, his mother is the same way. Only his dad is different, got a new lease on life after the divorce. His new wife is into New Age, so Vodka has been replaced by rainbow pyramids and incense.

We make casual conversation. I can't sit still. This is already too far into it. I miss Taylor terribly. The intense stimulation of our trysts is maddening for me. My heart may feel like that of a school girl in this love affair but my body is that of a woman and it's becoming more animal by the minute. I'm not used to just foreplay anymore. I anguish in the need to touch her, drink her in, bury myself in her. I keep having that vision of her dashing me against a brick wall, hiking up my skirt and having her way with me right there, standing up. Is this normal for a woman to think such things about another woman? I must be mad. I seem to have no self-control, either. I've not heard half the things my husband has said to me. So I excuse myself to the bathroom. I know the pay phones are right in front of them.

"God, I miss you," I gush unashamedly.

"I miss you, too."

"I wish you were here. I need you."

"Just one more day."

"You know, I bet the rest of the cast and crew are enjoying their day off. Me? I'm miserable."

"I know," she laughs along. We talk in centuries and circles. I've known this woman for many more lifetimes that this. Out of the corner of my eye, I notice our waitress going into the bathroom with a purpose. A silent alarm goes off in my head.

I check my watch. My God! I've been on the phone for a half hour.

"I gotta go. I'll see you tomorrow." I click the phone down and tiptoe very quickly up the stairs.

"Where the hell have you been?" My husband is livid. "I sent the waitress in after you to see if you were ok." I know your every move.

"You know," I say, thinking two steps before I speak, trying to come up with a logical explanation for why I excused myself for a half hour while out to a fancy dinner with my husband, presumably the only love in my life.

"I'm waiting," he thumps the table.

"I fell asleep on the toilet."

"You what?" he grins and I know it's working.

"Yea. It's all the late hours of rehearsing lately, I guess. Next thing I knew, I woke up on the toilet with my panties around my ankles." He's laughing, consoling me. The visual helped.

"Oh, honey, you need to find time to rest," he kisses my forehead. Another battle avoided.

.... 7 ....

The single 'Everybody Everybody' pulsed through the production trailer, heating up the tape deck on continual replay. In the back bedroom, the beds had no sheets on them, still covered in the heavy plastic. They weren't for sleeping anyway, just a place to lay down the clothes, bags, essentials for the shoot. Wardrobe everywhere, we slid it off the right bunk onto the floor.

And on those sheets of plastic, we finally, finally got together. Tearing off each other's clothes, licking and sucking anything we could get our hands on – necks, cheeks, eyes, shoulders, collar bones, sternums, nipples, belly buttons, backs of knees and toes. Falling on the bed in a crumpled heap, the plastic slick and sticky under us, the smell of sex permeating the compartment. Women's sex. And sweat.

They have a distinctly singular odour. We didn't penetrate that day. She asked me what I wanted and I knew immediately. Been dying to try it. I sat up over her and spread her knees. Then lifted my own knee over her perpendicular and lowered my rump.

Our cunts slid together like they were locked and I rode her, pushing in, gyrating, rubbing until I thought I would suddenly sprout a penis and enter her like a man. Didn't happen. Wasn't necessary. We came in waves anyway.

After, we got dressed, stepped out and sat on the steps of the trailer, looking over the parking lot in the dusk, shops all closed. If I closed my eyes, I could still see the film crew: DP, camera loaded; the PA's lallygagging about; curious on-lookers. It's not often that a movie is shot in this tiny suburb, so it's a sight to see.

Now I sit here, hair slicked back from sweat, smelling like cum, wondering how I can get inside the house and into the shower without my husband smelling me. He always wants that obligatory kiss 'hello.' And I know, this is just the beginning.

.... 8 ....

She drives me back in that big jalopy of a trailer. Curiously it hugs the narrow curves around my apartment complex' parking lot quite deftly. I hesitate to exit. We have all that we need right here – a whole apartment, if you will – albeit on wheels.

The term 'trailer trash' comes to mind briefly and I try to dismiss it from my consciousness. Hey, all the Big Stars live in trailers when they're on a shoot. I'm ok, then.

I kiss her good-night. I can still smell my scent on her lips. Wonder if her lover will notice. Doubtful. Too fat, self-centered and uninterested. She's right to say that none of her friends can figure out what the two of them are doing together. I can't either. They're like night and day. Maybe I don't know her that well yet, just first impressions. Though something in the back of my mind is gnawing at me: 'They've been together six years. There must be something there.' So I ask her. She tells me 'no.' Just gave up on life in general, is her reason. She herself hasn't been touched for six years. That's what she says. But she HAS touched her partner! Crusty, as she calls her, for obvious reasons. Yuck! Evidently she's told when the other wants something. She's told this by a gesture. No words. Under different circumstances that might be seductive. This sounds like a permanent master/slave relationship.

I feel sorry for her. I want to kill her lover. Literally. My husband and I may not be better matched, as lovers I mean, but at least there is mutual respect, societal admiration. It's an obscene coincidence that both my husband and her lover have the same name, Pat. What do you do with androgynous names? The long versions of Patrick and Patricia are different, but they've never been used by either of us. We just laughed at the irony of the situation. We already know, already feel that we're in this for the long haul. We're not thinking about the logistics, what it will take to get out of the situations we're in, and what it will take to keep us in a new reality that we will create. We're just enjoying the moment. Too much for anyone's good.

I can't even breathe when I'm away from her. She picks me up for the shoot in the morning, earlier and earlier each day. And the days stretch and stretch until the 12-hour shifts I promised my husband turn into 20-hour sojourns. And he is complaining, more vociferously each day.

On the 4th of July we get a day-and-a-half break. The first night, we're let off 'early.' Well, everyone else is. Taylor and I find excuses not to get home before 10:00p.m., even if those excuses are to go and dump shit from the trailer. The PA's are supposed to do that. We've concocted the excuse that we can't trust anyone but ourselves to drive the trailer because no one else is insured on it. I'm not insured on it, but we don't tell anyone that. We dump shit, then screw in the parking lot of the camp site like there is no tomorrow. Like this was the last person in the world we have to screw before the whole freaking planet explodes tomorrow.

I can't get enough of her. My first woman. My first lesbian. I want to try everything on her, and I do. This way and that. I've become an expert with my tongue. Yes! In just a few short weeks, given the right amount of pent-up lust and sleep deprivation, You Too can become a cunnalinguist! It's always better, too, when you're working on a time crunch. I have to get home to Pat. She has to get home to Pat. See the irony? I pat her quickly so she can get home to Pat and I to Pat. – To pat Pat? No. Haven't done that since after the first day she and I met. She says she hasn't either. Both Pats are pretty upset. Neither of us is around long enough to care. But we don't want to start the war until all our troops are in alignment, so to speak. So we play the game.

.... 9 ....

I get up, after a particularly wet session, straighten my clothes, wash my face and hands, re-blow dry my hair. The transformation into dutiful wife is complete. Handy to have a portable bathroom. I'll drive tonight. She recovers on the couch. We've moved away from the plastic sheets. Too many burns. And we can't put regular sheets on them. The crew will get even more suspicious than it already is. I mean, for God's sake, when the Director insists on dumping shit – something is VERY wrong! Luckily, this is an independent, we can get away with it somewhat. Although the more seasoned crew knows. They've seen on-set romances before. So this one happens to be between two women. Welcome to the 90s.

.... 10 ....

She drops me off at the apartment.

"I love you," I don't hesitate at all. Whoever said that a lesbian brings a trailer on a second date has never met us. We started in the trailer, so where does one go from here?

I gather up all my strength and leave her. Watch her drive away, the ache permeating my whole being. What is this? I'm not a teenager any more but I feel like this is my first crush. The adult in me knows that it's a lot more serious than that, though. I sigh heavily and turn towards the door. I practice my greeting briefly before I enter. Ten days on a movie set, I feel like I'm missing the essential pages from the script of my life. How am I to act now? This is a rude awakening. No one told me I'd be left to my own devices like this. Why is everything in life the main take without rehearsal? No wonder so many actors are so screwed up. The lines between reality and work blur so heavily in this profession, you don't know when you're on and when you're not. And usually, it's during the worst times that you wish someone would yell 'cut' and, cruelly, no one ever does.

'Hi, honey, I'm home. Hellooo. Anyone home?' Oh, fuck it! I unlock the door.

Familiar sound of Nick-at-Nite reaches me.

"Is that you?" No it's some other wife you have ...

"Yep!" I muster up a smile and walk into the living room.

"Hi Bunny!" His nickname for me. I melt into his embrace and try to hide my mouth so he can't kiss it. I feel like a heel. What woman wouldn't die for this? This woman.

"I'm stinky. I have got to go and take a shower."

"Ok. Then you want to go out to eat?"

"Ok." I walk into the bathroom, he follows. I take off my top and he buries his face in the crook of my neck.

"Really, honey. I'm salty and sweaty and ..." and I have another woman's cum all over me! So let me bathe before you figure it out!

"Hmmm. This is the smell I know. This is the smell I love. The smell I will live with for the rest of my life until you die – and then we'll both die." I want to fall through the floor. Why can't I love you back the same way? Mercifully, he leaves me alone in the bathroom. I climb into our bathtub, grateful for the time away. I touch myself under the shower, my flesh still pulsating from the caresses.

I enter me. My insides ache from the longing. All in good time, I think, the hot shower numbing my senses.

Biographies

Deborah Block-Schwenk lives in Boston with her husband and three cats and is a former co-editor of "Bi Women", the newsletter of the Boston Bisexual Women's Network.

Laurence Brewer has been involved with a number of Bisexual ventures, which also include writing for Bi Community News in the UK, as well as being involved with putting on the 6th International Bisexual Conference. Laurence enjoys listening to poorly played Punk Rock records (and inflicting them on other people). His greatest achievement to date was to play a track by the seminal anarchist-noise-punk outfit Crass during a tentative DJing set at the 16th UK Bisexual Convention in Cambridge. Laurence lives in London.

Wayne Bryant is a writer, software consultant, bisexual activist, and author of the book *Bisexual Characters in Film: from Anais to Zee*. He enjoys travelling in distant lands.

Mark Christian (Alice Blue) is a resident of San Francisco, California. His collection DIRTY WORDS: A COLLECTION OF PROVOCATIVE EROTICA is published by Alyson Books in 2000.

Dean Durber lives in Sydney, Australia. His first fiction novel, *Johnny, Come Home*, has recently been accepted in the United States. Several of his short stories will be appearing in a number of forthcoming American anthologies including *Bar Tales*. His one-man stage show about River Phoenix, *Rising From The Ashes*, received its premiere production in Sydney in February 1999. For the past five years he has been working as a freelance writer for a variety of publications around the world including The Sun Herald (Australia), Faces (USA) and The Daily Yomiuri (Japan). He is the author of the popular Icons column in Sydney's Capital Q and a regular columnist for the cruisingforsex website. He is a regular contributor to Australia's Capital Q, Blue and Outrage. He is currently teaching self-devised courses in Creative Writing at the Eden Creative Arts Centre (Manly, Sydney) and HaS bEaNs performance space (Newtown, Sydney). He is also involved in the writing of a biography and his first full-length screen play.

Paul Cowdell Paul Cowdell's most recent work has been with the Probation Service, for whom he has devised movement classes for young offenders. A keen 'cellist, he is currently compiling a compendium of werewolf stories from southern Europe.

D. Franklin writes left-handed, has been writing erotic fiction and poetry since 1989, and occasionally fantasises about writing a script for an adult film. Appearances include Forum, For Women, Eidos, The Journal of Erotica, Desire, and the Guild of Erotic Writers' 'Anthology No. 1' and 'Deadly Strangers'.

Jamie Joy Gatto is a New Orleans writer whose short fiction and photographs have appeared in *Black Sheets* magazine, a counter-culture anthology *Best of the Underground* by Masquerade Books, and other forthcoming anthologies. She identifies as a bisexual Tantric Priestess, a Dominatrix extrordinaire, a practising clairvoyant Wiccan, and feline lover. She may be contacted by writing to `sexcats@earthlink.net`.

Clint Jefferies lives in Jersey City, New Jersey, USA. Web page: http://www.brainlink.com/~cjeffer/

Lani Ka'ahumanu has lived, worked, played, organised and had many adventures, sexual and otherwise, in the last 56 years in the San Francisco Bay Area. Co-editor of *Bi Any Other Name: Bisexual People Speak Out*, her writing and poetry have appeared in books, magazines, and journals, while she appeared in *Women En Large: images of fat nudes* (BookInFocus) for her 50th birthday. Challenge your stereotypes, old women have hot sex.

Raven Kaldera is a gender terrorist, activist, organic farmer, parents, pagan minister, and pornographer whose writings are scattered hither and yon. 'Tis an ill wind that blows no minds.

Miodrag Kojadinović is the only person so far who got a Dutch Government's scholarship specifically for Gay Studies. His academic work has mostly been on gay spanking (eg final paper in Utrecht/Amsterdam and MA thesis in Budapest). His erotica has appeared in five languages in: *Best Gay Erotica 1996, MSM Koerier, Drummer Hardcore, Symposion, Angles, Keke* ©, *Powerplay, Zbornik o homoseksualnosti GAYto, Rough Stuff, Leuke jongens, Many Mountains Moving, Gay News Amsterdam* and *Henry Street*. As far as things *bi* go, he is bi-national (ie a dual citizen) ;-) See him at `http://fly.to/Miodrag/`

Kevin Lano (diversity33) has edited books on gender politics ('Beyond Sexuality', Phoenix Press, 1992) and polyamory ('Breaking the Barriers of Desire', Five Leaves Press, 1995) and has been involved in the bisexual community and the organisation of the UK Pride festival. His bisexual erotica has appeared in *Peacock Blue*, *Mind Caviar* and *Exquisite Darkness* magazines and the *Viscera* anthology (Venus or Vixen, 2000).

Isabelle Lazar 'Affair of the Heart' is an extract from a book of the same name. She has previously been published in Robinson Publishing's *The Mammoth Book of Lesbian Erotica*, Alyson Publications *Early Embraces II* and *Skin Deep: Real Life Lesbian Sex Stories*, and Philogyny Magazine. She is a resident of Beverly Hills, California.

Marilyn Jaye Lewis has been known primarily for her cutting-edge bisexual erotic fiction over the last decade. Her short stories have appeared in numerous underground zines, such as Bad Attitude and Frighten The Horses. While writing for RomAntics, Inc., she helped develop the award-winning DADAhouse – the first bisexual adult CD Rom game, featured on HBO 'Sexbytes.' She was also the original writer for the 'DADAhouse' cyber soap opera, which 'Entertainment Weekly' called 'kinkily engaging ... the Best Soap on the Web for 1997'. Her first book, 'Neptune and Surf', was published by Masquerade Books in March 1999. Marilyn Jaye Lewis edits and maintains the popular erotica web site 'other-rooms.com', the first non-commercial erotic fiction web site to be selected for PLAYBOY's online Hall of Fame. She recently launched marilynsroom.com, an online multi-media community for erotic filmmakers, photographers, artists and authors. She lives in New York, USA.

Rachel Martin is a marine scientist who writes comics, lives in Melbourne Australia, and is bringing up a beautiful baby whose father has forbidden her to ever write about him.

Trish Oak writes erotica under the name **Piglet** and lives in London, UK. Two collections of her SM bisexual short stories have appeared: **Pig tales** and **Pig tales II**. **Pig tales** won the Sexual Freedom Coalition's erotic Oscar for 1996. "Alice" previously appeared in Ungagged, the magazine of the UK SM Bisexuals group.

Katherine Park (not her real name) lives in Edinburgh with a silver inflatable alien. During the day she works for a charity, and in the evenings she pretends to be writing a highbrow novel but is probably scribbling some fanfic, when not driving her partner mad by constantly surfing between 60-odd cable channels.

Carol Queen is the author of *The Leather Daddy and the Femme*, *Real Live Nude Girl* and *Exhibitionism for the Shy*. "After the Light Changed" was previously published in *The Leather Daddy and the Femme* and is ©Cleis Press, reprinted with permission.

Alex M. Quinlan lives on the East Coast of the United States, with spouses, children and pets, of both the two and four-legged varieties. They all spend entirely too much time on the Internet – but not on the World Wide Web.

Thomas Roche is a resident of San Francisco, California. His erotic fiction has been widely published and his own collection, *Dark Matter*, was published by Masquerade Books in 1997. His web page is: http://home.earthlink.net/ ~thomasroche/. "What He Did" has appeared in: Cupido (Oslo, Norway), Vol 7/1995, August 1995; *Best Gay Erotica 1996*, edited by Michael Thomas Ford, Cleis Press (San Francisco), 1996; *Best American Erotica 1997*, edited by Susie Bright, 1997; *Dark Matter*, published by Masquerade Books, 1997.

Gabriella West lives in San Francisco. She has been published in several queer-oriented anthologies and literary journals. She is currently working on a historical romance novel set in Ireland in 1916.

Daniel Wolff loves the Pacific Northwest and the Australian Southeast, Irish fiddle, and the coffee at Café Greco, San Francisco. He has a passion for wooden boats and delights in embarking on strange adventures with good friends.

Printed in the United Kingdom
by Lightning Source UK Ltd.
116634UKS00001B/16-21

9 780953 881604